The Moulin Huge

Cover design by Lee Clevenger and R. Preston Ward
Back cover photo of Mr. Ward by Lee Clevenger
Edited by Lee Clevenger

LaMoulinRougeCarnival.com and NicevilleNewz.com were not valid websites at the time this book went to press.

ISBN Number 978-0-9788571-7-2
First printing, April 2007

Published by:

DIVACITY PRESS, a division of:

ThomasMax Publishing
P O Box 250054
Atlanta, GA 30325
www.thomasmax.com/divacitypress.htm

THE MOULIN HUGE

Robert Preston Ward

Divacity Press

ACKNOWLEDGEMENTS

The Moulin Huge was created at a difficult time in my life.

I thank my family for their support and love.

I thank Bill Jackson and Erin Littleton for their constant encouragement.

I thank Lee Clevenger for all his help in making this dream of mine come true.

Above all, I thank God. He knows for what.

With love and gratitude in my heart, I dedicate
The Moulin Huge
To:

Bruce, who helps me through the rain;
Brenda, who shows what love is;
Debra, who holds my hand;
Kevin, who shows me the world;
Lauren, whose encouragement moves me;
God, who put it all together.

THE MOULIN HUGE

1

"And that's all she wrote?" Lloyd, in his Marilyn persona, pouted as his hands trembled while he grasped the note from Lowla so very tightly. "That's all she wrote?" Looking around at his grand surroundings for which he had had to beg, borrow and steal, the note fell from his grasp onto the white leather Maralunga sofa. It landed on the spot where Lowla, also known as Evan, sat to meet the men that Lloyd lined up for him. The courting began every evening at dusk when Lowla was in town. He stood in one spot while his hands pressed against the leather armrest. Every being of Lloyd's body seemed to be frozen. The energy he needed just to move from the sofa . . . or just to sit down and comprehend what had happened . . . escaped him. He couldn't scream or cry. All he could do was just stand still.

It seemed like an eternity had passed since he opened the envelope. How exciting it was to have received correspondence from Lowla, especially considering Lowla had problems putting one foot in front of the other, not to mention joining sentences to form a paragraph. To have such high hopes only to find ugliness in the opening of a letter. Was it only a month ago that Lowla went back to Atlanta? Lloyd sighed very loudly as he caught his breath, turned and walked toward the balcony. He raised the floor-to-ceiling window and walked out to be surrounded by his sanctuary. He focused in on an unused pooper scooper hidden behind a plant. Lloyd paused for a moment while longing for the time when he had his beloved cocker spaniel pet, Churchill, and how they would sit together in his swing and what comfort Churchill brought to him and how he missed that comfort. He almost chuckled when he remembered how he would scoop up the dog shit off the floor with his pooper scooper and sling it out to the streets without regard as to might be below as he never walked the dog. Lloyd just let him do his "business" on the balcony. Although it overlooked the prestigious Four Hundred Block section of a busy Royal Street in the French Quarter of New Orleans, the hammock, the swing and all of the many plants made this his home away from home in the second-floor apartment. Here he could come for meditation, peace or to pick up a man off the street amidst the ferns, the fichus trees and the hanging ivy. Lloyd had an uncanny way of meditating in the middle of any noise level or crisis.

Instead of lounging in the swing, which was always nurturing to him, Lloyd stood in the corner and looked down onto the street, unable to focus because of the news he had received. He had great expectations that Lowla would come to his rescue to help him keep an eye on his unscrupulous partner of five years. Tears began to well up in his eyes, and he fought it with all his worth. Lloyd usually never cried unless it was in front of a man in order to manipulate him. Just when a single tear began to fall down his cheek, he noticed a pair of lovers engaged in a heavy embrace coupled with passionate kissing as though she were sending him off to the Navy in World War II. Holding on to the wrought iron columns that framed his sanctuary, he was envious of the pair, wishing it was he getting that much affection from his loved one. At long last they broke for air. Lloyd's eyebrows arched up as if he were doing an impression of Scarlet O'Hara in astonishment. The male counterpart in that embrace was his man. Torch was a gutsy kind of guy who continually pushed Lloyd to his limits. The smell of construction grew around him just like a vine to a tree. The couple embraced again. Lloyd watched, almost forgetting his present situation.

2

Dreams continued to rob sleeping hours while fantasies robbed wakened reality. There was no escape. The dark deep circles under his eyes and lack of energy were proof that this state of mind had torn him apart. When he first started to fantasize, it was for a secret pleasure . . . a place for him to go where he was in control of the needed situation, a place he had created because of all the time spent alone as a child and to cover the pain for seeming to be the only sissy in a small southern town. Not that he was an only child; he wasn't. Evan was a mistake that came late in life to his parents. The brother and sister were out of the home by the time he was three. His siblings had the looks of movie stars and the actions of corporate presidents. Evan had neither. His parents were always engrossed in his brother and sister as he grew up in shadows that would never move so that the light could shine on *his* face. But in his world of make-believe, his face was the only one that beamed the light. Over the years, that fantasy life had become a prison. The creative thoughts had become the jail where the sentence would be fulfilled, no matter how outrageous the daydreams became. His waking eyes would be the key to open the prison doors into which he walked every day — willingly.

It had been raining, but the sun had started to shine again. The rays of light were distorted as they shone through the glasses on the table by the window, where he had left them the prior evening. He thought he could wash them or go back to thinking about how his dual life was now taking a toll. His fantasy life made him happy. The dirty wine glasses did not. He looked around. It was hard to believe that this was his environment. Thinking of the past, he realized he had walked right in . . . hook, line and sinker. The floors were cluttered with plastic mail boxes full of God-knows-what. Extension cords outlined paths from one room to another, as his fantasy world dictated camera and sound equipment. He looked into the kitchen. The once-gleaming black-and-white tile was now more gray than white and a tattered black. The garbage had piled up; a mound of dishes littered the sink. He looked all around the house; he had so much of so little. Everything had its place and it all needed dusting.

Upon entering the living room, his reflection in the mirror

above the fireplace caught his eye. That was not unusual because he always like to look at himself as he performed, although he wasn't performing now. He was taking inventory of his depressed existence. But this time he saw a glimpse of sincerity . . . maybe maturity. Had he really come to look like this? The answer was obvious: *Yes.* He paused for a moment and reflected on memories of when he had kept up his appearance. As he tried to remember why he had let himself go, the weight from his face began to disappear. He had drifted into his imagination, a surreal place where he was safe and did not have to deal with the reality of his failures.

His reflection began to appear in another mirror, the mirror in his bathroom, which looked more like a dressing room for a cabaret singer. The five-by-eight-foot space had wigs, dresses and make-up scattered about, leaving just enough room for him to sit. On his make-shift vanity sat a vase of cut flowers that had been fresh at one time. He paused to smell the dead arrangement as he pretended he received them from an admirer. Evan was getting prepared for yet another performance to an imaginary audience. He began to slip out of his usual dress code: blue jeans and a sweatshirt. It would take a couple of hours to shave, bathe, and put on make-up and costumes. After his shower he would start the process of changing himself into Lowla. First he would slick back his hair and put on a base that made his face look like a blank canvas. With that step accomplished, the rest of the painting would take place as he drank and smoked. With each sip of cheap red wine and each toke of expensive pot, he would look more fabulous and sound even better than when he started. Since he preferred full, outlined lips as his signature, they were always the last to be done. They took the longest time and had to be perfect. It took him years to master drinking through a straw so that the lips would not lose their luster. When his pucker was just right, he chose a full, soft brush from his accessories, lightly dipped it into an open jar, and the final powdering was complete.

Once he slipped into his black cocktail dress, it would be time to go on stage to sing, dance and entertain.

Before he commanded his stage, he had to make sure the cameras were ready; the spotlights were on; the music was cued up, and all of the costumes, wigs and props were in place for changes between songs. People just did not realize the efforts he took to video his "specials" in his bedroom. The once-functional slumber room had become a film stage. Black sheets were taped to the walls and laid on the bed to give the appearance of a studio so that in viewing the final video one would think his show was in a professional setting. Looking at all he had accomplished he thought his show, *White Trash from Hapeville,* was pretty good. Evan was really proud of himself. Not only was he the emcee, but also the star, the director, the camera man, the lighting staff, the sound person and the make-up artist. Whatever it took to do the show, Evan did it alone. There were hours and hours of performances on film that he watched over and over again, not only for his personal pleasure but also to make improvements to his act. He only regretted that no one else ever saw his work. He was brilliant, but very shy.

The video camera which sat on top of the monitor was connected to the VCR. The monitor, aka the television set, was at Evan's eye level so he could watch himself perform. Tonight was a very exciting evening for him as he planned to film himself in blue spot lights with one white spot overhead. He thought the combination gave him a very good look. He began his final inspection. The lights were set. All of the other equipment had been powered on and were in the "pause" mode. He pressed the pause button on the video camera and immediately ducked. He sneaked out of the bedroom under the camera's lens in order not to be seen to make his entrance more effective. Once at the bedroom door, he hit "record" on a remote for the VCR to begin the VHS recording. Then he pressed play on the stereo remote so his background music would start. Being careful not to trip over the extension cords, he entered the arena, faced the camera and gave a big smile to an audience that wasn't there. As he acknowledged their applause, the background music started to play.

"Well, how do I look in blue?" he spoke in his best professional southern voice. "I don't know about me, but you all look *fabulous*." He threw his hands in the air. "Welcome to another evening of 'White Trash from Hapeville.' I am your *host*, Lowla! And that's L – O – W – L – A." He blew a kiss to the crowd. "Evan is so sorry he could not make it tonight. *But I'm not*. Hell, if he were here, I wouldn't be!" He reacted to their obvious applause. "Thank you. Thank you." Lowla stepped closer to the camera and posed. Viewing the monitor so the audience wouldn't catch on, he thought he looked really great. "Tonight is my tribute to blue. This is the episode of the Blue Light Cafe brought to you by Red Foxx's Beauty Cream." His hand touched his face. "Can't you tell?"

He walked away from the camera and went to a stool. In view, he picked up a joint and a lighter off the stool. "Pardon me while I light my cigarette. I hope you don't mind if I smoke, it makes me feel *effeminate*." He took his first draw from the pretender and then talked through the smoke. "Back to blue, hell, let's face it. I am blue. Lowla is blue." He sang, "You would be, too —" and then spoke, "performing in a dump like this! The paint may be peeling, but it's not in your cocktail." He returned to the stool to have a sip of wine which was already waiting. "Before I move on to our guests this evening, Kathleen Turner and Liza Minnelli —" He had to stop and smile. The applause for his guests was too loud for him to continue. "Yes, yes," he said as he also clapped his hands. "Go ahead and applaud the old broads. They deserve it. God knows they've had their blues, too! And their blues, as well as mine, will be exposed tonight at the Blue Light Cafe!

"Okay, okay, getting back to me, *Lowla*. I just want to enlighten *you* about *me*." Bob Fosse would have been proud of the pose he struck, and now that the music was cued up he started to sing and dance.

They're not going to whisper
They're gonna shout, Lowla!
Everywhere you look
You're gonna see, Lowla!
The name you read
On the marquees will be, Lowla!
Turn on your TV
And you'll be greeted by me,
L—O—W—L—A
I'll turn the fashion world upside down
While I make a million or two—

A noise intruded. He stopped singing. With the barking of his dogs outside and the buzzing of the doorbell, he quickly came back to reality. The spell was broken. *Just who the hell could that be?* He grabbed the remotes and turned off the music and the VCR. He walked lightly in his heels and headed toward the front bedroom to see who dared to interrupt one of his concerts. Besides he just couldn't let anyone in since he was dressed to the nines as Lowla. He stepped over piled clothes on the floor and peeked through the blinds to see a cop standing under his porch light. *Oh good, I just love a man in uniform.*

"Be right with you, officer," he yelled. The concert would have been fun, but this is really what he thought he needed . . . an encounter of affection for approval of whom he was. Evan ran for the front door, opened it and said, "I am so glad you came."

"My, oh my," Salvatore said, "you look absolutely stunning." The policeman walked into the living room and quickly embraced Lowla. "I'm sorry I came unannounced."

"Oh, there is plenty of time for you to announce that," Evan ersatz Lowla said as he pulled away from Salvatore's powerful grip and closed the front door.

"You weren't expecting someone else?"

"No. I was just practicing my show." Evan leaned

against the door, "You know, getting ready to do a number. I'd rather do you anyway."

"I got off my shift early, baby, and the missus is out of town. Why don't you go slip into something trashy and get me a beer? I'll be waiting by the fireplace, all dressed up and no one to arrest."

"Hold onto your handcuffs. I'll be right back." *How lucky am I to have that big Italian hunk of a cop want to fool around with me even if I'm in a dress,* he thought as he hurried to get that beer, slip out of the *Vera Wang,* pull off his wig, and put on his very best pair of ripped panty hose.

3

"All right already, I'm coming," Diva yelled as she paused to look at herself in the mirror before answering the phone. Oops, those lips need adjusting. She took her pinky finger and gently wiped the corner of her mouth. One more look in the mirror and she said, "*Ciao,* this is The Diva. Oh hello, darling. Yes. The Diva can do the phone interview now. Yes, yes, The Diva knows. The Diva is so sorry that it is raining, but The Diva can not get wet. Just a moment, darling, and let The Diva get adjusted. The Diva will put the phone down just a moment." She hurried over to get Mary, a name lovingly given to her smoking habit, and went back to sit on the couch nestled in front of a huge wall mirror. She took out a lighter and lit Mary, took a deep breath of smoke, then exhaled and said seductively into the phone, "The Diva is ready."

She had another puff of Mary. The Diva looked at her reflection as though she weren't on the phone. "The Diva would put you on the speaker, darling, but The Diva only likes to hear the sound of The Diva's voice." She cackled a clever laugh. "Yes, after all that The Diva has done, The Diva must say that publishing her first novel, *A Kept Reflection,* has been a high that no other source has ever given." She eyed Mary and took another puff. "And The Diva is so-o-o-o happy that it has been on the *New York Times* best seller list for three months now." Mary made yet another trip to her lips. "Yes it did have another name, *Reflections*, but she hears that The Diva looks like *Diana Ross* enough. Talk about a diva wannabe!" Looking at herself and not really listening to the caller, she smoothed out her eye shadow on her left eye. "The Diva begs your pardon? Plans for the future? Darling, The Diva always has plans; just look at what she has accomplished thus far.

"Good point. Let's start with the past . . . or the beginning, shall we say as The Diva has no past. Darling, The Diva's life is just one big circle," she said as she looked into the circular mirror to her left side for a different view.

"The Diva," she always referred to herself in the third person although due to limited education she thought she was referring to herself in the first, "was not your ordinary girl." At the tender age of two, she and her parents discovered her favorite joy in life, and that was looking into a mirror or any other reflective surface. "Most young children say 'da-da.' Not The Diva. She grabbed the mirror and said 'me-me.'" Again she roared her clever laugh while she ran her fingers gently over her bangs. "The Diva was considered genius at twenty-four months old when she created a mirror mobile that hung over her crib. Her mobile consisted of various shapes of mirrors that when in motion gave The Diva a panoramic view of her tiny shape that she still possesses to this day." She stood admiring her figure in one of the many mirrors adorning her living room; she had another puff of Mary.

"Yes, yes that is fascinating. Oh. You don't want to go that far back. Well perhaps it would be better to meet you for lunch as originally planned. It's hard for The Diva to concentrate with all the distractions around her." She smiled straight ahead, then turned to her left to smile again into a full length mirror by her hallway. "You could make it to *Sake's?* How thoughtful. It's in The Diva's building. Make reservations and The Diva will see you there in a couple of hours? Yes, darling. *Ciao!*"

Going back to her grand closets and bathroom, she thought how good she looked in the mirrors as she sauntered down the hall. Diva had maintained her relationship with mirrors her whole life. She claimed that by looking into a mirror she could practice her expressions and would know how she would look at all times, with or without the aid of a mirror. Diva used this talent greatly to her advantage. She could get anything she wanted with just one look. Some people said that she had to practice emotions in the mirror since she had no genuine feelings of her own. Once Diva overheard a similar remark and started to break down until she realized she had a compact on her and then quickly opened it to be consoled by a best friend: her reflection.

What should The Diva wear that no one has ever seen? Now that she was in her closet area, she stopped for a minute just to look at all of the reflections of her. All of the walls in her condo were solid white so that there would not be a conflict in the background when viewing herself. The white walls of her condo were home to mirrors, pictures of her, and framed posters of her movies. But the mirrors dominated the decor. Mirrors of all shapes and sizes were everywhere and at every angle. She had mirrors so she could see how she looked answering the phone, talking on the phone, how she looked throwing trash away in the wastebasket, how her shoes looked, how the back of her hair looked as she would stare straight ahead as she looked at herself looking at the back of her outfit. Smiling like a Cheshire cat, Diva suddenly felt a little faint. She went to her bedroom, in which all of the accessories were also in white. As she sat on her comforter underneath the canopy looking at herself in all of the mirrors, wondering what man would be lucky enough to share an evening with her and her and her and her and, yes, her too (directed to the mirror in the corner), something happened.

At once, Diva realized she did not know which side of the

mirrors was the reflected one. Surely this was a dream, other than the dream of looking at herself. Was she the one looking out or the one looking in? *The Diva has got to snap out of this or I'll* — *or The Diva will be late for the interview at* Sake's. *In or out? In or out? Oh God, please help The Diva.* The room began to spin and slowly Diva passed out. The reflection in the mirror remained calm and still. Too bad Diva didn't see herself fall to the floor.

4

The sky was set for the end of daylight, a signal for sadness to begin as love was about to depart. "T-o-r-c-h!" Lloyd screamed at the top of his lungs, "I need you, hurry, something terrible has happened." Slowly Lloyd disappeared into his garden in the sky.

"Sorry, doll, I have to be a going now. Got to go to work, you know. It's a full-time job just living with that one. Ah, don't frown, sweetie. I'll see ya soon." Torch turned to leave the lovely brown-haired girl who was now looking confused at being left alone. "Here's cab fare and a little extra. Compliments from the warden." He pointed upward to the balcony. As he turned to walk away he knew that she was watching him. He looked back only to verify that he was correct, which set his ego to growing again. *It's a tough job being good looking and hung, but heck, somebody has got to do it.* Even though he came to Lloyd like an obedient dog, he had no regard for Lloyd's feelings as to what Lloyd had just witnessed or anything else that he might have done that would have hurt Lloyd. Although he had the true heart of a Yankee carpetbagger, Torch eased his way up the block with a big, gracious southern smile to everyone he passed.

Hiding behind the hanging ivy on the balcony, Lloyd saw that Torch was headed home so he left the safety of his sanctuary and returned to the Maralunga sofa, the pivotal piece of furniture in what Lloyd called the parlor. Many forms of business had been transacted on that very spot, like the time he successfully secured being on an episode of *A Current Affair* for allowing the film crew to secretly video a movie in production from his balcony. He was having a lot of fun, until the very famous star of the movie, rumored to be Tom Cruise, caught on and called the police. Still, in that same spot, he managed to get out of the charge of "Intrusion on a Closed Set," which was a feat considering the residents of the Quarter had to sign a silence contract with the film producers. The parlor sofa was positioned strategically so that the soft hues of sunset light which came through the side window would beam only on the person sitting there. Lloyd knew exactly where to position himself since he had tested several locations in the room numerous times in order to achieve the very best effect for his looks. He was always dressed to the nines. Waiting for Torch, he dripped in Armani from head to toe. Even without being a fashion king, he was devastatingly handsome with a strong hint of prettiness and felt the natural light from the sun best displayed his boyish charms rather than the glare of the overhead chandelier. Lloyd had to look good at all times. With Torch in his life, he always had to give him his very best. After all, there were many standing in line, as evidenced this very evening. Reveling in his *noire* setting, Lloyd heard the buzzer. *How could he not have his key? Damn. He* jumped up and went to the intercom to buzz the door open for him. Hurriedly, he darted back to his seat, posed again, and tried not to look as though he had rushed, although a trickle of sweat dotted his brow. He wiped his forehead and licked his fingers. Lloyd thought his sweat to be like the morning dew on a fuzzy peach, a sort of nectar for the gods. Lloyd was not the skinniest person in the Quarter.

Torch kicked the door open and walked into the room expecting a confrontation. Lloyd sat there. His eyes were upon Torch like a searchlight, moving slowly up and down, taking in every detail. He always tried to make Torch feel like he was every bit of what he thought he was . . . beautiful in a manly way.   Towering over most, he stood six-foot-seven with dark brown hair, the bluest of eyes and a body that every man would envy and every woman would want.   He stood there staring at Lloyd, he at him. Torch motioned as if he was starting to speak.

"No, don't say a word."   Lloyd leaned into the couch. "Let me just look at you.   Let me just be grateful that no matter who you kiss on the street, you still come home to Momma."

"Stop acting like a woman. You are a man. I think."

"You treat me like a woman."

"I treat you like a pig. And you love it."

"Don't you even care that I said I needed you?   That something terrible has happened?"   Lloyd hoped that his lying did not show and that Torch would not see the note from Lowla.

"In some melodramatic fashion, you would have told me anyway."   He walked over to the bar.   "What is it this time? Did you take too much penicillin?"   He poured himself a shot of bourbon and drank it down.   In a show of strength, Torch threw the empty glass against the fireplace, just missing the original oil painting of "Mammy" which graced the wall above the mantle. The shattered pieces fell to the floor. "Or was there not enough money in the till at *Le Oui-Oui* for you to take? Huh? What, no popcorn box full of money for us tonight?"   Lloyd looked down to the floor, hurt that Torch cared more for humiliating him rather than consoling him. "Just go ahead and pout. I gotta take a shower. Then we'll go shopping at Neiman's. I need some new clothes."

His Marilyn persona evaporated and he was that little frightened boy, Lloyd Rochelle, frozen in the moment of degradation.

"Get off your fat ass and come take a shower with me," Torch said, commanding control over Lloyd.   "You'll enjoy buying me clothes a whole lot more."   He smiled and grabbed his crotch.

Slowly Lloyd got up, trying not to smile. "Do you really think I'm fat?"

"No, I know you're fat. But you're cute with your short blond locks and that schoolboy, uh, schoolgirl smile. Not bad for thirty-nine and holding." Realizing that he had Lloyd where he wanted him, he walked over to the couch to close the deal on getting his new clothes. "And I have grown accustomed to this way of life. You've spoiled me, now deal with it." Torch put his arm around Lloyd and walked him down the hall to the back of the apartment in the direction of the shower and bedroom.

5

Lowla paused in the hallway with Salvatore's beer in one hand and a glass of wine in the other. Salvatore was sitting in the high-back overstuffed chair in front of the fireplace. His hat was still on, cocked to the left side of his head. He looked so noble. He looked so normal. *What is he doing here? What is so wrong in his life that he comes searching for something he should be able to get at home? He is such a fine example of manhood only to be here with me. I don't get it.* Lowla cleared his throat.

Salvatore looked to the left to see Lowla standing in the archway of the door. The radiant glow from the fire illuminating just enough on Lowla's face gave an illusion of beauty. Lowla looked like a young Elizabeth Montgomery but was dressed in the manner of Stella Dallas. He didn't know if it was the tattered hose held up by a garter belt, or the one-piece brown velvet swimsuit draped with a see-through animal print blouse or those four-inch high heels that made his heart beat faster. Maybe it was that Lowla's dark-blond hair was shoulder length, which framed his features so perfectly that it made the whole package seem real. He was always relaxed and felt at home with Lowla. "Are you going to stand there all day or are you going to come and sit here?" he said as he patted his lap with his big hands.

Without hesitation Lowla handed him the beer and sat on

his lap. After sitting on his shapely thighs, he took his free hand and rubbed Salvatore's shirt to feel the muscular chest which lay underneath the cloth. They touched bottle to glass and raised them to the air. Then they kissed passionately as though they had known each other forever. It always amazed Evan how intimate he could be with a one-sided stranger. One-sided because all Evan knew about Salvatore was that he was a married cop who loved to visit Lowla. The kiss was over and they sipped from their respective urns.

Gazing at Salvatore, Evan remembered the first time he had met him. It had been at the gas station by the police department downtown. Evan thought he was asking for trouble by the way the cop stared at him. The next thing he knew he was inviting a policeman to his home. He was pondering if this was the right thing to do, being that he had left his pot in sight, not to mention that this could be a set-up or even a hate crime. But the cop was so handsome that Evan couldn't think of anything except how nervous he was, much less thinking of the pictures of Lowla that he had out. Salvatore came in the house, and as fate would have it immediately noticed the pictures of Lowla.

Salvatore looked at an elaborate framing of art on the wall. He stepped closer to see that the female's face in the picture had been changed to represent someone else. He turned to Evan, then back to the picture. "Who is this?"

"His name is Lowla."

"Lowla? Is that you?" He pointed toward Evan. "Do you dress up like this?"

"Yes, for entertainment purposes."

"Do you think that I could meet Lowla?"

The rest became history. Sitting now on his lap, Evan was glad for the history. Even though he was dressed like Lowla, he was glad to be in the company of Salvatore . . . a dream that Evan would not have experienced otherwise. Evan was thirty-five, but looked much younger, five-foot-eleven, blond and cute . . . but a guy like Salvatore would only pass him by in a bar and not even be aware that he was in the room. Salvatore was every gay man's dream of a masculine Italian. *Quit thinking about stupid things and just enjoy this hunk.*

"Lowla."

He answered with his eyes.

"I've got a present for you." He reached into his uniform shirt pocket and pulled out a small bag filled with a white powdery substance. "Think you could handle me all night long?"

Again, he answered with his eyes.

"Well then, I think it's time to get out of this uniform. Want to help?"

Lowla stood up and kicked off his heels so that he wouldn't be taller than Salvatore. Seductively he loosened the tie then pulled him to the bedroom where Evan had been filming his show. The video camera was overlooked as they walked into the room.

"I light the blue light," Salvatore said as he proceeded to pull the black sheets off the bed.

6

The sound of the phone awakened Diva. She was a little confused; the last thing she remembered was passing out in the bedroom. Now she was sitting at her desk with the phone ringing. She picked up the receiver. "*Ciao.* Yes, darling, The Diva is on her way. The Diva will be just a few moments and then she will be on her way. The Diva is sorry to have kept you waiting, but she wanted to look her very best." Hoping her excuse sounded reasonable, she put the phone down and studied herself in the mirror. The clothes she wore were unrecognizable, and she wondered why she was dressed in clothes she had never seen. Even the watch on her arm startled her since she never wore one. It was thirty minutes past the time she had agreed to meet at *Sake's. What happened?* "Is anybody here?" she yelled and proceeded to walk around the condo looking for the person who obviously had done this to her. No one answered. No one else was there. The door was locked and the key was still in the deadbolt. *Oh well, The Diva must not have remembered.*

This had happened a couple of times before but never for this long . . . and never had she changed clothes. Again, she paused to look in the mirror in amazement at the gold and black lamé jumpsuit she was wearing. Not something that Diva would wear, but somewhat tasteful. There was no time to change clothes. She was already late for her interview with *The Rising Star* magazine. On her way out the door, she noticed a matching wrap. Diva put it around her shoulders, grabbed her purse and headed to the elevator.

There at his usual table was the gentleman waiting for Diva. Although he was tapping the fingers of his left hand with force on the table top, he managed to patiently sip on a scotch and soda. He was a relatively small man although he carried an enormous presence. He was in his forties and looked every day of it. His thinning black hair seemed to grow into his beard. He was fierce, famous, and the most sought after Hollywood agent — ever. Everybody wanted him for representation. He had many connections, more than most mafia families. He was at *Sake's* to do the interview with Diva for two reasons. One, Diva would not talk to a reporter, and since he loved publicity, he was glad to do it for *The Rising Star* magazine, and, two, he wanted Diva. He wanted her for a client as well as to parade her on his arm. Diva had managed to refuse his advances over the years, which made him want her even more. There was usually never any love in his actions, just plusses and minuses in the what-can-you-do-for-me department. If there was to ever be a love for him, it was to be Diva. He felt their ruthlessness and hunger for the spotlights to be strong common denominators. His name was Aaron Archer, and he had started in Hollywood when he was fifteen years old. After all these years, there he was, waiting. He never waited. But there he was, waiting on the unobtainable goddess known as "The Diva."

The door to the elevator opened, exposing Diva. She had on her sunglasses so that no one would recognize her as she walked across the lavish lobby to *Sake's*. It would be hard not to notice her not only because she was so striking but also that she was quite tall for a woman. The maitre d' spotted her and quickly opened the door.

"Good Afternoon, Diva."

"*Ciao*, darling."

"Mr. Archer is right over there." He extended his hand to the far corner of the dining room and proceeded to escort her to the table.

"Yes, thank you, darling, The Diva sees him and The Diva will arrive there alone." Dismissing the maitre d', she removed her sunglasses and descended the center staircase. *This restaurant is so refreshing. So many reflective surfaces.* As she neared the table, Aaron stood to greet her.

"Hello, Diva." He took her hand and kissed the top of it.

"*Ciao*, darling. The Diva is sorry to be late."

Aaron smiled, "Your loveliness erases all memory of waiting. Won't you sit down?" He released her hand and pulled the chair out for her. "I don't think I've ever seen you look so beautiful." Once she was seated, he went to the other side of the table and sat in his chair. "I've taken the liberty to order for us. I hope you don't mind. I didn't want us to be interrupted." He tried to seem business-like and not to appear to be a love-struck puppy.

"Darling, how are you going to remember everything The Diva says?" she said, holding the wrapped cloth napkin seductively in her hands.

"By taping you, of course." He pointed to his hand-held recorder.

"As long as you don't tape The Diva while she eats." She laughed her clever laugh and began to open her cloth napkin. "What is it that you want to hear from The Diva? She doesn't want to bore you with all the details on her life."

Aaron loosened his tie and pressed the record button.

"Your whole life story would be heaven to hear, but considering we only have a column why don't you tell me about your newest venture, *A Kept Reflection*? Perhaps you can tell me all about The Diva later?" He took another sip of his scotch and soda. "Are the characters in your book based on anyone in your life?"

Again, she let out her naturally unrehearsed laugh as her fingers toyed with her bangs. "Darling, characters are as fascinating as those who create them." She stared piercingly into his eyes and continued in a seductive tone. "The Diva finds it very stimulating to transfer mind to paper and forming character to developed character." The waiter served her champagne. She sipped. "Thank you, darling." Back to Aaron as the waiter exited quickly, "This is what attracts The Diva to writing. Thinking of characters, scenes and dialogue is something The Diva constantly does so it is only natural that the people in *A Kept Reflection* seem familiar because, darling, they live in here." She pointed to her head. "It has taken The Diva a long time to realize why drama is important to her. It is an art form that goes in a circle. Every part is essential, and with The Diva's enthusiasm and your guidance The Diva hopes to visualize and materialize and eventually capitalize." A smile dressed Diva's face as she took her foot and rubbed it over his ankle under the table.

"I'll drink to that," Aaron said as he lifted his glass. "Perhaps we can work on getting *A Kept Reflection* to the big screen together."

Raising her glass to meet his, "Now, darling, whatever put that thought into your head?"

7

The morning rays of sunlight began to form on the muse's face as his eyelids slowly opened. Surely he was so blessed to be waking up in these surroundings with Torch by his side. Lloyd often thought of himself as the muse of excess, a muse he would eventually introduce to the rest of the intellectual community. But for now, looking at the lavish furniture and paintings and having the sun shine on his face made him feel divine. Looking through squinted eyes, he realized that it was the light from the lamp post outside his window that had beamed through and not the sun. Nonetheless, he felt beautiful in the moment. *I must look devastating.* He gathered the comforter around his chest and slowly turned to give Torch a good-morning kiss only to find an empty bed. Lloyd lay back on the pillow and wondered where Torch could be so early. It was five a.m. and he had been awake for at least half an hour waiting for the right moment to reach over and grab Torch. One thing about Torch was that no matter what was going on or what was happening or what time it was, he liked to fuck. And Lloyd never tired of getting fucked since he thought that was one way to keep him. *Perhaps he is still here and just out of bed.*

"Torch? Honey, are you in the shower? Torch!"

No reply came. *Oh well, I guess he is gone.* Lloyd decided to get up and have a cup of coffee in his sanctuary as he loved to do at sunrise every morning . . . and then go back to bed unless he decided to go to White Hawk Manor, his house. He lived in both his house on the avenue and his upscale apartment in the French Quarter. Although he held down three jobs, he never really worked. He was a school teacher for the gifted children of the community, or as his friend Evan called him, "the old maid school teacher from Louisiana." He taught the gifted children at a local school in the city, but what he taught them was a mystery to everyone. A mystery to everyone but Lloyd, who thought he taught them sophistication as they watched soap operas in the classroom instead of discussing the current events of the day. In addition to being a school teacher, he was the manger of the family's nightclub, *Le Oui-Oui,* but only went to work to take money from the register and flirt with the bartenders. Occasionally he rehearsed the cabaret show and auditioned dancers and singers as he was himself an actor and a director with qualifications a mile long, not to mention a Masters of Fine Arts degree in drama. As if he really needed to study the dramatic arts. He was a natural.

His degree, his credits and his résumé made him feel as though he were a true theatrical professional. He had lived briefly in New York City, and *Le Oui-Oui* was the answer to getting him back to Louisiana. After appearing on a few television shows and doing successful stand-up comedy, Lloyd was on the verge of making it in the show-business industry. When his father thought he was getting too serious, it became necessary for him to coax Lloyd back to New Orleans to keep his mother occupied so his father could do other things. His father, Anthony Rochelle, got Lloyd's attention with the allure of his own nightclub in the famed French Quarter as well as his own parade for Mardi Gras.

"Why not be a big fish in a small pond?" Anthony Rochelle said firmly to his son Lloyd. "Do you really think you are going to make it in this business of entertaining? Come back and be 'King' of the Quarter. I'll make sure you have everything you want." It was obviously an offer that Lloyd embraced. The Rochelle Empire seemed to have an endless supply of money and supporters. It never hesitated to use either in order to get what it wanted.

He also drew a salary from the Rochelle's main family business, Troubled Waters, which was comprised of five showboats that dazzled the tourists up and down the Mississippi River day and night. Giving tours, playing cards, serving liquor and dancing women helped the showboats stay busy throughout the year. Between the three occupations, he had lots of spending money and all the time in which to spend it. It often confused some people how he could get away with not working, especially in the public school system. As a result, a lot of folks were jealous of Lloyd. He was the subject of a lot of gossip as he always said what was on his mind: good, bad or sexy. He really thought he could manipulate God because he had a direct connection or it seemed that way to him. But Lloyd, or Marilyn to a close few, had a heart as big as Louisiana, not to mention a ton of contacts, and he made sure everyone around him had a great, unbelievable time. He was the epitome of the modern-day Evita. He robbed from the rich and from the charities and organizations of which he was president only to give to the truly poor who would never otherwise get to see the inside of a limousine or afford to go to the high-society events of New Orleans. If anyone in his reach needed a costume or a tuxedo or a dress, he would walk them into the world of Marilyn's closet . . . a closet that was a huge room filled with mostly old news, things he would never wear again and in varying sizes as his weight had fluctuated over the years. Whatever hung in the closet he would gladly share with the needy and let them do the choosing while he watched with delighted eyes the expressions of those less fortunate on their shopping spree. The closet contained something suitable for any occasion for almost anyone.

All of these amenities were justified because someone of Lloyd's stature needed an entourage and the entourage needed to look first class. It wasn't enough that he had his own parade, his own nightclub, and a host of people around him, he had to continually top his prior successes even down to the costumes he wore during the year to the various events he sponsored. Many people went to these parties just to see Lloyd as Marilyn make a grand entrance. Usually no one was disappointed. The time he had done Cleopatra, or Cleopa-trick as he preferred to be called, he had put on a stunning exhibition of decadence. He had a bevy of Egyptian slaves around him, thirty of them to be exact. The slaves attended to his every need. They brought him in on a "carrying chair" modeled after the one belonging to Queen Hetep-heres I, preceded by his ladies in waiting who escorted exotic leopards on leashes. When his Egyptian slaves lowered the carrying chair and Cleopa-trick stood up, the crowd screamed with cheers, declaring that the legendary ruler had risen from the dead. His costume was a visual delight. His hair was at least three feet tall with a gold asp weaving its way in and out of his wig. Two gold pyramids protruded over his tits, and the lower half of his body was covered with a shiny gold sarong. The rest of his followers fanned him with palm leaves. His entourage could have been a corporation. There were many so willing to please just for a chance to be involved in his glorious but tornadic life.

As he got out of bed, a note fell to the floor. Thinking it was the note from Lowla, Lloyd stepped on it en route to the kitchen to get his coffee. *I just love the aroma so early in the morning. Thank God Torch had the decency to make coffee.* Smiling like a June bride, Lloyd went into the kitchen and passed through the parlor. Out of the corner of his eye he glanced at a note on the couch. *That must be the note Lowla sent me. And it is odd for Torch to have made coffee at this time of the morning.* As if on a dime, he spun around and ran to the bedroom to where the other note lay. "What? Another note! Can't anyone talk to my face?" He hurriedly picked it up and recognizing the handwriting as Torch's, he ripped the envelope open. A look of disbelief came over Lloyd as he read the written words from his lover.

> *Baby,*
> *I know you did a lot for me, but I never asked you to do a lot for me. You showed me a good time and maybe I asked for that. I showed you a good time because it was the least I could do for all the times you got me out of jams and all the places you took me. Wow, Tahiti was really fabulous.*
> *But, Baby, I want more. I want a bigger fish than you are. And I have found one. Justin will be able to help me in ways that you can't. You know I'm destined for the great white way. And nothing is going to stop me.*
> *I will send you an address where you can ship me all of my things. Leaving in the night doesn't allow one to pack much. I didn't want a scene and I knew you would*

have thrown yourself at my feet and promised me the moon. But you already did that and it didn't get me anywhere.

Soon, you can come and visit me in Manhattan. I know we will always keep in touch.
Torch.

P.S. Don't take this personally, huh? I took the title to the jeep out of your safe . . . and the money, too.

Lloyd did not know whether to scream or to cry. He just stood there. *How could he? After five years and all I have done, the money, the college, the car, the hateful way he treated my family. He made me his wife and now he left me.* He walked over to the phone and picked up the receiver. He dialed Evan's number and stood there like he was posing for Edvard Munch's *The Scream*. His mouth was open but there was no sound.

"Hello," answered Evan, ". . . hello?"

Lloyd fell to the ground, his mouth still open, and tried to make an audible sound into the phone. Instead he curled up and was finally able to whisper, "L – o – w – l – a."

8

He moved underneath the covers as if someone or something was chasing him in a dream. Muffled sounds were emitting from his mouth as he turned from side to side. Beside his bed stood a very tall nightstand that was home to a lamp and his phone. The phone began to ring. It continued until Evan abruptly awakened. *Am I dreaming? Oh My God! It's the phone. At this time, is someone dead?* He managed to pick up the phone. "Hello." He heard nothing but silence. "Hello!" he yelled into the receiver.

"L – o – w – l – a," the caller said in a barely audible voice.

"Marilyn, is that you?" Evan pressed the phone closer to his ear, afraid that something was terribly wrong.

"A – a – a – h."

"Marilyn, what's the matter? Is it your mother?"

"T – o – r – c – h."

"What?" Lloyd was obviously upset over something else that Torch had done. "Has he cheated on you again?"

"G – o – n – e."

"Is he dead?"

"No. He left me," Lloyd said as he started to cry.

"Well, congratulations. It's about time that ladder climber took off so you can get your life back together."

"What am I gonna do? He's really gone this time. He left for New York. I haven't felt this bad since my daddy died and left my brother Johnny in charge of the companies," Lloyd wailed into the phone. "I'm lying on the floor and I can't get up. I don't think I am gonna make it."

"Of course you're going to make it. You'll need to reinvent yourself again, like Madonna. Who would have ever thought that she got that from you all those years ago?"

"Lowla, please. This really hurts."

"Now, Marilyn, it can not be that bad. It couldn't be any worse than what we have been through already."

"It is. It is the worst thing that could happen."

"That's what you said about the time we lost our only place to live in New York City, and we survived that." Evan laughed. "Remember when we found out that we were getting kicked out of the apartment on eighty-ninth street?"

"Yes," Lloyd barely whimpered.

"You started to cry when we were about to leave. We were standing, looking at the empty place when I decided to take all of the food out of the refrigerator and smear it all over the kitchen in order to make you feel better. And it did. You quit crying and jumped right in with the mayonnaise on the counter tops. We were in a frenzy for a while with the food being thrown everywhere." Evan began to laugh again. "I'll bet the landlord was pissed when he saw the raw eggs on the ceiling and the ketchup on the walls. Now, sister, that was a good time!"

"Lowla, how can you compare an apartment with Torch?"

"You're right, Marilyn. The apartment served a purpose."
Evan looked at the clock by his bed. "Do you know what time
it is? Do you know that I have to get up and go to work to a
job that I hate?"

Ignoring Evan's redundant comments Lloyd continued
very weakly, "Lowla, I don't think I will survive. Please come
here and help me through this. I know I asked you to come
here and spy on him, and I got your reply, by the way. You
hateful bitch. But this is different; I can't get up from the
floor. My family will scream, 'I told you so!' and they will be
right." Lloyd continued to lie on the cold hardwood floor.

"What happened?"

"He left me for Justin. You know, the rich guy from New
York City that I told you about? He said he needed a bigger
fish."

"Bigger than you?"

"How dare you make fun at a time like this?"

"A time like this? This is your freedom date, write it
down. You just don't know it. You put him through college,
bought him a car and let him pull a gun on your father. And
for what? Because he had a big dick and fucked you with it
and made you feel like a fake woman? Get real. Torch was
and is a user! I didn't want to tell you, but when you came to
Atlanta to visit last December, Torch made it very clear that
he was bound for the stage in New York City and you just did
not fit in." Evan rolled over on his side and adjusted his
pillow. "Don't you remember how it was for us the late
eighties? Don't you remember who you gave up when you
were star struck?" His intonation showed no urgency. His
voice sounded as though he had said these things many
times. "You know your problem is not that it didn't work out
with Torch, but that you could not put reins on him and you
gave up so much trying to control him in every way. Try to
give back to yourself what you have freely given."

"What a great way for you to talk, Lowla. You don't have
anything to compare my relationship with Torch." Evan had

stirred up some fire in Lloyd. "All you have in your life are married men that only drop by for a few minutes and then leave you alone. What do you call that again? A drive-by shooting? I was with him for years, not minutes."

"You know sometimes, Marilyn, I wish I had never confided in you."

"Lowla, my world is over."

"And mine never began. Maybe it won't work out and he'll be crawling back to you."

"No. He's gone. He's got someone who can help his career. I've been a fool. But I won't recover. Not this time. Please come and help me."

"Let me go back to sleep." Evan turned from his side and now was lying on his back staring at the ceiling. "I had a drive-by shooting last night. You know, one of my minute relationships. But this one stayed most of the night and he just left. We did not sleep. I can't wait to tell you all about that, but I guess you wouldn't want to hear it now." He shifted his tone to one of nurture. "Listen, Marilyn, you know I will see you through this. You just need to get up off the floor and calm down. Let me call you back in a bit when I am awake and have a good frame of mind. Maybe you'll feel better by then. Why don't you go sit on your balcony and have a cup of coffee?"

"Okay. I love you."

"I love you too, Marilyn." Evan covered his mouth as he yawned.

"I may kill myself!" Lloyd said in a desperate attempt to keep Evan on the phone.

"Well, be sure you take enough penicillin."

"You'll never let me forget that, will you?"

"That among many other things . . . and remember I have pictures for proof."

Lloyd hung up the phone without saying goodbye. This time it did not bother Evan, who put the receiver in the cradle and tried to go back to sleep.

9

   Diva could not believe that she woke up with no memory of what had happened after she left to meet Aaron at *Sake's*. There were a few flashbacks of looking at herself while she was at the restaurant but all she knew now was that it was the next morning. With a glance around the room, she noticed the gold lamé outfit on the floor. *The Diva never throws her clothes on the floor.* She pulled her white sheets from her nude body, got out of bed and leaned over to pick it up. *Did The Diva really meet with Aaron Archer yesterday in this? Is she really that desperate to get The Diva's book into a film?*

   All the years she had to scratch her way to the top just to become "Queen of the 'B' movies" couldn't have been in vain. She thought that maybe in a fleeting moment she had destroyed all hopes for her strategies to make a first-class film out of her book. Aaron could make her or break her and she knew it. But she had watched herself anyway in the mirrors at the restaurant instead of looking at him. Diva paced nervously along the hallway of her 'L' shaped apartment, wondering if her self-indulgent attitude had offended him. *If The Diva could only think of what he said or she said between the minutes The Diva remembers and doesn't remember. What did The Diva say?* She walked from the front of her place which was composed of the living room and kitchen area to the back which led to the bathroom, dressing room and her bedroom. The exterior wall along the hallway was adorned with her treasures. She stood in front of one of her many movie posters which accompanied the hanging mirrors. Diva extended her hand to touch the glass that shielded the poster of her greatest movie to date. The movie was a remake of an earlier classic that had been an academy award vehicle for Joan Crawford. She had believed with all her heart that this film would have made her a huge star. *Who wouldn't cheer for a story about a hard working African-American woman who makes good honestly? Apparently the public.* The movie had only played in a handful of cities since it was slated as "selected release" and not nationwide. Her hand caressed the image of her face as she mouthed, "Mildred Pierce." The story had been renamed "The White Elephant" against her wishes.

She looked at the poster and came to the conclusion that at thirty-five her empire was slipping and she needed to be back in the eye of the public again. Although she had been in an impressive number of films and plays, she had never been nominated for any kind of award, not even for "The White Elephant," which cut her to the bone since, in her opinion, it was her best work. Her worth at the box office had fallen, and that was why she needed to manipulate Aaron to get a movie deal. Even so, the Los Angeles-born Diva had managed to create an air about her which led one to believe she was truly a worthy star. Earlier in her career she listed on her bio that she was born in Antigua. She had learned to speak with a low-key British tone to her voice in order to give her an edge over the American models and actresses. Most of her money had come from fashion and the company she kept. But Diva Aneicia Borro always landed on her feet. As long as her hair was done, Diva could face anything except maybe last night.

Surely he would not have taken offense while she stared at herself and not him. After all, he wanted to interview her. Vanity never entered her mind as a possibility for her behavior and she did not understand why some people called her vain. The long sessions or the quick glances into mirrors or reflective surfaces were simply forms of maintenance and priority. To call her behavior obsessive was like explaining immigration to an illegal alien. Diva was simply The Diva, lost in her own world, a legend in her own mind.

Pacing around the room this morning Diva couldn't help but notice a tiny scratch on her arm. She stopped and stepped closer to the mirror for inspection. The scratch mark became intensified then blurred. Immediately Diva looked straight into the mirror but was not looking at herself in the same way.

The tiny scratch had become irrelevant. Her hands quickly rose to the back of her hair and she began to twist her weaves into a bun as she sauntered over to her vanity without even once looking at herself. Humming a snappy tune, she sat in the chair and with a free hand grabbed a hair comb and secured the bun to the back of her head. *Girl, you got to change this funky-ass makeup. I am going to take a shower, change and get out of this place. Why am I thinking inside of my head when there is no one here?*

"And I can say anything I want out loud since 'The Diva' bitch ain't here! Yes, I said it. You heard me. B – i – t – c – h! Oh, that feels so good. It just makes me want to shout and kick my heels up! Scream and holler. Oh, it is so nice to talk and not whisper. This getting in control of things is becoming easier, my dear." Talking to herself in the mirror, she said, "Let's keep it that way. *I*, yes *I — me — myself*, wonder what I am going to wear today since I premiered the gold lamé suit I got weeks ago. It was murder just waiting for a chance to wear it, bitch!" She started toward the closet. "And you are a stupid bitch, too. Didn't even read your credit card statement or you would have known why you woke up in that outfit yesterday. 'Oh, where did this come from?'" she said, imitating Diva's fake British accent. "But I guess you will never know why it was on the floor this morning." She laughed as she said, "But Aaron does!

"Oh, stop it! You are so wicked. Yes, Diva, excuse me, I mean, 'The Diva,' I am talking to you. You never made it to *Sake's*, well maybe for a minute or two just to look at yourself. I took over in the elevator and I did a damn fine impression of you, I must say. At least Aaron thinks so. Why, he smiled all the way through dinner and almost choked when I, 'The Diva impersonator,' suggested that he come up for a cocktail. Honey, he almost tripped over his tongue saying yes." She picked up a picture of Diva and held it in one hand. "Diva, I don't know whether or not you'll get anything out of last night, but you can rest well knowing that I gave all you had to give." She placed the picture back on the shelf.

She made her way to the shower acknowledging all the mirrors — all the reflections of who Diva thought she was. Turning on the water in the shower, she turned to the bathroom sink. Having her hair back like that, and with a make-up change, she wouldn't have any resemblance to Diva. Like Diva, she paused to study herself in the mirror. The difference was that she did not want to resemble the star. *I can be a new person with a new life. I don't have to be her. I can be . . . I need a name.* A big smile came across her face. She stepped into the shower to greet the water with visions of dreams in her head. *Finally to be let out of prison for a new life, a fun life. Maybe even a life of love.* With those thoughts, she settled in for a long hot shower.

10

Although Evan hung up the phone and closed his eyes, he was unable to go back to sleep. He was half hoping that Lloyd wouldn't suffer too long . . . Lloyd had a tendency to hold on to things, especially things that offered him a chance to star in his own tragic melodramas . . . and half worrying about his future and the way Lloyd talked about drive-by shootings. Evan could not figure out why he was always involved with married men when there was no hope for a relationship, except they seemed to be easier to get and always available. Besides, he needed some reassurance that he was attractive even if only as Lowla or as a temporary sex object. Evan hit his head! *Eureka, I am a fool.* Thinking he was a fool was something Evan did every day and lying in bed with those thoughts was not helping. He decided to get up and do something positive like call in sick to work. A mental health day was urgently needed. He dialed the voicemail number of his manager and breathed in a deep breath in order to talk through it when he left the message that he would not be in to work this day. It always made him sound sick when he spoke through held breath.

With that minor detail completed, Evan decided to get some old pictures and enhance them on the computer. Maybe then he would get started organizing his pictures into all of the empty photo albums he had. It would take a real effort; there were three large boxes of photos mixed with various pieces of his writings and nine photo albums, which might not be enough, but he didn't care because he probably would never finish it anyway. Before picking a stack of pictures at random, he put various show tunes on the compact disc player, pushed "play" and knelt there, listening for a moment. Evan danced his way back to the stack of work, spun and grabbed pictures. Without looking at them, he sat at his desk to prepare new masterpieces to join the ones on the wall that he already had done. His work was displayed with posters of movies and Broadway shows which adorned the hallway and other areas of the home. Evan took his favorite movies, posed as Lowla in the position of the star, then printed out his picture. As soon as the scissors cropped the image, he would glue it onto the poster so it looked as though he were in the film. After that, he would attach his name, starring Lowla, over the film credits. Among his cherished wall art were his versions of the 1933 movie poster of "King Kong," followed by the 1950 version of "Sunset Boulevard," which hung next to the 1935 movie poster of "Goin' to Town" and the 1958 movie poster of "Auntie Mame." His favorite was not of a movie at all, but of the *Wagons-Lits,* "The Golden Arrow." He thought that he looked best on that poster as the lady in the red dress that stood by the deco train, looking as lost as the heroine in *A Streetcar Named Desire.* He hoped that one day someone would notice his efforts and encourage him to be a professional photographer. He could not do that himself; he had no ambition or confidence in singing self praises of any kind. He was waiting for a man to do that for him. Admiring the creation of his photos gave him a necessary lift, and he realized he was at least halfway happy at the moment.

Smiling, he started going through the three-by-five-and-one-half's and stopped to focus intently on the second one. It was a black-and-white picture that he had taken when he and Lloyd were in Egypt. The sun was setting and they were in a Faluka, an Egyptian sailboat, on the Nile River in Cairo.

The picture activated his memory of that very day. He and Lloyd, also known as Lowla and Marilyn, had just returned from a tour of the Valley of the Kings. They stood at the bank of the river noticing all of the small boats for hire when an Egyptian boy came and asked the very American-looking tourists if they wanted to ride in his Faluka on the Nile. It was only "three USD" for the both of them to be carried on the famous river. Lloyd asked him his name and the boy replied, "Hapi, which means God of the Nile." The young man looked to be about fourteen and had been hustling other tourists to ride in his boat, impressing Lloyd and Evan with his ability to converse in several other languages before he came to ask them in English. Of course they accepted. Lloyd was anxious to get off the retainer wall plaza and get closer to the other men who were offering boat rides.

Once Evan and Lloyd were in the boat, Hapi pushed them off with a long pole pressed against the floor of the river and guided them into the majestic water known as The Nile. Evan and Lloyd immediately got lost in the moment as they both imaged themselves to be Egyptian Royalty sitting in the rear of the craft while their hands dangled off on the left side and off on the right. Evan was praying, saying to God how blessed he was to be able to touch the ancient water and how grateful he was for such a wonderful opportunity. In the background he heard Lloyd inquiring about a place called *Banana Island*. Apparently the young Faluka boy had told Lloyd that if it were earlier he would take them to *Banana Island*. "It is a beautiful island not far from Cairo in the Nile," he said as he pointed downriver. Hapi was encapsulated in a dark silhouette and Evan took the opportunity to take a picture to remember the beautiful moment. Hapi encouraged the pair to come back the next day. But Lloyd had a different plan.

Drifting back to the banks of the river was bittersweet. Evan wanted to stay on the water longer, but sunset was making way for the darkness. Getting out of the boat, he hoped that he would see this water again. On the way back to the plaza, the gold dust twins, as they called themselves since they were both blond and favored, walked by all the boats. Lloyd kept suggestively looking at the older young men.

"Stop that, Marilyn. You're going to get us arrested," Evan said as they neared the stairs. Just as he was getting to the first step he heard, "Want to see my boat?" He turned to the left and saw that Lloyd had stopped to converse with a boat owner. The man was pointing to the small doors at the stern of the boat.

"Banana Island?" Lloyd said innocently.

"You want to go to Banana Island?" He seductively slid his hands on his hips.

"No, I want to see Banana Island!" Lloyd yelled in his husky New Orleans voice as the boat owner roared with laughter.

"Lloyd!" Evan came closer to them. "I think it's time that we go back to the *Mena House*."

"Evan you can go back up on the plaza. I'm going to see Banana Island." Lloyd turned to the twenty-something-year-old man. "And what is your name?"

"Abasi."

"Abasi. That's very Egyptian. What does that mean?"

The young man looked confused and said, "What is your name?"

"Marilyn."

At that, Abasi extended his hand to help Lloyd get onto the boat. Once there, Lloyd sat on the bench located by the two-foot-high doors which concealed the tiny compartment in the stern. The young Egyptian slid the doors apart and crawled inside. By this time Evan had made it up the stairs to the plaza and was watching, from above, the smooth operator below he had lovingly come to call Marilyn. Evan snickered as Lloyd could not fit all the way into the compartment so he had to position his legs to hang over the bench while his upper body was hidden. Passersby on the riverbank and on the plaza watched with amazement and speculated as to what was going on . . . that maybe the guy was stuck and wiggling just to get loose.

The sweat was beading on Evan's forehead in worry that Lloyd might get them into some serious trouble, although he too could not take his eyes off of "tourists gone wild." *Why is it that I am the one always worrying and he is the one always having fun? Why can't I be like that?* Lloyd's legs stopped wiggling. *I guess it must be over.* Evan stood, slightly embarrassed although no one knew he was with "legs." He began to hear muffled noises from the direction of the boat. Most of the other Faluka owners began to gather and laugh. *He's stuck. I know it.* One of the men on the riverbank motioned for Evan to come down, and reluctantly he did so. When he got down to the Faluka, he could hear Lloyd screaming for Evan to pull him out. And so, there they were, on the Nile River, one pulling the legs of another while the curious watched and whistled.

Loud laughter came out of Evan as he held that picture tightly. If it hadn't been for Lloyd, he would have never been able to do some of the things he had done. Like that trip to Egypt. Lloyd paid for the air fare, the restaurants, the hotels and the tours. They ate at the best places and stayed at the Mena House in Cairo. Their hotel-room window had a fantastic view of the Great Pyramid and Lloyd made sure they arrived on the evening of a full moon. Lloyd was just crazy about moons, especially full ones. All Evan had to do was bring personal spending money. That was the kind of a friend that Lloyd was. Loyalty was all he really expected in return. Evan would be forever indebted for all of the generosity shown to him by Lloyd.

Evan and Lloyd were best friends, always, no matter the time or distance between them. Mostly Evan thought of Lloyd as Marilyn. Reason and need helped them to form a sisterhood that allowed no other sisters into their secret kingdom. They chose sisterhood because they had always been close to women and could not relate to brotherhood. Evan and Lloyd were not so much effeminate as much as they wanted to be pursued by men. Both of them carried large body frames with big hands and feet. They were actually beautiful masculine sissies. Although they could look out the same door and see different worlds, they believed that they were meant to be put on pedestals like husbands were supposed to do for their wives. Being a wife was something that they both aspired to be since they had been trained by their mothers to be subservient to men. They believed they could have sex with any man, either together or alone. Thoughts of their escapades went through Evan's mind. When he and Lloyd teamed together it was about the capture and not each other. He laughed thinking that they never touched the other as it was all about the attention they gave the victim. He sighed thinking that the biggest mistake was to look for husbands rather than take advantage of all of the wealth at their feet. *Why didn't we create a business instead of thumbing our noses at potential partners who could have loved and helped us? Why did we look for the one that would allow us a live-for-him syndrome?*

The next items Evan saw were two neatly folded articles he had written. They turned out to be *Ten Rules On How to Keep a Sponsor* and one which had been published in a gay rag magazine, *The Big Dipper*, entitled, *About My Sister, Marilyn*. He put down the other items in his hand and read what he had written seventeen years ago.

ABOUT MY SISTER MARILYN

About my sister Marilyn . . . well he could walk by

anything that showed him a reflection and would instantly stop to comb his hair and then smile like he was hanging on a wall in the "Met" or something. Sometimes he would strike a pose as the most desirable — the most beautiful — the most fulfilling . . . an imitation of a silent screen siren . . . or in a glimpse as the pretty boy he really was. At that time, my sister, Marilyn, needed a man who could fulfill him in the role of a woman or at least tame him with fried chicken or watermelon. You could be walking and talking with Marilyn only to find out that you are walking and talking alone because he had become occupied with food or a man.

About my sister, Marilyn, he taught his followers how to throw a man by the way side once you've captured then broken his heart. "Lowla, honey, answer the phone and tell my gentleman caller that I am in bed or sick or at work. Whatever, just sound sincere?" I always did what Marilyn told me to do even though, secretly, I wanted to tell his always handsome gentleman callers, "About my sister, Marilyn, he doesn't want you, but I do!"

One thing for sure about my sister, Marilyn, once he snagged a man, it was over; kind of like when he came he was gone. He had left many a puzzled man who thought they were just getting started in the love making process. Love! It was a conquest. He would only look back to see the hurt, wounded glances from his innocent prey.

Speaking of hurt and wounded, about my sister, Marilyn — he introduced me to Confederate soldiers a hundred years after the war! "Attention," he would say in a military voice as we would travel to scope out the soldiers. A Confederate soldier was any male that looked like he was straight and in the armed forces. We would usually hang out by the prison waiting for the newly released or in the ghetto trying to spot Mandingo. There was a definite art in getting a guy to come with us, not to leave out the fear there could be violence. There was much success in picking them up and then taking them to

Marilyn's house while we took turns "nursing" the soldier. There are even pictures of our prizes.

About my sister, Marilyn, he would always say, "Don't worry, I'm driving and I will always come out on top even if I have to be on the bottom to do it!" Considering his successes from Parades to Charity Events to Night Clubs to a celebrated emcee of the French Quarter, he has come out on top! He does have a heart of gold (I saw him buy it) as long as he is in charge. Always the perfect host, confidant and friend, his generosity had not only shown me the world but also how to share it.

You could always hear my sister, Marilyn, say, "I'm so ugly, it's no wonder that only hundreds of men want me instead of thousands," as he combed his blond locks and picked pubic hairs off of his beautiful face. Among the hundreds of men he had were airline pilots, priests, bank presidents, Emmy winners, bums off the street and even gangsters. He never let men's professions stand in his way of breaking men's hearts.

About my sister, Marilyn, I've seen him go from sitting in the ghettos to sitting on the Sphinx at midnight looking at all of the people praying below him, then asking an hired Egyptian guide with a gun for a cigarette, lighting it and saying, "Does anyone ever come here to fuck?" I've seen him grow from a lovely skinny boy to a defiant President of La Moulin Rouge Carnival charity in New Orleans to the loving grandchild of a rescued grandmother. I've seen him, once, actually give up a summer trip in order to feel more secure about life and his direction. I've seen him go from living with me to seeing me four to six times a year. I've seen him pursue his dreams just to stomp on the dreams of others. I've seen him feed the hungry. I've seen the hungry feed him. I've seen him loving, angry, and I've seen him go to other friends just to see him come back to me.

With my sister, Marilyn, it's hard being the ugly one, although he has never made me feel that way. Instead, he has given me so much and put up with too much from me. I can't help but wonder why I am so lucky for God to have given me my sister, Marilyn.

For my sister, Marilyn, I wish him the happiness and success he has never found although he searches endlessly. I wish that he never give up, and mainly I wish for his much awaited autobiographical novel to be released titled appropriately: Poor Little Marilyn, Everything At Last.

And in closing, if you are riding through the streets of the French Quarter and happen to see some well dressed whore hanging out of a balcony in the sky, you should know it is about my sister, Marilyn.

Evan remembered how mad Lloyd got when that article hit the newsstands in *The Big Dipper* magazine. He tried for years to explain that it was not a personal attack. It was a loving tribute to Marilyn. Lloyd's name was never mentioned. Even though it was all true, who would believe all that stuff really happened anyway? Evan was just trying to break into writing. He had been working on a book for twenty years now as well as several plays and articles yet to be published. Everything Lloyd touched seemed to turn to gold while everything that Evan touched seemed to turn out to be trash. It was a coincidence that *About My Sister, Marilyn* was the one that got published.

Evan had really wanted his *10 Rules On How to Keep a Sponsor* to be in *The Big Dipper* but was rejected. A sponsor was a name Evan gave to the current rich man in his life. They weren't interested in marriage, but the gifts and the money and the restaurants and the plays made the lonely nights worth it. They got what they wanted; Evan got entertained and educated. He couldn't help but go down memory lane again with the prose of long ago.

10 RULES ON HOW TO KEEP A SPONSOR

I. SPOT A SUCKER. Suckers are easy to find. Actually you probably will not have to look for one. He will introduce himself via drinks coupled with compliments about you.

II. ESTABLISH THE RELATIONSHIP IN YOUR FAVOR.

Let him know:
— That you are just friends.
— Although you are not a virgin, you do not sleep around until you "know" someone.
— That it takes you about ten years to "know" a person.
— That you have your youth and his is fading, rapidly.
Accept any kindness if:
— He knows there aren't any strings attached.
— You act very happy, but not indebted, to receive it.

III. NO MATTER WHAT HE GIVES YOU OR HOW DRUNK YOU MAY BE — NEVER SAY MUSHY OR ULTRA KIND REMARKS. ALWAYS KEEP YOUR WIT AND YOUR STYLE.

IV. OCCASIONALLY THREATEN TO LEAVE.

V. LEARN TO BE AN EXCELLENT LIAR.

Can you fake:
— A cold?
— A headache?
— A busy schedule?
— An orgasm?
— An enjoyable evening
— Any excuse?

VI. ACCUSE HIM OF FLIRTING AND HAVING OTHER AFFAIRS. KEEP HIM JEALOUS AND ENVIOUS OF HIMSELF.

VII. WARNING SIGNALS.

When he is irritable or tries to start an argument, you must:
— Act hurt.
— Turn the tables as usual.
He complains about spending money on you:
— Immediately say, "Did I ever ask you to?"
— Follow with "You know these gifts (or money) have nothing to do with our 'friendship.'" (Emphasize friendship).

VIII. ALWAYS FEEL YOU ARE RIGHT.

IX. NEVER FEEL ANY GUILT. SUCKERS ASK FOR IT.

X. ALWAYS LOOK YOUR BEST!

After Evan read his efforts from the past he sighed heavily, thinking that he could have done something with his life other than the niche he had carved so neatly into a rut. He became afraid that God would not forgive him for all of his mistakes and his split-second foolishness or for his thinking that love was pleasure of the flesh and control of the mind. Daily he woke up and found that he was lost and always had been lost. So where to go from here? Why bother? Misery had become the nature of his mental state while aging had become the nature of his body. The two never got along very well. His soul wanted to sing. His body wanted to garden. Addiction stepped in to pass the time; precious time. Time wasted is never refunded. Looking around at his pathetic prison of a fantasy life behind closed doors, he couldn't figure out how he was going to change. The feeling was too overwhelming, so Evan headed to the bedroom and lay down in the bed. He put his face into his pillow and thought about all of the things he had written, all the chances he had and all of the books, magazines, plays, and articles he had read. And yet he could not read the handwriting on the wall.

11

Still trying to think of a new name for herself, she stood under a hot shower and started to sing and dance, which was something Diva did not do. Surprised at the sound of her voice, she crooned louder until laughter erupted from her. Could it be that she was happy and in control of life? With that thought she shut off the water so she could go out and enjoy what life had to offer since she had to make up for lost time. She towel dried herself and looked at the clock, then looked at it again in disbelief. Two hours had passed since she started showering.

Other than to get dressed she did not know what to do first. *Get out of the house.* In Diva's closets, she walked back and forth looking for something to wear. Diva had three closets of clothes but nothing really appealed to her. Finally she found a form-fitting short sleeveless dress that was full of green sequins. Holding it up in front of the mirror, she decided this was it. It was something that Diva would never wear, as she always looked like a fashionable aristocrat and not some party girl in her twenties. She squeezed into the outfit and was pleased to look so youthful. She hurried to the vanity to add just a touch of make-up. Once the new face was on, she had to decide what to do with her hair. Since she had already pinned it back, she decided to look for a hat. The Diva's long hair had become a trademark and she needed to hide all resemblance of Diva.

On one of the closets' top shelf were several boxes just begging to be opened. The first produced an ugly hat, and so did the next and the one after that. The last box into which she dove was a delight as it produced several wigs. She snatched up the short-bobbed 'fro and put it on her head. Almost screaming with happiness she twirled around, thinking that she was the "T." There she was in a stunning dress and a stunning wig. All she needed were earrings and shoes. Rummaging through all of Diva's accessories, she found a cute pair of diamond earrings and a flawless pair of hi-heels. Putting the shoes on, she noticed the name inside the shoe, Beverly's of Rodeo Drive. Hurriedly she went to the full length mirror to see herself from wig to shoe. She stopped and stood there, dead panned at her reflection, almost wanting to release a tear. As Aaron had said the day before, a vision of loveliness stared back at her: tall, proud, and beautiful and, in her opinion, not favoring Diva at all.

This was the first time she had ever stood in hi-heels; Diva wore flats since she was so tall. She liked her statuesque physique so much that instantly a name popped into her mind, and *Beverly Heels* was born. Smiling, she knew that she was going to step all over Hollywood and "The Diva." Beverly practiced walking through the house in her spikes, getting accustomed to walking in them. She went from place to place in the house mainly trying to find money or charge cards. She discovered a total of three quarters when she remembered that Diva kept her money in a safe. Beverly did not know the combination but made a mental note to have Diva write it down if she ever showed up again. The only thing to do was to go out and take what she wanted. Yes, shoplift. Why not? If Beverly got caught, Diva would naturally have to pay. Such excitement awaited her. Beverly got a purse and filled it with the keys and the quarters. On her way to exit the condo, the view of the city caught her eye. She walked over to the window. Beverly looked out of the eleventh floor at the scenery which lay before her. She couldn't wait to feed her appetite for adventure. She then headed to the door to leave on a bound-to-be-memorial outing.

Inserting the key in the door, she heard the phone. *Should I dare answer it?* She listened to the rings. It was the fourth one before she decided to go to the phone bench and pick up.

"Hello, I mean, *ciao!*" she said, suppressing her laughter while trying to remember to enunciate in a British tone. "Aaron? Aaron, darling, how good of you to call — phone the Diva. I . . ." Oops — *remember who I'm supposed to be*, ". . .The Diva feels so wonderful today." Her hands moved up and down her dress. "Me too, The Diva feels it must have been last night. The Diva has not stopped smiling since. What is The Diva up to? You know that is not polite to ask. But for you, The Diva will tell that she is just going out to, uh, 'pick up' a few things." She suppressed more laughter. "Tonight? The Diva should say no on such a short notice but The Diva is compelled to say yes. Eight o'clock it is then. *Ciao*, darling."

Beverly hung up and proceeded out on her shopping spree, wondering what she would pick up to wear for her date with Aaron. *The Diva is just going to shit when she finds out.*

12

He walked into a restroom and didn't recognize his reflection. He saw men he recognized but didn't know their names. They asked him what he was doing in there. "Looking for a urinal," he responded as he pushed through the line of guys blocking his way. He stormed past them and found them all gone except one, totally naked, posing in front of Evan, enticing him to have sex. Just as the man had both hands caressing his face putting pressure on each one of his cheeks as to pull him down, Evan's father appeared. His father was about to speak when a ringing sound interrupted the somewhat-blissful moment.

He opened his eyes regretting that the dream wasn't allowed to continue. What really bothered him was not only that his father was in this dream but also that he had this dream about seven times now. Each time there was more and more detail but it never went any further than it had just now. *This better be good.*

"Good morning."

"Lowla?"

"Yes, Marilyn. Good morning."

"Are you all right?"

"I think so, why?"

"You haven't called."

"It's only been a couple of hours," Evan tried to infuse sympathy into his voice.

"It's almost been two days."

"I guess the dream I've been having is lasting a lot longer than I thought. I can not believe I have slept this long. I'm going to be in such trouble." Evan looked at the clock franticly and got out of bed. "I'm so sorry not to have called you. How are you? Any news from Torch?"

"Lowla, honey, I needed you so much yesterday morning. You'll never believe . . . on the way into the school building, you know the one I took you to introduce you to the principal that I wanted to hook you up with?"

"Yes, Marilyn, and if I haven't told you lately, I am grateful for all the hooking you have done for me." Silence was all Evan heard in the receiver. "Marilyn, are you still there?"

"Yes. As I was saying, on the way into the school I just lost it and threw myself on the grass lawn crying and having the students looking at me. I had my cell phone and I was leaving you a sobbing message. I guess you'll hear it when you get out of bed."

"You're kidding? You actually threw yourself on the school lawn during school hours? And called me? And I am out of bed, by the way. I've got to let my dogs out, poor babies, and feed them, too." Evan made his way to the kitchen as his dogs followed behind.

"It was wild. It took three maintenance men to get me to my feet and back to the car. I stayed in the car until I got my nephew to get someone to come help me. It was awful. I hope I still have a job. I hope you still have a job 'cause I'll bet you haven't called in sick for this day."

"I would be so lucky to be asked to leave that place. I will call as soon as I get off the phone with you." Evan opened the back door to let his pets out into the yard. "I called in yesterday so I will just tell them how sorry I am that I was so sick that I slept through the entire day, and if they were so worried why didn't they call me? Or maybe they did. I'll check my messages first." His stomach was empty. He went to the cabinet and took out a loaf of bread to make a sandwich. "What is that noise? Where are you?"

"I'm at school," Lloyd sighed.

"Can't the kids hear you?" Evan questioned.

"No, they are watching soap operas."

"Aren't you afraid that you are going to get in trouble letting those kids watch TV?" Evan spread peanut butter on his bread.

"No one ever checks on me and the kids would rather do this anyway." Lloyd said, catching a glimpse of the TV screen.

Evan took a bite of his sandwich, "So how are you coping today? Has he called?"

"No, not yet and I am sure he will. He needs his leather jacket. Do you want it? I bought that for him for our anniversary." Lloyd began to cry. "No. No more tears. That is one of the things I am calling about. Lowla, I am going to pick myself up. I can pick up any man, why not pick up me? Hold on, Lowla." Lloyd addressed the students, "Sit down and learn something. This is not recess. You can learn a lot from Erica Kane, trust me." He talked back into the receiver. "The only way I could ever get him to come home is to be happy and to be successful. So successful that he will come crawling on his knees to Mama."

"If any of my friends could ever make it, it is you, Marilyn. All that talent and all those smarts, you should be a millionaire on your own by now. I mean, come on, get something started so I can quit my job and come work for you."

"You could always come work for Troubled Waters or *Le Oui-Oui*."

"Your brother doesn't want me working for the family businesses."

"That's not true. Johnny likes you."

"Marilyn, I am not a dancing girl or a bartender and I am too old to be a bar back. Besides it wouldn't give me enough money to survive."

"Lowla, how many times do I have to tell you, you don't need any rent money. You can live with me." Lloyd leaned back in his chair and used his pencil to scratch his head.

"But I have my house here and . . . "

"You always have an excuse," blurted Lloyd, "so what excuse are you going to have for this?"

"For what?" Evan said curiously.

"You remember those people who do drag shows by the beach? The place I went last year and had such a good time? You know, The Miss Niceville Pageant. You should be the next Miss Niceville."

"I probably wouldn't win that contest. Those people are professional." Evan finished his sandwich and got a soda.

"First of all, it's a pageant, not a contest, Lowla. Well maybe there are a few title holders, but mostly these are college friends that have been going to Niceville for sixteen years now every year at Memorial Day. And year after year they put on a pageant on Saturday night and then on Sunday night anyone can perform. They all dress up in drag and you will have fun. It could be a lot of new friends for you because a lot of them live in Atlanta. You'll have a chance to perform and win. Lowla, you're going to be my horse. I want you to win. Then the following year you get to put on the pageant — with my help, of course. Most of the contestants will be so drunk that they would not even know their words. Last year, Craven Fame, who should have won, came in first as Miss Memorial Gay instead of Miss Niceville." Lloyd peered over the students.

"Craven Fame? What a name! I'm just plain Lowla."

"We can fix that. We'll make it Lowla something or another."

"I don't know, Marilyn. You know how I am in front of a crowd." Evan opened the can of soda.

"Lowla, you will love these people."

"Where is Niceville?" he said as he gulped his beverage.

"It's in Florida just north of Fort Walton Beach. Lowla, you'll be fourteen miles from the Gulf. You know you just love the beach. I'll pay your way."

"It's not the money, Marilyn, I am afraid to perform."

"You'll be great and they are the best to have as a first audience. Besides, you'll win Miss New Talent if anything. You have to be brand new to win that one, and all of the other contestants so far are the ones who did not win last year or the year before."

"How many contestants are there and if it is not a contest, why do you call the participants contestants?"

"Lowla, your last name should be Einstein. There are four and I don't know why pageants are not called contests, all I know is you'll fit right in and if not, there are the tree trails surrounding the park. You like those, don't you?" Lloyd spoke in a whispered voice to make sure the students did not hear. "There may even be a married man in the bushes. You remember that I told you it was mostly a gay trailer park, although some straight people go too, nestled in the park by Choctawhatcee Bay? Everybody rents a trailer that can hold up to four. All of the meals and the booze and the shows are in the Niceville Trailer Park Recreational Center. And you can't beat the price. It is cheap. Only two hundred fifty dollars for the whole weekend. You want to be a performer, don't you?"

"I am a performer," Evan said defiantly.

"I mean in public," Lloyd laughed, then shouted to his students: "I said sit down and be quiet. Listen to what Erica has to say!"

"Will they let girls enter in the pageant?"

"Sure, why not? Men and women go. Straight men and women, although there will be more gays and lesbians, but everyone is treated with respect. Look, I've got to go. These kids are driving me crazy. Besides it's almost lunch and I hear fried chicken calling my name."

They both laughed.

"You do love your fried chicken and your watermelon."

"Not to mention our Confederate soldiers!"

"Okay, Marilyn, I'll go."

"Good. The next time I talk to you I want to know what you are going to do for talent and presentation. The theme this year is 'Midnight at the Oasis.' Don't worry about your clothes; I'll have Chalmette make you everything." Lloyd hung up quickly.

Click was all Evan heard. Sometimes Lloyd never said goodbye, just disconnected. It really irritated Evan when he did that. *Wake me up and shake me up and then click.* He finished his soda and went into the bathroom. The light was on and he saw Lowla's things draped over the shower rod. He took this as a sign that entering Miss Niceville was a good thing. Besides, he really wanted some local friends and since a lot of the Niceville group lived in Atlanta, he felt it was a good match. He posed for the mirror, imagining how good he would look in his costumes handmade by Chalmette, the busiest and best costume designer and dress maker in New Orleans.

Whatever am I going to do for "Midnight at the Oasis?" He let his thoughts run wild since he would have Lloyd's money and Chalmette's talent backing him. Now all Evan had to do was come up with some great ideas. Still, he felt a little nervous. *Oh my God, I've got to call work.* As he hurried back to the bedroom to call his employer, Stars and Pipes, an industrial plumbing distributor, it occurred to him that he should invite one of his longtime friends to Niceville. She could even be a contestant. *It's been a while and she does want to be a stand-up comic. This will help her get her feet wet and I won't feel so alone being new all by myself.*

He dialed a number. Took in a deep breath. "Hello, Ross, it's Evan. I am so sorry I didn't call sooner" . . . he took in more air, ". . . but I just was in a deep sleep all day with this fever. I guess this flu really took it out of me." He inhaled once more. "Yes, sir. Thank you, I really appreciate it." He breathed again. "I'll be in tomorrow. Thank you. Bye." He laughed as he again pulled the wool over his bosses' eyes.

Hitting the "new-call" button, he dialed his good friend from years ago. *This will be great. I can't wait to hear the Diva's voice.*

13

They came from the bayous of Louisiana to become a family of *nouveaux riche* who had worked hard and gotten lucky. The father was a genius at starting businesses. The mother was simply beautiful, which was all she needed at the time. Nothing pretentious about them; whatever they thought, they said.

He arrived at seven to endure the evening at his mother's. Lloyd had expected it to be just the two of them, but his brother and his nephew were there as well so it was the usual fare of good food and loud arguments. When Lloyd, his mother Renee, Johnny and his son, Johnny Ray, were in one room together, they usually argued. Mostly the Rochelles argued about money. In a way, they were the poorest of rich people, always saying they never had anything when it was evident they were not hurting. It usually was Lloyd that caused the friction because he felt as though he had not been represented fairly since his father's death and that he deserved a fairer percentage in all the family's businesses. "You're making me survive on a school teacher's salary," Lloyd screamed at Johnny.

"We pay your car note, your car insurance, your groceries and your utilities. And you have a grand apartment in the French Quarter by the nightclub so you can sleep there when you work late so you won't have to hurry to school. Ha. Ha. You don't work at all. Tell me any other school teacher that makes forty grand a year and lives and dresses like you do, drives a new car and has a house on Saint Charles Avenue and a two-thousand-dollar-a-month apartment in the Quarter? Your excesses have to stop. That apartment has to go." Johnny started to leave the room.

"All of you use the apartment, too. White Hawk Manor was a deal and you know it. It takes money to run a house of that size and have a maid to take care of Grandma. I was the only one who took her in." Lloyd pounded his hand on his chest.

Turning back to Lloyd, Johnny spoke in a low tone. "Grandma was part of the deal for you to get that house. We sold her house as a down payment for yours."

"And my monthly house note is a whole lot cheaper than a nursing home, isn't it? And what about your friends and your business associates over at my house enjoying every Mardi Gras parade that comes down Saint Charles Avenue? I'm the one who has all the food and booze and has the viewing stand built. Every frigging holiday is spent at my house for that matter."

"If we gave you any more money, you would only spend it on someone like Torch," his nephew screamed as he jumped to his feet.

"Johnny Ray. Shut up. Why should you have anything to do with what I get or not? Or how I live? I don't see your ass suffering any. And your friends are always there, too"

"All you do is take and take. You never think about anybody but yourself." Johnny Ray moved closer to Lloyd's face. "Your friends seem to make it on their salaries."

Lloyd just looked at Johnny Ray. He was almost an identical image of his father: dark hair with a pleasing face. One would never know just to look at his medium frame and his masculine looks that he could be so ruthless. "You have really grown up to be the man, haven't you?" He pushed Johnny Ray back a few steps. "All college educated and big business experienced and you know what's best for this family and this business, don't you?"

"Yes," answered Johnny Ray. He pushed his uncle back,

and with a big smile on his face, added, "And that is why Grandma and Daddy made me President of Troubled Waters Incorporated this morning while you were having breakfast at Tiffany's. Because this company is in trouble and I am the only one who can save it!"

Lloyd felt as though he had just been slapped. "Mother, is that true?" Lloyd said breathlessly, glaring at Renee in a state of disbelief.

Renee looked up at her sons and her grandson. "You all are driving the nails in my coffin. What do you want me to do? I thought I was doing the best for this family and for this company."

"Doing the best for this family? What? By listening to Johnny and Johnny Ray until they have succeeded in getting me totally out of the picture? Mother, how could you do this to me? I thought you loved me? This ain't over yet." Lloyd grabbed his jacket and headed toward the door. "This is not over yet!" he shouted in reiteration. "Not by a long shot. I still have some shares in this company and I am smarter than any of you! You are going to pay, somehow, some way."

Lloyd heard his mother wail loudly as he slammed the front door behind him. Walking to his car, he could not believe what had happened. *How could they do this to me and get away with it?* He got into his car, put it in gear and headed for White Hawk Manor, a name he gave to his home. He had named his home because everything about him had to have some magic to it, such as Marilyn's Closet or the Lowla Suite, which was the guest bedroom upstairs in White Hawk Manor.

Speeding through the streets of the city he maneuvered in and out of lanes, and at one red light he drove the car up on the sidewalk and went through the intersection, causing tourists to scatter. Lloyd did not worry about traffic tickets or minor misdemeanors; the Rochelle family was heavily involved in politics and the police, and even if he got a ticket, it would somehow magically disappear. At last he was on Saint Charles Avenue. He began to think how lucky he was to have a home on this avenue. The avenue of New Orleans where most of the rich society of the town lived and all of the tourists would visit to see first hand the grandness of architectural genius. He loved living on the avenue so much that he could easily give up the apartment in the Quarter. Lloyd only had the apartment because Torch wanted to live where the action was and the rest of the Rochelles could use it for visitors or guests of *Le Oui-Oui.* Thinking back, it was easier for Torch to be deceitful living there. He had caused him so much heartache and cost him so much money.

Looking at the houses along the way, he remembered as a child that he had vowed to live on this street one day. Passing the multi-million-dollar mansions on each side of the divided avenue, he came to the conclusion that his was probably the smallest, least grand house on the block, but he was on the block even if he had to force his family to get him into White Hawk Manor. It would help the reputation of the Rochelles as far as society was concerned. After all, they were new money and needed to break into the circle of society slowly. Lloyd figured that by the time Johnny Ray's children would be born and grow up that all the things they had done would give those kids an easy arrival to the elite. *How can they think I am selfish when everything I do is for them? My house is for them, they are just too stupid to realize it.*

Nearing the house, Lloyd signaled to make a left turn across the median but had to wait for a streetcar to pass before he could cross over to the side of the avenue on which he lived. The streetcar stopped to let off some passengers. Lloyd looked them over and found a few college-looking students appealing. *Maybe that's what I need to calm me down since I already have eaten fried chicken tonight. Maybe fried chicken after?* The trolley riders moved about the street and the trolley moved on down the tracks. Lloyd went across the median and immediately turned right, down the side street so he could pull to the back of his house. Sitting in the driveway, he looked at White Hawk Manor in all its glory. It was a white three-story house with the first floor serving as a basement. The entrance of the house was on the second level for both the front and the back. The front landing that faced the avenue had two columns on either side of the huge steps that led to the lead-crystal cut-glass front door. It might be modest but it was grand to Lloyd. He pondered what he was going to do to make sure that somehow he would come out on top of his current situation. He got his things and climbed the steps toward the screened back porch.

Once inside the screened porch, he opened the backdoor which exposed a long, wide hallway. He put his things on an antique sideboard which was immediately to his left. Lloyd faced the lead-crystal door at the opposite end. He stood there looking at the main floor of White Hawk Manor. On his left were three doors that lined the grand hallway of the house. One was to his bedroom, one to his study, and the other to his grandmother's room. The other side of the hallway housed doors which led to the kitchen, basement, the stairs and the archway to the living and dining rooms. The brilliance of that sight always made him happy. It was decorated with antique chairs, a twenty-four foot mirror, and southern historic art. Smiling he called, "Mimi."

Peeking out of his grandmother's door, Mimi answered. "Yes, Mister Lloyd, I'm here." Mimi came out into the hallway, shut the door and continued. "Your grandma is sleeping and I have fed her and she took her medicine. And I've got to go. You are late, you know, and what about my money?"

"Is that all you think about? Money?"

"No, sometimes I think about my husband," laughed Mimi.

Digging into his briefcase, Lloyd pulled out an envelope and handed it to her, "It's all cash in there, baby. Can you come earlier tomorrow?"

Breathing heavily Mimi replied, "What time?"

"Eight o'clock."

"I will, but you're killing me." She gave Lloyd a hug and was quickly out the door.

Lloyd went into the kitchen and got a can of cold tea from the fridge, popped the top and headed to his grandmother's room. "Ruby," he called gently as he opened the door. His grandmother was snoring. She looked so peaceful and happy. She had been living by herself for years and had morphed into a silent hermit until Lloyd had her moved in with him. Being at Lloyd's and enjoying his friends and the fuss they made over her had helped her blossom into a character of interest. She was eighty-eight years old and full of herself. He prayed to God to watch over her as he knew he was getting ready to go out and look for intimacy and would have to leave her alone. He loved his grandmother so much. She had never denied him anything. He smiled and shut the door.

Down the hall behind his grandmother's room was his suite of rooms. It consisted of a bedroom that opened into a bathroom which led to a study with a fireplace that he used as an office. Usually he would seduce suitors in his study by the fireplace before bringing them to the bedroom. Everything in his life had a purpose, and the fireplace was for romance. He walked into the bedroom and took off all his clothes and threw them on his enormous four-poster bed. Slowly he looked through his closet until he found his newest tuxedo. Hurriedly he dressed in the tux, went to the window and looked fondly at the full moon. *You'll never let me down, will you, La Luna?* One more look at Ruby and he was out the door.

Fifteen minutes later he was at his special spot along the levee. He loved to go to the levee, especially on the night of a full moon. He got out of the car and disappeared into the trees that lined the river. Once in the shadows of the trees he took off his shoes and his pants and began to expose his bottom to the many textures of the wood and the plants. The feelings he experienced were so intense that they increased his sexual appetite. After romping through the overgrown pasture by the river for an hour, he put his pants back on and went to the Marilynmobile, a white convertible BMW, the color chosen to match his white house. He cranked the car and carefully looked around on both sides and in the front and rear vicinities. Seeing that there wasn't anyone in the area, he took off his pants once again, still in the car. He prepared to drive the streets and pick up a Confederate soldier who would be surprised to see a pantsless Lloyd in the driver's seat. This wasn't a new thing for Lloyd, and as outrageous as it might have been, he usually was successful in his endeavors. Tonight would not prove to be different.

He decided to head toward the prison, but on the way he spotted a young, handsome, tall man walking down Esplanade. Lloyd pulled up alongside the pedestrian, stopped and put down the window and asked, "Do you need a ride?"

"No, do you?" the big man replied flippantly.

Lloyd wasn't used to hitting the jackpot so soon. "Yes, get in."

The man appeared to be in his late twenties. Surfer boy looks, light brown hair, clean and very handsome. He had a familiar look as though he could be a distant Rochelle relative. He got into the passenger's side of the car. "Whoa. You don't have any pants on."

"Scandalous, isn't it? Do you want to get out?"

"No, but why do you do that?"

"I love to see how men react when they get into the car." Lloyd pulled back onto the road.

"You've done this before?"

"Yes, a few times. Tell me how you knew what I wanted?"

"It doesn't take a Ph.D. to figure out what's happening when a car like this stops you on the street. Men usually don't stop and ask for directions," he said, putting on his seat belt.

"Oh, so men have stopped for you before?"

"A few times."

"My name is Lloyd, what's yours?"

"Rex."

"Rex, wanna fuck me at my downtown office? You can knock everything off the desk. There'll be plenty of room."

Without hesitation, Rex smiled and said, "That would be my pleasure."

Lloyd grabbed Rex's thigh and said, "With an attitude like that, you're sure to get a big tip." He moved his hands onto Rex's crotch. "And with equipment like that, I'm sure to have a big, good time. And let me warn you. After you've had my pussy, you won't want anybody else's."

"Oh, yeah? Let's go find out."

"I think we are going to have a good time, Rex." With that, Lloyd floored the Marilynmobile and moved like lighting through the traffic to get to the offices of Troubled Waters Incorporated. *My family thinks they know everything. But I wonder how they would feel if they knew how many men I fuck on top of their desks?*

14

Beverly had been out shopping all afternoon. She toured all the stores on Melrose Avenue to North La Brea and received a lot of attention. She thought it was because she looked so fabulous. In reality it was partly because she was dressed in evening attire at three o'clock in the afternoon and partly that she evoked a faint recognition of familiarity to someone that shoppers could not place. It wasn't unusual to spot stars in that area of town.

It was as if she had never been shopping. Beverly picked up each item, carefully inspected it and then replaced it perfectly to the spot from which it came. The clothing she had touched that day was beautiful and complimented her caramel shade of skin. The fashions did not compliment her purse as most items were above her means to afford. She took many dresses from the racks just to try them on and dream of when they would all be hers. Although back at the condo, she had had high hopes of snagging a few outfits without paying, Beverly just could not work up the nerve to do so. It just wasn't in her. She would have to be creative with her outfit for the date with Aaron later. Reluctantly, she took back the clothes to the racks. A final look around the store filled her with hopes that one day she would have Diva's credit cards again so she could buy what she wanted. *I'll be back.*

She hit the street like she was walking the runway. The green sequined dress sparkled in the bright California sun which made it possible to see her from a great distance. At a closer inspection, she looked as though she was moving to a beat, although neither were there no tunes to be heard nor did she have any kind of music accessory with her. She picked up her pace when she had made it to Beverly Boulevard. *If I only had a camera, I would have a picture of Beverly on Beverly.* She stopped under a street sign for about fifteen minutes, waving to the motorists that waved at her and blew their horns. In her mind she was celebrating having a boulevard named after her, not realizing that the people who waved, whistled, blew their horns or spoke were actually acknowledging Diva. Time passed so quickly that she did not realize how far she was from home until she was at the intersection of Beverly and Fairfax, across from CBS studios. When she saw CBS, excitement rose from her body like lava from a volcano. Standing there, she was lost in a dream about having her own talk show. With Diva's clout and her personality, she began to plot what she could do if the both of them could work together. *Working together could be beneficial after all.*

Estimating that she was at least an hour away from home, she decided she could not make it back without something to eat. Feeling a little weak took her from her talk show fantasy, so she turned to walk back home. She clutched her purse, remembering the three quarters she found while digging through the couch earlier. That would at least get her something to drink. The pangs of hunger, though, were a different matter. Beverly smiled and sashayed with a different attitude. Perhaps it was because she was out for this long for the first time and had a chance to see that Diva's life wasn't all that bad. At least Diva could afford to purchase any article of clothing . . . or food.

After walking about fifteen blocks she landed in front of Trader Joe's and decided that was where she would get something to drink from a vending machine. Instead, the *Los Angeles Times* headline of "Feel the Pulse of the City" caught her eye. Now that she was determined to behave in a respectable manner rather than in a radical one as previously thought, Beverly decided to get a newspaper. She opened her purse, took out fifty cents and purchased a newspaper in order to get a feel for what was out in the city and to find out where the happening spots were. *At least I can go inside and get some water out of the fountain.*

Beverly entered Trader Joe's with the *Los Angeles Times* tucked neatly under her arm, unknowing that a man who appeared to have great interest in Beverly's movements for blocks had followed her into the store. She inquired at Customer Care as to where she could find the restroom. A cute young man told her the restrooms were on the left in the middle of the store added with, "You look very nice this afternoon, miss."

Miss. "Thank you so very much," said Beverly. She took that to reinforce her feeling that she was headed in the right direction with her thoughts of fashion. Walking through the store, she stopped at the book counter and picked up Diva's book, not noticing that someone was very closely observing her movements. After thumbing through *A Kept Reflection* she spotted the water fountain and put the book back on the shelf. She hurried over and proceeded to drink enough to sate a camel. Although the water was nice, it did not relieve the growls now coming from her stomach. On the way out she had to pass the deli area of the store. Unaware of the people around her, she paused to look at all of the pre-wrapped choices of ham, roast beef and egg salad sandwiches. Without thinking, she picked up the egg salad sandwich, tucked it in the Times and then headed out the door.   Beverly immediately walked across the street, darting through the traffic towards Plummers Park, hoping that she escaped without notice.

Scanning the area, she picked out a park bench where she could eat and try not to think about what she had done. While eating the egg salad, she vowed that she would repay Trader Joe's for this most delicious lunch . . . so, justifiably, she really had not stolen the sandwich.

"Where's the rest of your picnic?" asked a stranger.

"This is just something to tide me over," Beverly said curiously.

"I'd like to take some photos of you, with your permission, of course." He took his shoulder pack off his arm, put it on the ground near Beverly and began to open it.

"Photographs of me? Why?" She scooped some egg salad off her lip with her tongue.

"It's not every day that you see a . . ."   He paused, appearing to rethink what he was about to have said, " . . . such a vision of loveliness, dressed to the hilt, sitting on a park bench and devouring a sandwich like it was the first thing she's had to eat in a while. Even a seasoned fashion photographer could not come up with this setting. Actually, I've taken some pictures of you already. I just wanted to get a little closer."

He began to snap a few shots as Beverly finished her last bites. She then stood up, threw the wrapping away, got her newspaper, turned to walk past the photographer, paused and said, "Get a few poses of this," patting her rear end. She turned back to him and pointed her finger to his face. "Don't you have enough manners to leave a pretty girl alone in her own park? This is my neighborhood, you know, should I yell for help? You're not a freak, are you?"

His thinning blond hair was beginning to blow in the wind. He was eye-to-eye with Beverly. "No, I'm not a freak. But I am not going to pass up an opportunity to sell my photos. Thanks, at least I'll be able to eat this week, too." Hurriedly he grabbed his bag to leave.

"What do you mean, *sell photos?* You don't have the right to." She was talking to him as he was walking away. "Hey, I'm talking to you. Stop!" He began to pick up his pace and soon disappeared into a sea of people on the street. "What the hell is going on?" Beverly left the park. She needed to hurry home and get ready for her date that evening.

Walking through the doors of her building, she smiled to the doorman, "Good Afternoon, Joe."

The doorman showed surprise to get a salutation first from Diva, as she usually did not speak. "Are you okay?"

"Yes. Why?" she said looking over her body to see if anything was out of place.

"I was just on my way over to the park when I saw that photographer obviously bothering you with his camera. I know how you feel about the *paparazzi*. You never go out and the day you do . . ." He put his hands in the air as though he was using a camera, ". . . pictures. Those kinds of lowlife hang out in this area just for celebrity shots. I'm sorry I didn't get to the park."

"You can see the park from here?" She turned to the window. The lobby was elevated a few steps; she had a birds-eye view of the bench that she had chosen. "Oh, my God, The Diva didn't think anyone would recognize her."

"Miss Diva, you look very nice today and not dressed like you usually do, but those vultures are out looking at everyone under the microscope. A lot of famous people try disguises but usually wind up in a magazine anyway. Oh, I almost forgot this just came for you." He retrieved a box from behind the concierge's desk.

Taking the large white box from his hands, she said,

"Thank you so much and thank you for almost coming to The Diva's defense. I really appreciate it."

The doorman watched Diva as she went to the elevators. Something was different. It wasn't so much that she talked to him for a change, but it was also her tone and her sincerity.

Beverly couldn't believe she had been so careless. Maybe there wasn't any reason to worry since she wasn't doing anything wrong, and who would believe it was Diva anyway? The elevator stopped, the doors opened, she exited and took out her key. She went into her condo and looked at the clock on the wall. It was six o'clock; she had two hours to get ready for Aaron. Immediately she put the box the doorman gave her on the hall table and pulled the ribbon while she placed the envelope to the side. Taking off the top of the box, she was exposed to at least two dozen beautiful sterling lavender roses. She put the roses down and opened the envelope to read the card.

> *Diva,*
> *I can't believe what has happened between us. What a merger this may turn out to be. Dare I sign . . . love?*
>
> *Aaron*
>
> *P.S. The minutes will seem like hours until I see you tonight.*

Beverly smiled and put the card to her heart. She took the roses and put them in a vase of water and went to get ready for the evening. Walking to the bedroom, she noticed that there were two messages on Diva's answering machine. She pressed the play button.

"You have two new messages," the machine said in a monotone voice. "First message. Thursday, four-oh-two p.m."

"Diva, this is Evan in Atlanta, remember me? Long time, no hear. It's been at least a week since we've talked. Where are you? You are never at home when I want to talk to you. Call me. I want you to go to Florida with me for Memorial

Day to a pageant where you will have a chance to do your routine. I need you to go with me because I am in the pageant and I need your support. It's been too long since we have spent any time together anyway. Call me, call me, and call me! I'll explain it all when you call. Love ya! Call me!"

"Second message. Thursday, five o'clock p.m."

"You know who this is. You know what I want. You know that I will be there at eight. Be sure to have the doorman let me come in without being announced. "

"End of messages." The machine turned off.

Beverly picked up the intercom phone and dialed a three digit extension. "Hello, Joe, it is Diva." She had dropped "The" before her name in an unexpected personal gesture and continued her instructions without saying her name at all. "I'm expecting Aaron Archer this evening at eight. Please just send him up. Right. No need to call me. And, Joe, thank you again for your help this afternoon. Next time I go out alone, I'll see if you think I can pass for someone else."

15

Lloyd, now clothed, and Rex made it up to the fifteenth-floor offices of Troubled Waters. Standing in the hallway just out from the elevator banks, Lloyd saw that Rex looked a little nervous.

"Don't worry, baby. We own the whole floor and there is no one else here but me and you. Let's go inside." Lloyd took out a key to open the double doors to the main entrance of the office complex. The doors were made out of tinted glass, each having a three-foot-high letter attached at the end of the door when closed simply stated TW. Once the doors were opened, the room revealed a sight of the city that was most impressive.

"Wow. This view is fantastic," Rex stammered.

Looking at Rex, he answered, "Yes, it is. And the view of the city is not bad either." He paused to notice Rex's reaction to his compliment. "We use it to intimidate our clients. With this office and this setting, most people think we are pretty powerful. You know, like the Ewings of Dallas." He put his hands on his hips. "Just call me Crystal. Linda Evans and I look a lot alike," Lloyd said laughingly. He gestured for Rex to pass him and go into the office. Once Rex was on the inside, he closed the doors.

Rex smiled and walked closer to the windows. He intently stared out as if he had never seen any big cities before. Not only was the view breathtaking but the office also gave a sensational statement of fashion mostly seen on television series and not in real life. He looked over the huge room. There were executive-type desks with leather chairs and there were leather couches behind coffee tables that were filled with amenities for visitors such as miniature showboats and boxes of candy. Along the near wall were large portraits of former rulers of the Troubled Waters Empire. Against the far wall was a bar that looked as though it came out of a castle. It was mahogany with intricate carvings on the lower portion of the wainscoting. Large columns went from the top of the bar to the ceiling which housed a rack where glasses of all liquor possibilities hung. Rex thought it was like a magical kingdom up the in clouds above the city. He found himself standing in front of the bar looking at his reflection in the mirror.

Lloyd walked up behind Rex and put his hands on the stranger's shoulders. "Looking for something?"

"A needle in a haystack."

He ran his hands down the nape of Rex's neck. "Maybe I can help you find it."

"Maybe," Rex muttered as he turned to Lloyd and then looked at him quite seriously. "I'm not just some hustler that you picked up on the street. I'm not looking for a tip either, like you suggested earlier."

"And I am not just some pervert, either. Frankly, I'd be happy not to have to pay you."

"Sometimes I don't know what comes over me and I'll do

things just for the excitement value of it all," Rex said expressively with his hands.

"Trust me. I know exactly what you mean, for instance, tonight."

"So that's why you ride around in a BMW without pants looking for a trick?" asked Rex. "I'm not trying to offend you, but it seems as though you should have everything." He motioned with a wave of his hand the perimeter of the office. "And if you wanted something, all you would need to do is call and it would come to you."

"It's not that easy, baby. You can't trust anyone really." A manipulative tone came from Lloyd.

"You just told me to trust you."

"Trust me." He placed his hand on Rex's arm. "I wish I had someone to call." Walking toward the windows, he continued, "It is for the excitement of the moment. Coming to this office with you makes me feel like I own the world, that I am the '*king*' and I have the power to be naughty at the office and," pointing out the portraits on the wall, "the family doesn't even know it." He continued as though he was teaching a class while using his arms for expression and emphasis. "A fleeting moment. I survive on the energy I create by living from season to season; from event to event; from social soiree to soiree, and then I fill the empty gaps with hunts of the night when the moon is full." He looked out at the city and at the moon. "Mostly, I'm lonely. Even if I am surrounded by a crowd, I'm restless."

"Are you wondering why I got into the car with you?"

"Why?"

"I'm restless, too. Searching, maybe a little lost." Rex moved some frames and sat on top of a desk, still facing the view. "Sit down and let's talk, if you want. I still want to make out. I find you attractive and I find you comforting. I'd like to talk some more. Sex is great, but without conversation, you might as well have it alone."

"You must be lost and lonely to actually want to have an

in-depth conversation with someone you just met for sex."
Rex looked at Lloyd as though Lloyd had pierced his heart.
He continued in a condescending tone. "Conversation with
sex is special if you're married or have a lover, I know.
Talking with a trick is a waste of time. All they want to tell
you is about their problems or how much money they need."
Lloyd pushed a chair beside Rex and sat. "It's exciting for me
because I go after Confederate soldiers only."

"Confederate soldiers?" Rex pondered.

Feeling a little pity for him, Lloyd eased his demeanor.
"It's a nickname that my best friend and I have for men who
look unobtainable. It doesn't sound as cheap as saying a trick
and a lot easier to remember instead of a name." He spun
around in the leather chair. "So why are you in New Orleans,
Rex? Are you going to college? Working here, what?"

"I'm on a mission. Not currently working and I don't
know how long I will be able to stay or if I want to be in this
city. I think I saved up enough money to be here for a year.
It's only been a couple of months and my leads seem to go
nowhere."

"A mission? Leads? Who are you, Cary Grant in *I'm No
Angel?*"

"It's a long story." He looked down.

"I've got time. Tell me." He continued to look at Rex,
who seemed to be at a loss for words. "Give me a quick
review or something."

Trying not to sound rehearsed, Rex started his tale.
"When I was about thirteen, my mother told me she wasn't
my real mother, but that she loved me like I was her own. She
was unable to have any children naturally and could or
would not tell me how I came into her life." He picked up a
framed picture of a group shot of what appeared to be a
family photo. "Is this your family?"

Lloyd nodded affirmatively to Rex.

"There was no father around when I grew up. Since Mom
was good to me, I never thought to venture off to find my

roots or badger her for an answer. Just the mention of my beginnings upset her, so we never talked about it." He put the picture back on the desk. "Until recently, I had no idea that I was born here at Charity Hospital."

"Charity hospital? I'll bet she's not happy that you're here."

"She died five months ago. The fact that I am here cannot hurt her now. "

Lloyd sprung out of the chair and hugged Rex as a caring gesture. "I'm sorry. I know how that hurts. Losing my father was the worst day of my life."

"Well, it also hurts that there doesn't appear to be any avenues to explore and no one to help guide me. Charity can't help me. The state can't help me. I don't know which adoption agency even handled my case or what year or even if I was stolen." He peered at Lloyd with a sad look on his face. "It's seems as though there is no known birth certificate." Rex slid off the desk and walked to the window. "After my mom died, I went through everything she had searching for an answer. There was private schooling and I never did without. I don't know where the money came from as she did not work. There never seemed to be any issue with my validity. Now that's all I have left; finding out who I am and who I belong to, if anyone. If I needed a birth certificate, I don't know what I would do."

"How did you find out you were born here, Rex?" Lloyd was still in the same spot, studying Rex's shadow which was surrounded by the light of the city. He was dressed in tattered jeans and a tight tee shirt. Imaging him in slacks and a sweater, Lloyd decided Rex's wardrobe would be the first thing he would change.

"My uncle finally told me in a tense confrontation that the only thing he knew is that I was born in New Orleans at Charity Hospital. My identity is the needle in a haystack." He turned back to Lloyd. "I asked all my other family members and no one knew anything. I can not believe in the small town of Plain Dealing, that there wasn't any gossip."

"Plain Dealing? Where's that?" Lloyd said joining Rex.

"It's just twenty miles north of Shreveport, Louisiana. You'd heard of Shreveport, haven't you?"

Lloyd smiled at Rex's sarcasm.

Rex smiled back and continued. "So, I come to the *Big Easy* and find closed doors. People look at me like I'm crazy. Like how could you not know your parents' name or your real birth date? Maybe I should hire a detective, but I don't have much information to give. And I wouldn't know who to turn to anyway." Rex stood as he looked directly into Lloyd's eyes.

"Did anyone ever tell you how beautiful you are?"

"Beautiful. Not handsome?"

"Handsome is for the un-tortured soul," Lloyd smiled, "and I could look at you all night."

Rex shyly smiled back at Lloyd.

"How 'bout it? I have a swing on my front porch. We could sit there, rock back and forth and talk and watch the streetcar go up and down the avenue." Lloyd pointed in the direction of his house. "I'd make sure you got home. I wouldn't make you walk."

"I've got a car. It's not much, but it's paid for," Rex said with a sigh. "I walk a lot to clear my head."

"Funny," Lloyd said, "I like the feel of plants to clear mine. I'm just nuts about nature."

"Do you live alone?"

"My grandmother, Ruby, lives with me, but she has her own room and it's a big house. She'll love you when you meet her. There's nothing to worry about."

"You don't have a lover, Lloyd?" Rex asked as he went back to a desk chair to sit, anticipating that this evening might take on a new direction. He sat regally in the chair as though he was the head of the office.

"I did, and I was still lonely and restless because he didn't actually love me." Lloyd left the window and went to the chair where Rex was sitting. "It took a long time to figure that even though I was involved, he was not. He only wanted what I could give. I don't think we ever had a conversation like the one we're having, especially before sex or after. He wasn't interested in how I felt nor did he ever care to tell me about his life. There was one word in his vocabulary: himself. That's another story we can talk about when we're swinging. I wasn't happy the last few days being single again, but maybe it's a good thing now."

"For some reason, Lloyd, I feel as though I can talk to you." He got up from the chair and moved closer to Lloyd. "For some reason, I feel instantly connected to you. Sounds crazy, doesn't it?" He took Lloyd's hand. "I'm thinking despite the surface of our meeting, deep down you are quite a wonderful person. Don't play with my head and I won't play with yours." Rex squeezed Lloyd's hand tightly.

"Deal." Both gentleman shook hands. "I won't play with your head, but you'll have to give me something else to play with." Lloyd looked into Rex's eyes and smiled. "Let's go to White Hawk Manor and get something to eat along the way. Do you like fried chicken?"

"At this time of night, I'd prefer Chinese." Rex let go of Lloyd's hand. "What is White Hawk Manor?"

"It's home and you'll love it." Again, Lloyd took Rex by the hand and led him out of Troubled Waters.

16

If anyone had told Evan that he would one day work for a place called Stars and Pipes, he would've thought it was a porn shop, not a plumbing house. It was just another Friday to him as he pulled into the parking lot. His car stereo had been blasting with tunes he had picked out, hoping to find something suitable to do for the pageant in Niceville. Alas, nothing had caught his fancy that morning. It was still early though, six a.m. Evan usually was the first to come in to work and the last one to leave. He was an inside sales manger who supervised ten people who did not really seem to care if they worked or not.   And they were backed up by the management. It seemed to Evan that if you were straight in this job, you could get away with everything.

Evan felt that all the work was dumped on him because he could handle it with few mistakes, plus the customers just loved him. In fact, after seventeen years, he had become their confidant and personal problem solver over the phone lines. His customers would call him, give an order, and then ask what they should do about their troubled relationships. He loved how he would dish out advice, knowing that he had no real experience to back up what he told them nor did he practice what he preached to others. Upon getting out of his truck, he took off a weathered jacket that he called his smoking coat and proceeded to spray himself with an aerosol of a mango scent. He did this so he would not smell like marijuana. He justified smoking pot before work because the work was unfulfilling and he knew he would ultimately go nowhere in this company due to his sexual orientation. Although he never spoke of his "life", he assumed it was assumed by the office staff that he was "gay." So he smoked on the way to work, at his morning break, at lunchtime, and his afternoon break. It amazed him that he still could work circles around everyone else who apparently never smoked at all.

Evan threw his smoking coat back into the truck and slammed the door. Still humming a tune, he went inside to his desk and put his things down, then went to the bathroom to brush his teeth and spray his beautiful thick long hair into place so it wouldn't get in his eyes as he typed. Returning to his desk, he sat down and wondered why he was even here. It took him an hour to commute in the morning and sometimes twice that long to get home. *Oh well, it pays the bills.* He was hoping that something would happen that would allow him to escape this prison. He chuckled to himself because he thought he should blackmail two of the men who worked there. He was ostracized from the "good ole boys" at the company and was never included in their golf games or fishing and hunting outings. How fitting it would be to expose the facade two of them presented. It would be nice to have them give him large sums of money since he had slept with them, and that would not go over well with the corporate offices or their families and their buddies. But dealing with the men of the plumbing industry could result in a death, like his. He thought he was so clever to hide his video camera and videoed the secret meetings when they happened at his house after office hours. No matter how much Evan fantasized about doing such a thing, he knew deep down he could not go through with it. Being an adulterer was enough guilt.

Evan logged on to his computer to start his daily routine. Instead of keying orders right away he decided to work on his talent for the Miss Niceville pageant by writing an original song and performing it live rather than lip-syncing. He took his order pad and started writing. Usually at the job in between phone calls, he would flip a few pages over and draw. He loved to draw, especially eyes. He had a box at home full of masterpieces from this job. As he was sitting there scribbling an idea dawned upon him. *Oasis. Desert. Mirage. That's it! Our love is like a mirage.* With that in mind he began to write.

He was so caught up in the moment that he did not hear anyone enter into the office.

"Good morning, sunshine." A hand brushed over the back of his head and then lightly pulled at Evan's long locks.

Evan looked up to see the towering Rick over him. Rick was one of the two men in the office to whom Evan was unable to say no once his advances were made. "Good morning, Rick." He moved his head away from the pull. "What are you doing in town today? I didn't think you were here until Monday."

"I finished early this week." He moved to the front of the

desk. "Tennessee was very agreeable to me. No one said no to any of the spiff orders."

"Great. Did you bring them? You know I need more work to do today since I was out the last two."

"I know. I hate it when you're out and I have to deal with the others in here. You always get the job done, not to mention the fringe benefits."

"How would you like to work with them every day?" Evan laughed as he tucked his song away under his order pad, ignoring Rick's comment about fringe benefits.

"I wouldn't. I really wouldn't. I got here early this morning hoping you'd be here, Evan." Rick bent over to Evan's ear, "Let's go upstairs."

"Are you crazy, Rick?"

"No. Just horny. Come on. It's been awhile since you've been good to me."

"Maybe after work," Evan suggested as his heart started to beat faster.

"I'll be out of town with the family. It's been a long time or it seems so to me. We got a little while before anyone else will get here."

Evan looked at Rick, and although he thought he was "through" with everyone, especially married men, he found it difficult to say no. He took a deep breath. "This is the last time."

"Yeah, right, like you can say no to me."

"That day will come when you least expect it."

"Don't be mean to me, it's not becoming to you and you shouldn't let anything detract from your charm." Rick smiled and continued to whisper, "I'll go up first and unlock the office. Don't keep me waiting, unless you want me to drag you upstairs by your hair. Why don't you put it in a pony tail so it won't get in our way?" He then exited the office by the stairs in the back.

The upstairs was composed of private offices for the outside salesmen of the company. Usually they were empty except on Monday when the salesmen were there to plan their weeks or when the office would hold a meeting or a training session in the conference room on the second floor. Evan slowly got up from his desk and put his song into his knapsack. He thought of the day he first saw Rick and how attractive he had been to him. Rick was six feet four with dark hair and an athletic body, a great package for a guy in his early fifties. He sighed heavily and decided that he was going upstairs and tell Rick that he would not be a part of this any more. It was not his problem that Rick needed a little extra something that he did not get at home. *Why is it that married men do not seem to get what they need at home? Why in the world did I ever think this was glamorous?* Evan looked at the clock on the wall. *6:30 a.m. There's not much time.* He took a rubber band from his desk drawer for his hair then disappeared up the stairs to heaven.

17

Beverly and Aaron woke up in each other's arms. He was staring intently at her, caressing her head and shoulders.

"I never thought it could be like this between us."

"Neither did I. Our stroll in the park was so romantic, the fabulous food and this bracelet that you bought me." She held her arm in the air. "I don't know what to say to you, Aaron, except thank you."

"What amazes me is the transformation you've made since we have been involved romantically. Maybe you have always been like this, but didn't show it to anyone, especially me."

"Transformation?" Beverly gasped. "What do you mean?"

"Diva," he said, kissing her hand, "you must admit that you have let your guard down. You laughed and let me do most of the talking. You acted like a schoolgirl in love. Most of all, you did not refer to yourself as 'The Diva' at all. I mean, is it me or is it that you want a movie deal that bad?"

Aaron put his hand on her waist.

"The Diva should be insulted by your insinuation," Beverly laughed, "but I guess I can understand what you mean. It's just that holding on to something, like an image of oneself, can be draining. Very draining. And it takes such energy and effort to always remember that you are 'The Diva' and she does this and she does that." She sat up in the bed. "In the end, The Diva realized that," pointing to herself, "*I* am the one left out. There is no more *me*. But it's like an avalanche. The Diva just keeps on rolling. How do you stop it? It was like I was on the inside looking at life on the outside. I say to myself, 'why?' Why can't I let go and not worry about what anyone says or that I will fall on my face or that somehow I will hurt my career." She caressed his face. "Oh, Aaron, I want to have a movie made of my book and I want to star in it. I think that it would be of utmost personal satisfaction. But more than that, I want to be a woman who has a man who loves her and is devoted to her. There is a certain freedom that comes with that, I believe, and I want to be free."

"Baby, you're looking at your freedom." Aaron took Beverly by her hair and kissed her passionately and deeply. The two embraced and again engaged in love making.

18

"Are you awake, yet?" Seeing that he was, Mimi said, "Good morning, Mister Rex," as she entered the room with a tray of breakfast delights. Mimi looked to be in her forties. She sported braided hair with beads at the end of each row.

"Good morning . . . "

"Mimi. It's a pleasure to meet you, sugar, I hope you're hungry. Mister Lloyd had to get up early this morning so it's just me and Miss Ruby. You haven't met her yet, have you?"

"No, ma'am."

"What manners. You don't have to say ma'am to me. It makes me feel old." She put the breakfast tray on the bed with Rex and lifted the lid off of the plate. "Hope you like eggs, grits, and ham and fresh biscuits. I made it just for you. Mister Lloyd had an early appointment with the family this morning. He told me to take care of you. He'll be back soon. We're hoping you don't have to rush off, but if you do he left cab fare for you to get home." She went to the window and pulled back the drapes. The dark room filled with the sunshine of the day.

"No, I don't have to rush." Rex adjusted to the light beaming into the room. "I didn't know it was so late."

"I'm glad you rested. Now you enjoy your breakfast. There are clean clothes in the armoire and fresh towels in the shower should you need them. Give me a holler if you need anything, okay?"

"Okay and thanks."

"I got a feeling we all will get along just fine," Mimi said as she exited the bedroom and closed the door behind her.

Rex looked all around at the lovely antiques and art in Lloyd's bedroom and thought how nice Lloyd had been to him. It was a great feeling to sleep in a good bed for a change rather than in the lumpy mattress at the motel. They had talked most of the night and did not even have sex. It was refreshing just to have someone listen to him. He hoped that maybe this time he had found a true friend and not just a predator that was looking for Mr. Here and Now. There was a definite comfort to being at White Hawk Manor. Perhaps he could rent a room here and get out of the motel he was staying at on the Airline Highway. He wondered if it could be possible to actually meet a nice person like the way he met Lloyd. It all seemed to be too easy at this point. Deciding to play it by ear, Rex sat up in the bed, careful not to disturb the breakfast tray, said grace and then ate the delicious meal before him.

Stuffed from the good food, he got out of bed still in his clothes from the night before and went over to the armoire and opened it. It was amazing to see the clothes inside. It looked like a display right out of Barney's of New York that he had seen in fashion magazines. Although he did not think anything would fit, he looked through the available wardrobe anyway. To his surprise there were a few very nice things in his size. Even though he thought the smaller sizes had to have been old clothes, they were nice old clothes and did not look like they had even been worn. He picked out a pair of slacks and a pullover sweater and put them on the bed. First he decided to take his breakfast tray to the kitchen.

Once in the grand hallway, Rex called out, "Mimi."

Peeping her head out of the kitchen door, "Yes, Mister Rex."

"I'll make a deal with you, Mimi." He moved toward her, "I won't say ma'am if you don't call me Mister Rex."

She put out her hands to take the tray. "Okay, Rex, it's a deal."

Rex walked past Mimi to the kitchen, "Since you made breakfast for me it is only fair that I do the dishes."

"Now if Mister Lloyd comes in he won't like dat."

"Well, Mister Lloyd will have to get over it." Rex put the tray on the counter and started to rinse the dishes. "So, are you from New Orleans?"

"Yes, I've been here all my life. Don't think I'll ever leave either. You?"

"I'm from Plain Dealing in North Louisiana."

"I know where dat is. I have an uncle dat live dat way." She took the silverware and glass Rex had rinsed and put them in the dishwasher.

"Really? Most people don't know where it is. Sometimes, I wish I didn't."

They both laughed. "I knows, you just can't run away from yourself. You can try, but you'll never get very far." Mimi took chicken meat out of the refrigerator. "I'll be making some stew for tonight. Hope you'll be here to enjoy it, I'm a good cook." She put the chicken on the butcher block.

"I'll say . . . and I forgot to tell you how delicious breakfast was. What a treat. Breakfast in bed. That has never happened to me before. It is a first."

"I'm glad I was the first," Mimi said with a satisfying grin. "You're sure not like the others."

Rex was holding his breakfast plate under the running water as he turned to Mimi. "The others?"

"Mister Lloyd has some high falutin' friends that don't even know my name even though I serve 'em every holiday and between some." She left the butcher block and took the dish from Rex. "They don't even say hello or thank you. Why, Mister Rex," she closed the dishwasher door, "I mean, Rex, this is a morning for firsts."

Rex shut off the water and smiled. "Now that the dishes are done, where does the tray go?"

"Right here, sir. This is how I serve Miss Ruby's meals on this tray. She should be awake in a while. She loves company and she will love a sweet-looking boy like you."

"I hope so and thanks for the compliment. I'm going to take a shower now and then I don't know if I'll head home or wait for Lloyd."

"You should wait for Mister Lloyd. His study is in the back and he's got lots to look at and read. He'll be home shortly. Those meetings never last too long." She started to pull the chicken meat apart.

"Isn't he a school teacher, though? I mean, it is Friday and school time." Rex asked standing in the doorway.

"Mister Lloyd has lots of jobs and things to do. He probably done been to school and through for the day. When you teach smart kids, he say, you don't have to spend a lot of time with 'em."

"All right then, Mimi. I'm off to the shower."

"Okay, Rex. When you come out, I'll introduce you to Miss Ruby if she's awake."

Rex left the kitchen and headed down the hallway into Lloyd's bedroom and closed the door. He could really get accustomed to this way of life, he thought as he went into the shower. But like everything else in his life that had gone bad, he was expecting the bottom to drop out at any minute.

19

Evan stopped at the mail box at the end of his driveway. He was glad to get home late — when it was dark — because he was ashamed of the way his house looked. His yard was just beautiful, especially in the springtime.   He lived in Hapeville, Georgia, located very close to the main airport of Atlanta and which bordered the city limits of Atlanta. He had bought into a changing neighborhood because it was the only thing he could afford "inside the perimeter," the area inside Interstate 285 which looped the city of Atlanta. The house sat on a double lot and was fenced so his dogs could roam freely. It had a fireplace and hardwood floors. The house had a deco flair, built in nineteen thirty-three.   There were nine pecan trees on his property so he named his home, "Nine Pecans." He fancied that he was not too far from Twelve Oaks, which was made famous by *Gone With The Wind*.   But he was embarrassed that he had neglected the outside of his home. There was never any time to fix the house up since all of his free time was occupied by his fantasy performances, smoking pot . . . and the occasional married man.

The paint was peeling, and from a distance the house looked like it had the measles. *This was really no way to exist,* he thought as he got his mail and got back into the truck to pull it into the detached garage. Closing the door to the truck, he ran to the front door, hoping none of the neighbors would see him.   Evan avoided any kind of contact with his neighbors, not because he thought he was better than they, but because they had no common interest. Besides he didn't want any of them to ask him when he was going to paint. One day he vowed that his house would be the nicest on the street. He had lived there for eight years now and when that would happen was anyone's guess.

Once inside the house, he fed his dogs, Princess and Cher. As usual, their tails were wagging as they were happy to see Evan, but he was usually in a bad mood, which he blamed on his job, and too many times he told the loving animals to leave him alone. "I feed you and that is enough. Momma doesn't have time to show you attention." Truly, Evan felt bad that Princess and Cher suffered from his unhappiness and wondered what kind of a person he was to not have time to fix his house or to pay attention to the ones that loved him most. He had to rush home from work on a Friday night just to drink, smoke and perform his "White Trash from Hapeville" show. When he got his buzz on, life was good.

After getting his glass of wine and his joint ready, he went to the computer to log on to see if there were any emails for him. To his surprise there was an email from someone called Doyle-Leigh with the subject being "Miss Niceville Contestant Survey." Evan quickly opened the email and read the message:

Lowla, we are delighted that you are entering the Miss Niceville Pageant this year. Marilyn sent me your email address and tells us that you are very excited to be entering the pageant this Memorial Day. Please visit our website, NicevilleNewz.com, to get a feel for what we are about. As you know, the theme this year will be Midnight at the Oasis. You will need a one minute presentation, a talent not to exceed five minutes and a formal dress for evening gown competition. Your tuition, as we call it, is also due for the weekend event and it is two hundred fifty dollars per person. Please answer the questions below as we will use the information to introduce you at the pageant. Also, we are having a pot-luck this Sunday and insist that you attend. You can bring your money, your answers and any others questions you may have. Oh, please make out your check to Manny Lewis, also known as Faux Pas, as he is the treasurer. You will also have a chance to talk with the current Miss Niceville, Crown Jewel. I am assuming that you will be rooming with Marilyn. Your accommodations can hold up to four, so you need to discuss with Marilyn who will be in your trailer or if it will be just the two of you. Please let us know what and who you will bring to the pot-luck. A dessert would be good since we will have the entrée taken care of. Be prepared to perform if you would like as we always are in the mood to do drag. Of course you will need to bring your music, your make-up, and your clothes. I have several rooms in the house that you can get ready in. Directions to the house are attached. I look forward to seeing you there. If for any reason you can not make it, please let me know. Doyle-Leigh.

Evan went immediately to the website and was delighted at what he saw. The site had pictures from the previous years and most of the people looked normal. Although the costumes and make-up were good, they were not out of a magazine. That calmed his nerves to think that he could actually compete. It amazed him that he spent so much time at the NicevilleNewz site that it was almost too late to do his show. He decided not to film himself, but to practice some more songs to see if there was one that would fit. He suddenly remembered the song he was working on in his knapsack. He took that out and began to work on the song along with the questions he needed to answer for the pageant. The questions ranged from "what is your name" to "what is your hobby" to "what is your favorite thing about the desert." Evan had not been this excited since he'd received a bit part in a play for a local theater group in Atlanta fifteen years ago.

He took another sip of wine and picked up the phone and dialed his friend in New Orleans. "Marilyn, is that you?"

"Marilyn?" the voice answered back, "Do I sound like a Marilyn?"

"I'm sorry. I thought I had called Lloyd Rochelle."

"You've reached the right party, but this is not Lloyd and I don't know any Marilyn."

"My name is Evan. Who is this?"

"My name is Rex and I'm looking forward to meeting you one day. I've seen a lot of your pictures."

"You've seen my pictures and you have never heard the name Marilyn?"

"No, but I'm going to ask about that. Lloyd is right here trying to grab the phone." Rex was running around the room while Lloyd was reaching for the phone. "He let me answer it because he saw it was you on the caller ID. I hope to get to meet you soon."

"Me, too, Rex. Nice to talk to you."

Lloyd took the phone from Rex. "Hey, Lowla," he said with a lift to his voice.

"I hate it when you do me this way; you know how shy I am. Who is Rex?"

"Just the most wonderful person I think I ever met."

"Is he new?"

"Yes, a breath of fresh air. You'll love him." Lloyd patted Rex on the head.

"That's what you said about the Niceville people and that is why I am calling. I got an email from this Doyle-Leigh and she is excited that I am in the pageant. I guess you must have entered me already," Evan said as he rolled himself another joint.

"Yes I did and you'll be a hit. Now that I have Rex to take up my time, you won't have any competition from me. I'm not going to enter this year. Like I said, you are going to be my horse, baby." Lloyd and Rex playfully chased each other around the room.

"You sound like you're out of breath. I didn't interrupt anything did I?" Evan asked.

"No. We are just playing. Stop it, Rex."

"I have these questions I have to fill out and email back and then there are the dues we have to pay. Who all is staying in our trailer?" Evan lit the joint.

"So far, you and me and Rex. He doesn't know it yet, but he is gonna be there. I need for you to come down so Chalmette can take your measurements and get your costumes ready. But back to your questions that you got from Doyle-Leigh . . . what are they?"

"Just questions about the desert and my hobbies. All

related to the pageant. I can forward you the email and you can answer the questions for me and then email them back to Doyle-Leigh if you like."

"Would you please, Lowla?" Lloyd heard silence. "Have you thought of a song yet?"

"I'm hoping to write a song and perform it."

"What?"

Evan repeated, "I'm hoping to write a song and perform it."

"Lowla, please. Use something that is already done so that way you don't call crying to me at the last minute."

"Now why would I do that?"

"Because of your nerves and you can't decide on anything. Remember all of the other attempts you have made at show business? That's all you do is attempt."

"Then all of the things I have done must have been because you stepped in and showed me the way. Thank you, Marilyn, for my accomplishments which I am sure will bring me comfort in my old age."

"You're welcome, Lowla." There was more silence to be heard. Lloyd decided to show pity to his best friend's empty life. "Lowla?"

"Yes, Marilyn."

"I think it's a good idea to write your own song. That way you will be original."

"I can't wait for you to hear it." Evan brightened at Lloyd's approval. "I am also hoping that you will get your friend, Michelle, to write the music and then have Chalmette sing it and record it for me. I want to sing live, but I think I would lose for sure." He laughed and had a toke. "I think for the talent costume I want to borrow your Cleopa-trick outfit. I think that will go with the oasis theme."

"Another great idea, Lowla. It's in Marilyn's closet. Then all we will need to do is make you an evening gown and like I said don't worry about the money, Marilyn is driving. Can you come down next Friday?"

"I don't see as how I can avoid not to."

"Great. I'll get my travel agent to take care of the details and Fed-Ex you a ticket next week. Now you make sure you go to their party this Sunday and remember to work it."

"You seem to know everything."

"And don't you forget it. Look, Rex just left the room. He is gorgeous. I will call you back when I can talk and tell you all about him." Lloyd looked out the door to make sure Rex wasn't listening. "I think this maybe the one I was looking for all along."

"What about Torch?"

"Nothing like a rush of fresh air to put out a flame. I finally heard from him and he is waiting for his things. I guess he'll get them when material items learn to walk. I gotta go, we are about to meet my family out for dinner. Call me tomorrow."

"Wow, so he is meeting the family already? He must be really nice. I thought you and your family were fighting over the business."

"We are. I figure Rex might as well get broken in. I haven't prepared him for the arguing that might happen. At least he is very polite and very well behaved. Not anything like Torch."

"Marilyn, I was thinking that I wanted to invite our friend, Diva, to come."

"Diva? You think someone like her would actually come to Niceville?"

"Yes, she wants to try her hand at stand-up comedy." Evan went into to the bathroom and pulled out his make-up.

"Okay, Lowla, that'll be fine, she can stay with us or y'all can share a trailer, but they have to know pretty soon who all is coming. She can do her stand-up in the Sunday night show. I guess those girls will love having a celebrity around instead of the usual doctors and lawyers in drag. It'll be good to see her high-maintenance self again." Lloyd spied that Rex had come back into the study. "Rex is back and we have to go, will call you tomorrow." With that Lloyd hung up.

I just hate it when he does that.

20

"*Ciao,* darling, this is The Diva."

"Well it's about time. And you can drop 'The Diva image' and 'The Diva accent,' relax, it's just me. One of your best friends since childhood."

"I was eighteen when we met."

"That's exactly what I mean," Evan said laughingly into the receiver, "since childhood. What's been going on? I haven't heard from you in days. You used to call me twenty times a day and now nothing. Has your big head finally gotten the best of you?"

"Child, you would not believe what is going on in my life, and no, the big head hasn't gotten the best of me," Beverly said, sitting at her kitchen table looking through magazines which had become a highlight of her day.

"Don't forget who put it up on your shoulders."

"That's one thing, Evan, I'll never forget. You've been a true friend. You always tell me like it is."

"Again, what's been going on that you couldn't return my message?" Evan began to put on his base while he stood in front of his bathroom mirror, getting ready for his late-night show.

"You just wouldn't believe me, even if I told you the truth," Beverly said, turning a page.

"Don't make me beg. I'm not one of your men."

"Am I that bad?" she questioned.

"Yes, Diva, you are. Why in the world do you think your parents named you Diva? You acted like a Diva even before you became a Diva. And you couldn't be satisfied with just Diva, so you had to call yourself 'The Diva.'"

"Stop, stop. More, more," Beverly let out with a grin in her voice. "I did receive your message and have been meaning to call you but something just kept coming up and I just had to sit on it." She roared with laughter.

"At least I hope this one is not crazy like the others."

"That's not funny, Evan. Not funny, but true. This one is Aaron Archer, can you believe?"

"After all these years, you mean you finally threw him a bone?"

"No, honey, he threw me one."

There was silence on the phone. "Diva, I meant pay him some attention for your career, I didn't mean that way."

"Well, I meant it that way." Beverly got up to smell the roses that Aaron had sent. "He's great and he has been treating me like royalty. I would have never thought that we would have gotten together. I'm glad I finally gave him a chance. And if you play your cards right, I may even let you be an extra in the movie of my book that Aaron is going to get produced for me, starring me, and directed by me! I'll be a regular Streisand," she said braggingly.

"How wonderful!" Evan exclaimed loudly. "I am so happy for you and I'd love to be on the big screen at last. If he needs a screen test, I have a ton of videos that I can send. It's been a long time since I met Aaron. I'll be sure to wear my best Hollywood smile. When will the filming start?" He smoothed out the foundation base on the right side of his face with his fingertips.

"You know how things go slowly here at first. Probably within a year. So, I may be able to squeeze in Florida; tell me all about it."

"You'd actually come?"

"For you, I would. But I'll need to check it out with Aaron."

"That serious, huh?"

"I just can't leave if my face is needed for filming. This movie has to be perfect. We need it for the future," Beverly said. She left the roses and went to the refrigerator.

"We?" Evan questioned, "You and who else?"

She paused for a moment to test Evan's reaction. "Me and The Diva. Don't you know there is more than one of me?" she declared as she looked at the pictures of Aaron and her that she had clipped out of the entertainment section of the paper and then taped them to the door of the icebox. She smiled at the fact that she had managed to get publicity when spotted with Aaron around the town. Beverly opened the door and found nothing inside except baking soda.

"That would explain a lot about you." He sat down in front of his bathroom mirror and chose colors for his eye shadow.

"All right then, it's Memorial Day in Florida, right?"

"Right."

"And when and where will I perform?" she asked, taking a glass out of the cabinet and filling it with water from the sink's faucet.

"It's a three-day weekend, Friday, Saturday and Sunday or Saturday, Sunday, and Monday, depending on how you look at it. You'll do your routine on Sunday night before Memorial Day in a town called Niceville not far from Fort Walton Beach, Florida." Evan put the rest of his make-up back in the drawer. "From what I understand it's just a bunch of friends that come from all walks of life that go to this trailer park every year at Memorial Day and throw one great big party and a pageant and I am entering the pageant. I'll need your support. And by friends, I mean friends, but I also mean gay and lesbian friends. There will be some straight people there so you won't be so out of place." He added enthusiastically, "Besides, the crowd will go wild just to see a celebrity right there in that trailer park."

"Evan, don't take this wrong, but I thought this was some kind of a club thing. I don't want this to blow up in The Diva's face," Beverly said very coyly. "Perhaps I can come as a Diva impersonator and be so over the top that I believe I am The Diva all the time."

"You know, that's great. I was worried that you would

have reservations. But this way, no one will know who you really are. We'll have to give you a new name. I know it's a lot to ask and I'd love to see you again." He looked at himself from different angles to make sure the make-up was perfect.

"And it will be good to see you." She drank from her glass. "I need a few days away from sunny California with my best bud. I can't wait to hear more about it, we'll have fun. I'm learning to throw caution to the wind. I will ask Aaron tonight and then I will call you tomorrow. And don't worry about a new name for me. Use this one, Beverly Heels."

"Diva, did you make that one up all by yourself? How fabulous."

"Yes, child, I did. And I need to go get ready for tonight. Call you tomorrow?" Beverly smiled at her own cleverness.

"Promise?"

"Yes, The Diva promises," Beverly again said with a smile.

"Diva, tell Aaron I said hello. Can't wait to see you."

"Me, too. Love ya."

"Love you more!" Evan hung up the phone. His smile was so big that he actually felt his cheeks swell. He finished his lips and moved from the bathroom to start filming and to be the best that he could be.

Beverly put down the receiver and smiled. The conversation with Evan went well. She looked into the mirror across from the couch. "Diva," she said as she put her hand on her heart, "Beverly is going to show you how to live, baby."

21

Nestled in the heart of the French Quarter was a restaurant that catered to anyone who could afford to go there. Usually the very rich to the very famous would come for three things: to be seen, to be treated like royalty, and to enjoy the really good food. The patrons of *Bon Mot* would dress in high fashion. Although most would be in formal dinner wear, there were those who would be in jeans, sporting sunglasses. But no matter what the attire, according to *The Times Picayune,* the ambiance and the food were undoubtedly number one. In the center of the grand dining room sat a group of people who resembled a happy family. Seated on one side of the table were Johnny, Johnny's daughter, June; beside her, her brother Johnny Ray. On the other side of the table Renee sat between Lloyd and Rex. All had just received wine, *Luna di Luna Cabernet Sauvignon,* which was Lloyd's favorite only because of the name. Renee lifted her glass to toast her family, "I toast that we all have a good evening and a wonderful meal together."

Rex was the only one who raised his glass.

"Well then, to you, Rex." She looked at her children and then back to Rex. "Thank you for not embarrassing a mother." Renee's and Rex's glasses touched.

"They're so very lucky to have you in their lives." Rex put his glass back on the table.

"How sweet. Thank you." Renee leaned over and kissed Rex on the check.

"Be careful, Grandma, Aunt Marilyn might get mad at you," Johnny Ray said.

"Stop that with your filthy mouth. I swear I can't go anywhere with you all. I don't ask for much, just a nice night out with my family." Renee slammed her glass on the table.

"You're right, Ma." Lloyd lifted his glass. "Will everyone please join me in a toast to Mother? A person which, without, we would not be here. Thank you, Mother, for all that you have done."

This time all the family at the table lifted their glasses in unison. A smile came over Renee's face. "That's more like it." They toasted and drank. Renee turned once more to Rex. "Rex, I enjoyed talking with you earlier. Maybe you should talk to Johnny about getting you some help to find your birth parents. That's just so sad." She put her hand on his shoulder. "Bless your heart."

"Mother!" Lloyd shouted.

"What, Lloyd?"

"That's really nice of you to say that, Mrs. Rochelle." Rex unfolded his napkin into his lap.

"Call me Renee." Her long fingers toyed with her large pearl necklace. Everything about Renee was exaggerated. She looked like an Italian Dolly Parton.

"What do you do for a living?" June asked Rex.

"Nothing." Rex's face reddened, but he quickly continued, "I've saved up some money and I just wanted to find out about myself so I'm not really working right now. But that probably will change." He shifted uncomfortably in his seat.

Lloyd followed, "Rex is not on trial so leave him alone."

Renee looked at Lloyd. "There's nothing wrong with being curious." She looked to her right at Rex. "You can come work at the club with me. You can help me seat the people." Renee put her elbows on the table, put her hands together and rested her chin on top of her knuckles.

"What club?" Rex asked unknowingly.

"Lloyd hasn't told you?" said Johnny.

Everyone at the table looked at Lloyd. Lloyd said in defense, "I haven't gotten around to everything yet. There are things more important than talking about myself."

Everyone at the table laughed except Lloyd and Rex, who sat still, not knowing exactly what to say.

"You all are real funny. I wanted Rex to meet all of you first before I forced a job on him. Rex, Mother is right; you ought to work at the nightclub we own with Ma. She only works a few nights a week and I work there, too." Lloyd said, his tone proud.

"When?" asked Johnny Ray, downing his glass of wine.

"This crowd is a real riot. I'll be glad when the food is here so we can eat and go," Lloyd declared.

"Where are you going?" Renee turned to Lloyd.

"We're going to a movie, Ma."

"I needed a ride across the river." Her voice was raised.

"Can't Johnny take you?" Lloyd looked at his brother.

"Sure, I'll take you, Ma," mumbled Johnny, "but I'll have to drop off June and Johnny Ray first."

"Great. Now that's settled. Oh look, here comes the food, at last." Lloyd said exasperated as he fidgeted in his chair.

"But you will take me places I need to go sometime, won't you, Rex?" asked Renee. "You see, I don't drive."

"It would be my pleasure" answered Rex.

Lloyd suddenly remembered Rex had said the same five words to him the night they met.

The waiters served the main course to the Rochelles and their distinguished guest. After a long meal and polite conversation, Lloyd got up and said, "It's been great, we gotta go."

Rex took his wallet out in order to pay for his share of the meal.

Renee waved at Rex. "Now you put that away, you are our guest. Okay, honeys, both of you give Ma a kiss."

Lloyd and Rex gladly showed Renee a sign of affection. "It really means a lot to me to be treated so kindly by you, Renee. In a way, you remind me of my own mother," Rex said to Renee as he grabbed her hand and looked her in the eyes. Rex noticed that Lloyd was watching them with interest. The boys bade goodbye to the rest of the family. Rex thanked them again for a wonderful meal. Then they headed out the door of *Bon Mot's.*

"Gosh, I have never eaten in a place like that before. It was wonderful and your family is super. A little volatile but super," he said with a wolfish smile. "Thank you for sharing with me and for being so nice. I haven't had such a good time in months," Rex said between gasps of breath. He broke into a trot to catch up with Lloyd, who was walking at a rather fast pace.

Suddenly Lloyd stopped in his tracks which caused Rex

to almost bump into him. "It looks like you are trying to win my mother."

"Of course I am." Rex answered him in a harsh tone.

It was a sound of Rex's voice that Lloyd had not heard which made him think that there was more to Rex than the corn-fed image he showed people. "You are?"

"Yes," Rex said soothingly as he touched Lloyd's shoulder. "I want your mother and your family to like me because of the way I feel about you."

Lloyd smiled and began to trot again. "The best is yet to come. We're going to enjoy life together. I just know it. Now that you know we own a nightclub, let's go there so I can get some money." Lloyd pulled out the inside of his pants pocket, which was empty.

"Is it far from here?" Rex pulled out his pants pocket also, forgetting that he had pulled out his wallet at the restaurant.

"No, it's on Bourbon and Saint Anne. It's *Le Oui-Oui.*"

"You own *Le Oui-Oui?*" Rex's face showed tremendous surprise.

"Yes, and let's make a move on it or we will miss the movie." Lloyd started walking faster still through the crowd of the Quarter.

"I wanted to talk about getting my things from the Alpine." Rex yelled to Lloyd.

"What about them? Later, okay, not at the club," Lloyd said as they arrived at *Le Oui-Oui.* The club had a stage, which was decorated to resemble a street in Paris, at the far end of a large room with a piano and a set of drums. Bistro tables sat throughout the rest of the area which led to a bar and an elaborate popcorn machine from decades ago. The design of the inside of the place was very French with pictures of the Eiffel Tower and the *Follies-Bergere.* When the employees noticed their boss, they fell all over Lloyd, asking him questions like "Who is that cute boy you got with you?" Rex smiled. The bartender offered to fix Rex a drink. Lloyd encouraged him to accept, as it would take him a minute to get the money out of the register. Rex watched Lloyd as he took an empty popcorn box and filled it with cash. Once he was done, he told everyone to work hard and have a good show and that Renee wouldn't be in that evening.

Walking out the doors of *Le Oui-Oui* Rex said to Lloyd, "I can't believe that you own *Le Oui-Oui.* I've heard and read that it's the best club in the Quarter."

"It's the only club in the Quarter where there is respectable entertainment that shows a little leg from all the can-can girls. You'll have to see the show one night. I guess if you start working there, you'll see it soon enough." Lloyd was heading in the direction of the Marilynmobile, clutching the popcorn box tightly to his side.

"But what would I do?" Rex yelled over the noise of the Quarter from the tourists, the horse-drawn carriages, the jazz houses and the drunks in the street.

"Nothing, just keep Momma company. Help her seat people. It'll be a breeze." He walked a few steps until he saw a man slumped down in the archway entrance of a closed shoe shop. *"Hey, you.* Are you asleep or just passed out drunk?" Lloyd shook him. There was no response.

"What are you doing?" Rex asked surprisingly.

"I often talk to the street people who have no place to sleep." He reached into his popcorn box and took out a one-hundred-dollar bill. "It's so sad. I had trouble once with a guy who used to sleep in my doorway. When we started talking, I understood more what he was facing and we didn't have a problem after that." Lloyd slipped the bill underneath the man's worn jacket. "Buy yourself something to eat."

The guys went back to walking. "That was really nice of you."

"I do it every time I can. I don't always have this much money on me. Sometimes it's just a twenty. I think about their reaction when they discover the money and have no clue how it got there." Lloyd and Rex reached the spot where

Lloyd had parked his BMW. He unlocked the door for Rex and went to get in the driver's side. "Rex, did I tell you how good you look tonight?"

"And in your clothes, to boot."

"No, really. It felt good to be seen with you." Lloyd said, getting in the car and putting the popcorn box under his seat.

"And it feels good to be with you," Rex said as Lloyd cranked up the car. "Also, I really appreciate you giving me new things to wear." He touched his chest to feel the material of his shirt. "Fine clothes are different. They fit better. But, I need to go by the hotel and check on my things and get my car. I haven't been there in days."

"Don't worry about it. It is all taken care of. I had Mimi and her husband go by and pick up all of your things, including your car, and pay your bill at the Alpine on the Airline. You're too special to stay there. She took your stuff to the upstairs bedroom at White Hawk Manor this afternoon when we were out, and your car is in the garage. Congratulations on your new residence. I was going to tell you tonight after the movie." Lloyd smiled triumphantly at Rex.

"How could you do that without asking me? Did you expect me to live at White Hawk Manor?" Rex's raised his voice to an obvious deaf ear.

"Of course, where else?" Lloyd said, reaching into his pocket and pulling out a tiny wrapped package which he handed to Rex. "For you."

Rex opened the wrapped package and discovered a set of keys attached to a metal ring with a medallion inscribed White Hawk Manor.

"Happy new beginnings," Lloyd said enthusiastically.

Rex's hand closed around the keys, "Oh my God, how Sunset Boulevard."

22

Ignoring his inner feeling of not wanting to face people,

Evan decided not to let his nervousness ruin a possible gold mine of fun times and new friends in the Atlanta area. He packed his make-up, his outfit and his home-made lemon pie for the pot-luck affair, hoping that he would make a good first impression as he left his home to go to the Niceville group gathering. His questionnaire regarding the pageant was neatly tucked away with his things. Most of his answers, he thought, were witty and would bring a few laughs for the theme of "Midnight at the Oasis." One of the major things that made him happy was that he had changed his name from plain Lowla to Lowla de la Vie, which meant "the life of Lowla."

Actually Lowla wasn't a plain name at all. It was another one of Lloyd's gifts to Evan's life. "Lowla" was born in New York City when Lloyd and Evan were living there. Lloyd told Evan he felt "Lowla" suited him better since he always stayed at home and was depressed. Evan immediately replied to Lloyd that "Marilyn" suited him better since he didn't date anyone other than politicians or writers. From that moment on, the names "Lowla" and "Marilyn" became part of their identities.

After going through the unusually light traffic of a Sunday afternoon in Atlanta, he turned into the subdivision according to the directions he had printed off the internet. He hadn't been accustomed to visiting the neighborhood of Peachtree Hills. Looking at all of the houses along the way, he wondered what the people must do for a living to afford such grand elegance. Evan finally arrived at the house of Doyle-Leigh. The home, which looked more like a mansion, had a manicured yard with all the trimmings he expected of a million-dollar dwelling. The sidewalk was made out of marble stone and had statues of lions on each side of the doorway. His first impulse was to leave because it was obvious he wasn't in Doyle-Leigh's league. It was also obvious that his truck did not fit in with the top-of-the-line automobiles that decorated the street in front of the house.

He took one more look at the brick façade, took a deep breath and gathered his things to go inside to meet the people. Entering the foyer, he was greeted by a butler who took his dessert and then escorted him to the party. It made Evan feel a little better to see that the house was overdone and sparse. All the rooms were enormous with hardwood floors and furniture in all the colors of the rainbow. He could understand why this was the place to have a gathering as there was plenty of open space in which to perform.

A man from the party noticed that a new arrival had joined the crowd. He made his way to Evan.

"You must be Lowla."

"Yes and you must be Doyle-Leigh," he said with an extended hand.

"Oh, give me a hug and follow me." Evan complied and then followed Doyle-Leigh into the fold. He noticed that his host looked like a faded Doris Day with about the same height and build as Evan. He was told to make himself at home and not to be a stranger to the rest of the group which looked to be about forty people. Evan quickly glanced over the place. *At last, I have arrived.* But whenever he thought like that, stupidity usually took control. Evan obliged his host and made his presence known one by one around the room. Everyone had a guy name and a girl name so it was hard to learn both, especially since most called each other by their feminine handles. There were people of all shapes, sizes and professions. Laughter rang out explosively all during the afternoon. The only somber moment came when the prayer was said before lunch. Evan was especially touched with the ending of grace when the host thanked God for everyone in this chosen family and how fortunate they were to have found each other.

He spied an empty seat next to a guy with short blond hair. Evan guessed they were the same age. Like most of his colleagues, he was a little on the heavy side. His sideburns ran from the top of his ear to the bottom of his jaw. Evan decided to go sit next to him. "Is this chair taken?"

"No, and neither am I."

"My name is Evan. I mean, Lowla."

"Florence Tightintale, at your cervix."

Evan laughed politely. "Do you make house calls?"

"Only if there is a doctor in the house," Florence laughed back.

"Are you registered?" Evan quipped as he sat down.

"At Saks."

On the other side of Florence was an unoccupied love seat. Another party attendee plopped down and said, "I am so glad there are egg rolls on the buffet. I've been craving them."

"Quit performing." Florence pointed to Toule Lyps. "Toule," he pointed back to Lowla, "this is Lowla and vice versa, whatever."

Evan noticed Toule was the most muscular of the group. *He must look weird in drag.* He was a handsome dark-haired good-ole-boy type. "Pleased to meet you."

"Likewise, I'm sure." Toule smiled. "Quick somebody come sit by me, here comes Craven Fame," he yelled teasingly.

Craven Fame walked with swinging hips. He was tall, skinny and had black curly hair. "Make room for Momma. Craven Fame here."

Toule motioned to Evan. "Lowla, there."

Craven sat down and the conversation began. Honey dripped from them like sap clinging to a tree. They were so nice to him, expressing sincere interest in every word Evan said. Crown Jewel dropped in on the four and took Evan's questionnaire and discussed Niceville during the afternoon brunch. As time progressed, more and more of the group gathered around Evan. The chatter mostly centered on what he did for a living, where he lived, what he drove and what he did for fun. He thought it was impressive to tell them about Lowla and Salvatore. Evan noticed that Doyle-Leigh left before he could finish his story. Although he was concerned that he might have offended Doyle-Leigh, he continued while the others listened to him intently.

When the luncheon was over, the chosen family divided up and went to different rooms in the house to get ready for entertainment and pictures. He had asked earlier if it was okay to go and smoke on the terrace before he got ready. A few of the group joined him; most just looked from inside the house. He could only imagine what they must have been saying and maybe he had gone too far. But in his opinion it was best to be who he was from the very first. He had wanted to smoke just to help him through this drag outing. The people on the terrace were passing another joint when Doyle-Leigh opened the sliding glass door, gave a mock cough and called, "Hey, hippies! Get ready." The crowd put the smoke out and went inside to change.

After getting dressed in the upstairs master bedroom, Evan stood in front of the mirror. He thought he looked good in his one-piece white-laced bathing suit, white hose, white heels, blonde wig and a wedding veil. Twirling around, practicing his routine one more time, he heard his name called for pictures. He didn't realize when he had been invited for the afternoon festivities that these pictures would be used for the brochure at Niceville for the upcoming pageant. If he had, he probably would have worn a different outfit. It was his turn to perform. He held his breath, went out into the archway and lip-synched Madonna's *Like A Virgin.* His performance was very simple and the group politely applauded when he was finished. Overall, Evan thought his Lowla debut went well which provided him hope for the pageant and a new interest to go to New Orleans to finish his outfits, music and to be with Lloyd and meet Rex.

23

"It seems as though I'll need your services once more," Renee said, holding the phone so it wouldn't mess up her hair. "Yes, him again and I thought that June would be the one to grow up and cause problems.

"There is a new boy in Lloyd's life. I was hoping that after the Torch fiasco, he would have waited and gotten to know someone a little better. I just don't think I could stand another five years of an impertinent, ungrateful gold-digger sucking the family dry." She looked around to make sure no one else in within earshot of her conversation.

"This boy appears to be nice . . . too nice and too eager to give a good impression. On the surface, he presents himself as the kind of a young man you would want to have as a son, except things, in my opinion, just do not add up. He states that he is in town solely for the purpose of finding his real parents. There seems to be a question of his origin. He has no job, although I've persuaded him to work with me a few days a week at the club. I thought it was a good idea to keep him close." Again she moved the phone while she fixed her hair.

"He has already moved in with Lloyd, but that was Lloyd's doing. Lloyd is convinced the guy is an angel sent from God. No, I am not convinced. All I know is he says he is twenty-seven, claims to be from Plain Dealing and goes by the name of Rex Greenfield.

"Why don't you drop by, let's say next Friday around ten p.m. That's when I usually stand outside greeting people as they come into the club. I'll make sure Rex is by my side. He's about six feet and blond hair and in a masculine way he favors Lloyd. Don't mention this to Johnny or anyone. I wouldn't want my kids to know their mother is constantly aware of their moves. I prefer to remain naïve. I don't want to be outsmarted. Besides, they really like Rex. Actually I do too, but I've been around enough to know that if it is too good to be true then it is too good to be true. There is just something about this situation that troubles me and I just can't figure it out as to what it is.

"Thank you, Johnston. As ever, I am indebted to you. Hope you find out some information soon. Bye now." Renee hung up the bedroom extension, opened the door and called for Johnny to take her to the club. Carefully she put back the earring she had taken off to talk on the phone. She grabbed her purse and looked in the mirror, admiring her hair. She was an Italian woman who had married a Frenchman but wore her hair like a country singer. Once again, the image of an Italian Dolly Parton stared back at her from the mirror. She smiled, thinking how wonderful she looked at sixty as the bedroom lights lit up her sequined jacket. Quickly she picked up a can of hairspray and sprayed her hair for a while then exited out the door.

24

Sitting on his red velvet chair to the left of his queen-size bed, twisting the telephone cord as he spoke, Doyle-Leigh, aka the Executive Directrix of the Niceville Group, talked about the upcoming Miss Niceville Pageant to another of the founders of the group. Faux Pas, a Miss Niceville entertainment legend even though he rarely performed on stage, was eavesdropping in the doorway of the master bathroom. Faux Pas had gone in there as the phone rang to try on Doyle-Leigh's wigs with hopes to use them for the Miss Anorexia-At-Large Pageant in July. Although it was strictly for charity, that pageant was important for someone of Faux Pas' hugeness to win as he thought of himself as thin and was desperate to win a normal title. Rumor had it that he actually was responsible for starting the "At Large" pageants. Some speculate it was coincidence that his first and only title was "Miss Blue Bar At Large," the first known "At Large" pageant. He stood around five-foot-seven and carried about two hundred and thirty pounds and was bald. Most of the Niceville performers were also overweight thirty-something men who tried to pass themselves as fit and trim. They also tried to pass themselves off as talented. Struggling to hear the conversation, he took the wig off and without looking tossed it.

Suddenly he realized the conversation had come to an end. He turned to pick up the wig he had tossed aside and almost gasped aloud when he saw it had landed in the open toilet. Immediately he picked up the semi-wet wig, opened the shower door, threw the wig in and then closed the shower door. He got another wig from Doyle-Leigh's elaborate wig stand, put it on and turned back to the mirror as if nothing had happened.

"Sister, you'll never guess what Rouge-Red just told me!" Doyle-Leigh said in a teasing tone as he pushed through the half-opened door.

"Were you on the phone? I didn't even hear it ring," Faux Pas replied as he finger-curled the front hairs of the wig he was wearing. "I hope you don't mind, I just don't know why you had bangs on this hairdo. They may look good on your forehead, but not on mine."

"Oh just style my wig anyway you want. My hair is your hair, darling."

"Thank you ever so . . . so what did Rouge-Red say?"

"Oh, just talking about the 'talent-less' Lowla entering our pageant this Memorial Day. Honestly, next thing you know, Babe the pig will compete."

Faux Pas screamed, "At least we could barbeque Babe."

"Well, aren't we roasting her?"

"No, that's something you do to someone's face. Either way, all Lowla is going to give us is indigestion. Not even entertainment." Faux Pas stood back from the mirror admiring himself. "On second thought, Babe has a lot more charisma than Lowla."

"Oh, stop!" *Oh* was a major part of Doyle-Leigh's vocabulary. "Oh, get this — she has even changed her name from 'Lowla' to 'Lowla de la Vie' according to her answers on the questionnaire. She must have been really stoned when she filled that one out. Did you see the cloud of smoke around her on the terrace at the pot-luck? She brought the pot and tried her luck." He giggled as he imitated Evan saying his drag name. "Lowla de la Vie."

"De la B?" questioned Faux Pas.

"No, V as in vulgar." Doyle-Leigh said as though a light bulb had gone off in his head. "Oh, the 'de-la-Vie' must be the talent part."

"Don't be mean, Doyle darling." He took off the wig and tried on another. "Just because you're trash and get high doesn't mean you're not talented. I'm sure at one point even Bette Midler bought her make-up from the dime store and got her clothes from a thrift shop." Faux Pas walked from the mirror to get a better view of the new hair on his head.

"Oh, Faux, how true. But I hear her talent is doing something other than lip-sync with that Mick Jagger mouth of hers. I hope Lowla knows that trashy whore is not a winning talent."

Faux Pas put his hands on his hips in an effort to be dramatic. "It's not? I thought that's what you did the year you won."

"Oh no Faux, I didn't want to be accused of following in your footsteps!" Doyle-Leigh darted without hesitation.

"Perhaps Lowla can give you a few pointers so you could get a man or at least get one in bed." Faux saw that he had wounded Doyle-Leigh with those harsh words. "Is that it? There was some talk going around at the pot-luck affair about Lowla and a certain cop. Lowla did the man you wanted, didn't he? The man you keep talking about, yet he has never been seen. What was his name again? Sal . . . something?"

With a simple tongue lashing he could make Faux Pas really mad. But, that was just not done. There was going to be enough fallout when Faux Pas found out he had been sleeping with Faux Pas' lover. "Oh, no . . . no, my man, who must be protected from many things, is not that desperate or ethnic. Besides, I know how to jump for my man."

"Yeah, you jump right to your knees."

"That seems to work for me." *Maybe you should try it some time on your husband because he really likes it.* "It's just that

Evan . . . "

"Her name is Lowla, Lowla de la Vie," sang Faux Pas.

"Well she sure ain't no showgirl and she is living proof to the second half of that song. I don't know why she didn't change her name to *Lowla Lowlife*. That freaky way she spells Lola." He imitated Evan again, "Hi, I'm Lowla Lowlife and I'm high, but low."

"Doyle, maybe you should suggest it to her. It's catchy." Faux said as he laughed.

"Oh, Lowla is making such a big deal about her drag debut at thirty-five in the Miss Niceville Pageant. After seeing her *Like a Virgin* at the pot-luck, I can understand why she has waited so long. What I can't understand is why she is even bothering. That is one act that will open and close on the same night."

Laughter emitted from them both. "Seriously now, Doyle, you know we really need the Lowlas of the world to make our pageant look legit. And the extra cash always comes in handy." Trying on another wig, Faux said, "I wonder what everyone is doing for talent this year? Those who have talent, that is."

They both laughed again until Doyle-Leigh turned to Faux Pas and seriously stated, "Don't you tell anyone I told you . . ."

"I won't. You know I won't. My word is as firm as jello."

"Ohhh-k! I hear that Florence Tightintail is debuting *Judy*."

"Damnation!" Faux slammed down his hairbrush. "You had to tell her I was working on Judy Garland, you bitch. Florence always finds a way to steal my ideas."

"Calm down, Faux. You know that I am most faithful and loyal to you. I don't know how she found out, honestly." *How am I going to get out of this?* "But just imagine how good you are going to look doing your 'Judy' after hers. And just think how you will look when I personally take care of your outfit and make-up. No one will ever know we knew."

Faux Pas smiled as he knew he needed all the help he could get when it came to make-up, costumes, and wigs. He depended on his "sisters" for those items. It seemed that he never had any "props" of his own and would arrive at the last minute demanding that everyone stop what they were doing and take care of his needs.

Doyle-Leigh continued with the closer: "Listen to me, she'll think twice before she puts her nose around your business again."

"Doyle, hon, I am s-o-o-o glad we're not like that."

"Oh, me too, Faux, me too!"

"Don't you think we ought to call Toule Lyps and Craven Fame?"

"Whatever for?"

"Think about it, Doyle. Momma didn't send you to Blonde School for nothing, did she?"

"Oh!" A big smile came over Doyle's face as he realized where Faux was headed with that train of thought. "All of us together can make sure that Florence looks like the amateur she is."

They looked at each other for a moment, then raced to the phone to spread the joy that only a pageant can bring.

25

Friday afternoon and rush hour were upon him. He was worried that he would miss his flight as he pulled into the weekly parking at Hartsfield International Airport. Since it was just for a weekend Evan's entire luggage consisted of a carry-on. He found a spot, grabbed his bag, and headed for the gate to depart for the fun city of New Orleans.

He arrived at the counter just when the final boarding call was announced. He was grateful that Lloyd had Federal Expressed his ticket with a seat already assigned so all he had to do was hand the ticket to the counter attendant. Making his journey down the jetway, he thought of all the times he had spent on a plane to and from *The Crescent City*. It seemed as though he loved *The Big Easy,* but it never worked out for him to stay there although he had tried many, many times. It didn't work because he could not leave the fantasy world he had created in Atlanta. He always felt uncomfortable being away from it. Coming up to the open hatch, Evan paused and put his hand, palm out, on the body of the jet. He stopped to pray for the blood of Jesus to protect the plane as he always did no matter if he held up the line or not. He didn't care. He prayed for the blood of Jesus to protect everyone on the plane, as well. *If they knew that, they wouldn't mind waiting a second.* It was the only way he could fly and halfway relax. Flying usually brought out the worst of his nerves. There were times when he would take four white Xanax and then drink wine on the plane, only to still be wound up. It was one of the few times when his palms would actually sweat tears.

Making his way down the aisle, half looking at the row numbers and half looking at who was on board, he finally came upon row number twenty-eight, seat F. At first the gentleman sitting in seat E looked vaguely familiar. Staring into his direction a little while longer, Evan realized who the man was. He stopped and put his carry-on in the overhead bin. "Excuse me, sir; I need to get to my seat."

The man looked up from his magazine, smiled and got up to let Evan in the row and then returned to his seat and looked at Evan. "So you're the reason we haven't departed yet?"

"No, they just started calling the final boarding when I arrived. You know how Friday afternoon traffic is in Atlanta. What are you doing here?"

"Going to a convention, and you?"

"Lowla is getting fitted for an evening gown and costumes by the best fashion designer in New Orleans. Speaking of which, I almost didn't recognize you without *your* costume on." Evan fastened his seatbelt. "What do policeman need a convention for anyway? Pep rallies for arrests?"

"Actually I am a detective. The uniform is a decoy I use

sometimes."

"Are you here alone or are you traveling with other detectives?"

"I'm on my own," Salvatore said, grabbing Evan's arm.

The jet began to back away from the concourse while the flight attendants began their speeches about airline safety and the precautions one would take should there be an emergency.

"This is quite a surprise. How long are you going to be in New Orleans, Lowla?" he emphasized loudly.

"Keep your voice down. Until Tuesday. How about you?"

"I was slated to come back on Sunday. This is just your weekend seminar. Maybe I can stay until Tuesday. That is, if you think you can work me in your busy schedule. I'd love to see Lowla get measured." Salvatore suggestively began to fasten his seatbelt.

Evan said with high hope in his voice, "And I would love for my friends to see you. I don't think there would be a problem for you to stay at my friend Lloyd's house or his apartment if it's not already occupied. That is if you do not have any other plans for lodging."

"Nothing I can't get out of. It looks like after Saturday afternoon, I'll be all yours." The jet had made it to the runway and was revving its engines for its ascent into the sky. As the pressure of the building speed pushed them deeper into their seats, Salvatore looked at Evan with a serious glare. "There is one thing I'd like to ask you, though."

"What?" Evan said with an unexpected smile.

"Are you a member of the mile-high club?" Salvatore's smile widened.

26

Beverly got out of bed and could not believe that she had slept so long. She began her search to find the combination to the safe because she was totally out of money. She had only been able to eat because Aaron had taken her to many a restaurant since they became an item. And what she didn't eat at the restaurant she would take home in doggy bags for lunch the next day. Sooner or later she would have to figure out a way to confess to Aaron that she had let the combination to the safe slip her mind. Surely he would have to believe her, especially since he seemed to be totally smitten by her "new" charms. Beverly had already been through every drawer, box and coat pocket in the house. The only place she hadn't looked was in the tank of the toilet. Figuring The Diva would not put it there, she didn't bother to lift the lid to check for herself.

Feeling a little antsy, she decided to get the newspaper from the corridor outside the condo in order to calm her nerves. Usually a warm bath did that for her, but she had spent so much time in the tub lately. She was feeling uneasy because it had been a long time that she was in control rather than Diva. It was a great feeling, but in the back of her mind she thought that one day soon Diva would surely appear . . . and then what would happen to her? Not to mention the shock that Aaron would experience. Aaron had been so good to her and she had built a deep caring for him in a short period of a time. She retrieved the paper and looked over the first section. All the same old news: inflation, war, and higher prices on the home front.

She decided to go out to take her mind off of things while she waited to hear from Aaron about their movie deal. She thought that maybe she would go to a free museum this afternoon, alone, with a scarf around her hair, accompanied by sunglasses this time, like Diva wore when she went on an outing. He had told her all of the work he had done on the project during mad throes of passion the night before. If anything, Diva should be grateful that Beverly had succeeded where Diva had failed. She got out the entertainment section, which produced a big shock. There — in color — on the first page was Beverly in a series of three pictures. The caption above the pictures was *THE DIVA will work for food: The desperate attempts for attention of today's celebrities.*

The pictures were laid out horizontally. The first was of her opening the sandwich, the second was of her consuming the sandwich, with the third being when she patted her rear. The article further went on to say the photographer did not see the transaction of The Diva buying the sandwich, just that she had come storming out of the store with a newspaper tucked underneath her arm. The reporter, who was also the photographer, went on to say that maybe "attention pangs," not hunger, had driven The Diva to dress the way she had and blatantly pose for pictures on a sunny afternoon while eating. The article closed with the statement that some people will do anything for publicity when their careers had faltered.

This enraged Beverly to the point of tears. *How could that son-of-a-bitch do this to me? What is this going to do to my image? What is this going to do to Aaron?* She broke into uncontrollable sobbing. Wailing, she walked from one end of the condo to the other. A few times she would stop, look at herself, then scream as she continued walking through her home. Feeling a bit light headed, she sat down. She looked into a mirror and said aloud, "You really fixed things this time didn't you, Beverly?"

"Yes, darling you did," came the reply, apparently from the mirror.

"What the . . .?" said a startled Beverly.

"Yes, darling, it is The Diva, talking to you."

Beverly pinched herself. "Oh dear God, I've lost it, this can't be happening. I'm hallucinating."

"Yes, you are a figment of The Diva's imagination and The Diva wants to come back. Only The Diva can get you out of this one." The reflection in the mirror calmly stated, "Let it go, Beverly, get out of The Diva's head and let The Diva have her life back."

"No. Never. You're too weak to come back or else you'd be here. You don't know how to live."

"The Diva would have never let herself be photographed or dressed that way. The Diva has class, or have you forgotten? And The Diva would never have slept with Aaron just to get a movie deal."

"You mean you know everything I've been doing?" This was surprising to Beverly even though she knew what Diva did when she was dormant.

"Yes and it infuriates her that The Diva can't get back." Diva had a hand on each side of her head. "Stop. You are ruining The Diva's life. Get out of her head."

Beverly looked the mirror squarely in the eye and said, "If it weren't for me, you would not have a chance at a movie deal." Pointing to The Diva, "*You* get out of *my* head. This is my life now. You don't know how to have any fun and you don't know how to love. And for your information 'class' cannot snuggle. I have a chance to have someone wonderful in my life and if you are in my head, you'd know it. The lovemaking Aaron and I have done has been a beautiful experience. You should stick around to see how it actually feels for someone to touch you."

"The Diva goes away when that happens. Just the thought of being touched makes her sick to her stomach. And do you think Aaron will want you now? Honey, he is Hollywood royalty and he will not want a common ghetto tramp like you."

With that Beverly snapped and grabbed the first thing she could reach and threw an alabaster egg into the mirror. Pieces of reflection flew over the floor and onto the table. Beverly didn't stop there. She proceeded to break as many mirrors as she could while she screamed, "You will not make me go away. Damn you. Damn the photographer. Damn the world."

The ringing of the intercom broke the sound of falling mirrors and moaning. Beverly went to the intercom and pushed the "speak" button. "Yes, what is it?" she said in a snappy tone.

"It's Joe, the doorman. Aaron is here to see you."

Beverly took a deep breath and decided to face the music. "Please send him up." If the heat got too hot, she could always slip away and leave Diva holding the bag. But Beverly really felt attached to Aaron and did not want to lose him . . . or her existence. She frantically tried to pick up the pieces of the broken mirrors when she heard the knock on her door. Beverly dropped what she had in her hands. She went to the door, opened it and found Aaron standing there.

After an awkward silence, Aaron put down his briefcase and hugged her, "It'll be all right, baby. I'm here and I will take care of you." The two just stood in the doorway and he was holding her tight. "Let's go inside."

"I am so sorry that I let that happen. I just wanted to get out for a change. I wanted to see how people lived and shopped around here. How did I know some sleazebag was following me? You have seen the paper, haven't you?"

He looked at the disarray of the room. "Yes, and I see you have made quite a mess. Why are you so upset?"

"I thought that once you saw the paper and how I had messed things up and how that man says I stole a sandwich, and that my career had faltered, you wouldn't want me any more." She attempted to pick up more broken pieces. "I couldn't take that right now."

"When I saw the paper, I thought you might feel this way." He knelt down to help her. "We have really become in tune with each other. Don't be silly, Diva, I'll always want you." He took his hand and lifted her chin. "As far as those pictures go, there is no such thing as bad publicity, and with your movie deal this probably happened at a good time. It's just you all dressed up eating in the park. Besides you look great in those pictures, I must say. Here's my handkerchief. Dry those beautiful eyes, darling. I have great news."

"You're not mad?" Beverly said in disbelief as she sat down, drying her eyes with his handkerchief.

"Not at all. Didn't you hear me? I have great news. It'll

make you feel better. I promise."

In between tears she cried, "What is it?"

He got up and put the last pieces of mirror on the table. He went to his briefcase and pulled out a long folder. "Contracts for us to sign!" Aaron did a little victory dance. "Paramount is offering us a two-movie deal . . . as long as I am involved, of course."

"Two movies?"

"Yes, my darling. *A Kept Reflection* is one and we have a year to work on an idea for the other. So dry your eyes, we have to get to work."

Beverly instantly grabbed his face and pulled Aaron closer to her so she could kiss him. "I don't know what to say. What would I do without you?"

"Wait, there's more."

"More. How can there be more?"

Aaron stepped to his briefcase and pulled out a small box and then got on his knees in front of a seated Beverly. "I know this is kind of fast. But heck, this is Hollywood and it's not like I haven't tried from years before. I don't know what clicked, but I think we make a great team and I think the future is ours for the taking." He opened the box and produced a diamond ring. "Diva, you are what I have been looking for my entire life. Please complete me. Will you marry me?"

Beverly started to cry again, "I just want you to know, with or without the movie, for richer or poorer, I will marry you."

Aaron slipped the ring on her finger, stood up and then picked her up in his arms and took her to the bedroom.

27

The Louis Armstrong New Orleans International Airport was quite crowded as Lloyd, Rex and Chalmette hurried to meet Evan at the gate of his arriving plane. Dodging tourists and business people throughout the concourse, Lloyd stopped in front of a television monitor. He pointed to the screen and yelled, "The plane has already landed. I'll bet Evan is on his way to the baggage claim."

A voice came from over their shoulders, "I would be if I had baggage like yours."

Lloyd and his group turned around to see Evan standing behind them, accompanied by someone they had not met. "Lowla! You made it! You're here." They embraced as the airport patrons watched while moving around them. Pulling away, Lloyd introduced Rex with enthusiasm in his voice. "This is Rex."

Extending his hand, "I've heard a lot about you, Lowla."

"Yeah, but you can't prove it." He took Rex's handshake and turned it into a hug. "It's great to meet you. Chalmette, I can't believe you came to the airport, too."

"You know me, get me while you can." Chalmette said.

Evan gave her a hug also and said, "You're looking good." All the while, Salvatore stood patiently in attendance. "Everybody, I want you to meet a friend of mine. Lloyd, Chalmette, and Rex, this is Salvatore."

"Salvatore," Lloyd's mouth was almost watering. Taking in every inch of him with his eyes, Lloyd proceeded, "Now that's a Stanley Kowalski if I have ever seen one. I've heard a lot about you. Lowla isn't under arrest, is she?"

Salvatore put his hand on Evan's shoulder. "House arrest. I'm afraid I'll have to escort Lowla wherever she goes on this trip." He laughed and continued, "Actually I am in town for a meeting. I was blown away when I saw her coming down the aisle and then sit right beside me. Neither one of us knew the other was going to be on a plane not to mention the same plane. It was something right out of a book."

"It's a small world in so many ways." Lloyd took Evan's arm, removing him from Salvatore's grip. "Let's get to baggage claim 'cause we got a lot to do and Chalmette needs to get your measurements tonight."

"All I have is a carry-on," Evan stated as he moved his arm from Lloyd and walked closer to Salvatore.

"Me, too, so we are good to go," Salvatore said with a smile as Evan stood beside him.

"How long are you going to be in town for, Salvatore?" Rex said curiously.

"Hopefully until Tuesday. That is if Lloyd will let me stay at one of his places. I had planned to camp out at the Marriott and was going back on Sunday until fate intervened." He looked lovingly at Evan. "Lowla suggested that maybe I could be a part of your weekend." Salvatore picked up his bag and slung it over his shoulder as they all started to leave the airport.

"Let's hurry," Rex ordered. "We're double parked."

As they walked Lloyd made plans for the evening. "I hope we can all fit in the Marilynmobile. Chalmette and I will sit in the front and the three of you will have to squeeze in the back."

"As long as I am in the middle," Evan giggled as they went out the sliding doors.

"Salvatore, do you need to call and cancel your reservation or do you need to get to your meeting or what?" Lloyd questioned.

"Yeah, that would be great to call and cancel with the Marriott. Thanks for letting me stay. This will be the first time I have ever stayed in New Orleans in someone's home."

"Okay then we will head back to White Hawk Manor." The quintet piled into the car, sitting as instructed earlier by Lloyd. "I'd prefer we all stay together rather than you and Lowla in the *Quarter*. You can make your calls and Rex can help you get settled. Lowla, Chalmette and I will go to the theater and get Lowla's measurements out of the way. Then we can all meet at the club and go have dinner." They all agreed as the convertible Marilynmobile darted up the freeway into the city toward Lloyd's home. Once they were at Lloyd's, Rex and Salvatore got out of the car, and the others went to the theater at which Chalmette worked.

"I can't tell you how much I appreciate you making my evening gown," Evan said to Chalmette. He stripped down to his underwear so that he could be measured accurately. "It's a shame there is not a best gown award because I know I would win that."

"Don't worry, Evan, you'll look great. Just don't gain or lose any weight. Once I sew it, it's gonna stay a size sixteen," Chalmette said, taking her measuring tape and putting it around Evan's chest. "Do you want big boobs?"

"Yes, of course Lowla wants big boobs and big hair. Just like my momma's," Lloyd said as he looked through the costumes in the seamstress room of the theater.

"What are you looking for, Lloyd? Don't mess my costumes up." Chalmette wrote down Evan's chest measurements while glaring at Lloyd.

"I'm looking for something to wear to the ball. This is great." Lloyd pulled out an Elizabethan dress trimmed in maroon and gold.

"The ball is far away, now put that up. Actors are picky about their stagewear. And you're not going to get me in any more trouble." Lloyd continued to parade the dress in front of a mirror. "Put it back!" Chalmette ordered, looking at Lloyd with her hands folded across her chest.

Evan looked around the room, taking in each costume creation and the row of sewing machines used to create such enchantment. He couldn't help but to look at Chalmette and wish there was some way he could look like her. She was twenty-nine years old with black flowing hair, high cheek bones, Creole features . . . simply beautiful. "I don't understand why you aren't a star. You can sing and make anything with a needle and thread. And you are so pretty."

"Don't worry, Evan. Lloyd has already paid me," Chalmette said with a warm smile. She took the measuring tape and placed the top on Evan's rear and let the remainder fall to the floor, "Don't move."

"I'm meaning it sincerely." Evan spoke as he stood stoically. "Really, you are a wonderful person and always have been."

"You too, Evan, and that is why I am making the gown for you. If it were for Lloyd, I wouldn't do it."

Lloyd was taking more costumes off the racks. "Why don't you ever make me anything like this, Chalmette?" He held another elaborate costume to his chest and admired himself again.

"You need to tell me what you want rather than letting me make all the decisions." She wrote down more of Evan's measurements. "That's it. Done. Now I got to get to work." She turned to Lloyd. "I told you to leave that shit alone." She walked over to take things out of his hands and started hanging them back up.

"You're not going to eat with us?" Evan asked.

"No. I'll be working all night. I've got this wedding on Sunday and I have a few dresses to finish. I hope you like black satin." She looked at Evan with her hand on her chin. "A strapless black satin dress with elbow-length gloves would look great on you. I have a lot of that material left over from a show so it's free material." Chalmette went to a cloth bin and began to look through it.

"That sounds really great. Kinda Rita Hayworth in *Gilda*. Could we bring you anything or can I stay here and help?"

"No, Evan, I have some friends coming over to help me, but you can order us pizza. That would be nice."

"Done, what kind?" Evan turned to Lloyd. "Do you know a place we can call?"

"She knows. She can order. I'll leave her some money. Look, we gotta go. Our men are at home alone and I am beginning to get nervous." Lloyd said as he opened his wallet. Handing Chalmette money, he said, "Here's fifty dollars. That should be enough pizza. Come on, Lowla."

Evan quickly got dressed and rushed to hug Chalmette. He and Lloyd left the theater and got into the car. "You don't have to worry about Salvatore, unless Rex likes to put on a dress."

"No, Rex doesn't do drag and I may never do it again. Rex brings out the man in me." Lloyd looked into the rear view mirror. "Did I say that? But that Salvatore is really handsome. I can't believe you got him." Lloyd cranked up the car.

"I don't have him. He just uses me because I let him. He's married or so he says. And he really doesn't like me. He likes Lowla and this long hair of mine." Evan folded his arms. "But I do have a video tape of us having sex."

"You're kidding? How did you do that?"

Evan smiled. "Well, we went into my bedroom where I film and I kinda turned on the VCR to record when he went to the bathroom. You know, that video might come in handy one day." He laughed.

"I can't wait to see it." Lloyd said eagerly.

"And I can't wait to show it to you. You might learn something."

"Remember I taught you everything!"

"But don't mention the tape, he doesn't know." Evan smirked and sighed. "Did you get me any weed?"

"Even though I don't smoke it, you know I did. Look in the glove compartment. It's already rolled."

Evan lifted up the glove compartment, took out a gold cigarette case, opened it up and pulled out a joint. He lit up and inhaled the first smoke from the joint as though he hadn't had pot in a while. The two friends headed for the house as Evan smoked and Lloyd listened. "Rex is really cute. There is something familiar about him, like I've known him for a long time. He seems nice, too."

"He is. I don't know what I would have done without him. It's like a present from God so I won't think about Torch. We have become really, really close. And I think he likes me for me. We talk all the time like we did when you and I first met, except Rex and I have sex." Lloyd stopped for the red light.

"We would have sex together if either one of us had been a top. We were just meant to be best friends for naps and such." Evan took another toke. "It really is going to be weird to be here and not sleeping with you. Usually we spend all of our time together like we are stuck with glue. Now you have Rex. I guess that must be part of the safety net with us." Lloyd looked at Evan. "We love each other and love the same things, so when we spend time together it's not about sex. It's about true friendship and you have so many friends. Yet, you still hang with me."

"Don't be silly. You are my only friend. People like me don't really have friends. I have surrounded myself with people who want to go somewhere in life and think that I can make it happen and when I don't, they become enemies and leave."

"But you can make it happen. Look at what all you have made happen for me and I am still not on the social ladder of success, but I still love you after all these years. You know, I have always liked you for the person you are and not the money you have. I am still just me, the shy person you met at an audition a lifetime ago. The country boy you saved from a life of normalcy." Evan sighed as he took a deep toke.

"Lowla, put that joint down. Do you want everyone to see?" The light turned green and they were off again.

"Sorry, I sometimes forget myself. I'll take one more toke and then put it out. Thanks for getting it for me."

"Anything for my sister. And you don't have to put it out."

"I don't want to give Rex a bad impression, Marilyn, unless you have already done that for me." Evan took the joint and ground it out in the ashtray.

"I let you handle those things all by yourself. I've been so busy; I forgot to ask you how it went at Doyle-Leigh's. Didn't you fit right in?"

"I hope so. I had a great time. They were all real nice and

they all talked to me like I was a celebrity," Evan beamed.

"They all wanted to get the four-one-one on you. That's all. Don't be fooled. They all want to be Miss Niceville, past or present."

"But not any of them were pretty, I thought, or that talented either. But I guess that is not a fair thing for me to say. Who am I to judge pretty or talent? Maybe I did fit in, except for the pretty part. My performance was terrible and so was my costume." Evan threw his hands in the air. "Like a virgin, hey."

"They won't be able to say that this Memorial Day. You have got to practice and practice. At least I know you'll look good. Don't disappoint me, you are my horse and you are going to win." Lloyd put a fist to the air. "It sure is hot tonight."

"Yeah, but it feels good. Look, I can see your house from here. It is great to be back in the city."

"Too bad you don't live here, Lowla."

"It's too bad I don't live at all," Evan said.

Lloyd looked at Evan and rolled his eyes as they pulled to the front of White Hawk Manor. Sitting on the swing were Rex and Salvatore. "Ah, what a sight, two hunky men on my porch. You Confederate soldiers hungry?" Lloyd said as southern as he could.

"For you," said Rex, getting out of the swing.

Evan hurried up the steps to the front porch to stand by his soldier. "Make all your calls?"

"Yes," Salvatore said. He got up to greet Lloyd and Evan. "I'm all unpacked in the Lowla Suite. It's nice. Can't wait to break it in."

"The bed or Lowla?" Lloyd said.

"I broke one in a long time ago. I bet you can guess which one." Salvatore put his arm around Evan, who smiled as though he believed he was actually happy.

"Is Miss Ruby okay, Rex?" Lloyd said as he went to the front door.

"She's been fed and is asleep. Just lock the door and let's go." Rex handed Lloyd the keys. The guys headed down the steps to the car. "I'll drive. You and Evan can sit in the back this time."

"It's Lowla," Lloyd said to Rex.

"It's confusing that everyone you know has more than one name," Rex teased Lloyd.

"It's just nicknames and you'll get used to it." Lloyd responded.

Before they knew it, Rex had maneuvered them into the Quarter. "Is this your first time here, Salvatore?"

"It is my first time here like this. Usually every time has been so rigid with the wife or other policemen. I feel like I am far away from myself," Salvatore said, getting out of the car and pushing the seat up for Evan to get out.

They walked to *Le Oui-Oui* and went in as the show was about to start. Lloyd walked to the bar and ordered drinks for them all. The emcee entered the stage, and the dancing girls followed. They twirled, spun their skirts high in the air and had naughty-but-nice fun with the customers. The club offered clean entertainment, fun for all ages to enjoy, which wasn't the case with most clubs on Bourbon Street. Lloyd made his way to the stage manager and whispered into his ear some instructions for the performance now underway. The stage manager got the attention of the star of the show and glanced towards Evan's friend. The show stopped and the Madame was scouting the audience, looking for the perfect man. She eyed each man until she came to spot Salvatore. Before he knew it, Salvatore was up on stage blindfolded and was made to take a garter off a dancer with his teeth. The audience loved it. From the look on Salvatore's face, he did too. Upon leaving the stage, he went directly back to Evan. "We have a new thing to do, Lowla." Salvatore said, wiping the sweat from his brow.

"Are ya'll ready to eat?" Lloyd said as he got a popcorn box to do his routine of taking money from the cash drawer.

They looked at him and said in unison, "No."

"Would you mind if Salvatore and I walked along the river at the Riverwalk for a while?" Evan said to Lloyd and Rex.

"You remember where the apartment is, right?" Lloyd said, filling his box carefully with ten and twenty dollar bills. "Meet us there in about an hour and we will go eat."

"See ya later then. Let's go." Evan turned to Salvatore and they were out the door. They started walking through the French Quarter to the River. The night was a bit breezy but very humid. Evan didn't care. He was delighted to be seen with such a prize. He couldn't actually believe he wasn't the third wheel as he usually was when he was with Lloyd. People were shouting, and on the sidewalks some mimes and tap dancers were entertaining the tourists. Throughout the area, there were artists sketching likenesses of people or painting originals of the Quarter's famous sights. In spots, the air smelled like urine, the usual fare for that time of night as people came to the city to drink and to be rowdy. The two of them just walked, taking in all the sights and shops until they reached the Riverwalk at the Mississippi. From there, they could see the lights of the downtown buildings as their reflections shimmered on the water. The noise from the Quarter was music in the background. Evan looked at Salvatore just as the Cathedral's chimes started to ring eleven.

"What are you thinking?" Salvatore put his hands in his neatly pressed dress pants.

"That I wish this wasn't a fleeting moment. That I wish this was real. That I wish I could just enjoy our time together and not think of Tuesday when it will end. That I don't know why you are here, with me." Evan looked up at the sky then back at downtown. He and Salvatore had walked near the end of the Riverwalk and were at some steps that led down to the river. "Look. I can go touch the water." Evan ran down the steps as though he were a child and touched the water of the Mississippi as it splashed up on the steps. They heard a riverboat in the foreground blow its whistle. "Oh, that's one of Lloyd's family's showboats. I wonder which Troubled Waters that one is? Each one has its own name. There are five. Let's see, 'The Bridge Over,' I know that one is a real cute name, huh. Get it, the bridge over troubled waters?"

Evan looked up and saw that Salvatore was beginning to come down the steps. He quickly looked back to the river. "There's 'The Showboat On' . . . "

Salvatore had made his way to Evan as he was rattling on about Trouble Waters; he took his hand out and turned Evan's face so he could see it. "And which troubled waters are you?" Evan became silent. "You're not very happy, are you?" Salvatore leaned in to Evan and kissed him as the sounds of the river and the city blended into the background.

* * * * *

Rex was standing among the plants on the balcony of the apartment in the Quarter. He looked at all of the people on Royal Street at eleven-thirty on a Friday night. It was amazing that inside the apartment he really couldn't hear much of the street noise. Lloyd came out to join Rex.

"What are you thinking?" Lloyd stood behind Rex and put his arms around him.

"I'm thinking how lucky I am to have met you and I really don't understand why we clicked so fast. It's funny. I feel as though I've known you my whole life and yet we have only known each other for such a short time. You and your family have taken me in and taken care of me. Especially you." Rex turned in order to face Lloyd eye-to-eye. "I mean, you've given me keys to your home and let me move in, rent free, and your mom has given me a job, and all my cares seem to have evaporated. I wanted to know where I came from and I wanted to belong somewhere." Rex went to sit on the swing. "I never felt this comfortable growing up. It was like everything was all wrong in Plain Dealing. Plain Dealing never dealt me a fair deal."

Lloyd went to the swing and joined Rex. "Don't analyze

it. Don't hurt me and I won't hurt you. I have always heard that when it was right, you'd know it. I think I know it. You feel . . . we feel right to me. I never felt that way in the five years with Torch. You have even listened to me talk about hurting over that bastard. You and I have stayed awake all night talking about our deep feelings and our dreams." They swung back and forth as the night air caressed their souls. "You don't laugh at me when I tell you the things I want to do. You really care about me, Rex. I know that. You appreciate me and that is important to me. You have taught me how to care about someone other than myself and my needs." Lloyd ran his fingers through Rex's hair and they embraced in a kiss.

The door buzzer sounded and broke the moment between the two on the swing. "That must be Lowla." Lloyd got up to let them in and the three returned to the balcony.

"How was your walk?" Rex got up from the swing.

"Really nice. But we are hungry, right, Evan?" Salvatore knocked Evan on the shoulder lightly.

"Evan? That's the first time I've heard you call him that. What happened at the river?" Lloyd put his hands on his hips in a demanding-to-know gesture.

"We had an epiphany, so to speak. I can't just talk to Lowla all the time. Evan needs some attention now and then. Where do you want to go eat, dear?" Salvatore said to Evan.

Without hesitation, Evan said, "La Paniche."

"Of all the places to go and you want to take Salvatore there?" Lloyd said, walking back into the apartment.

"Salvatore has never been there and it is a fun place. I need some red beans and sausage." Evan said, closing the window behind them once Rex and Salvatore were inside.

"You can have all the red beans you want, darling, but I'll give you the sausage you need later." Salvatore grabbed Evan's waist.

"All right, let's go. I like that place too." Rex said.

The guys got in the car and drove to La Paniche, which

was located near the Quarter, not far from the Fauburg Mariny. La Paniche was a small, crowed restaurant that had a big menu. The décor was not fancy but the patrons were. People from all walks of life ate there. It was a place to have a delightful meal at an affordable price. Lloyd and Rex questioned Salvatore about his police career with enthusiasm. "So do you handcuff Lowla?" Lloyd asked with interest as he stirred his tea.

"You mean Lowla hasn't given you all the details?" Salvatore said, finishing off his last bite of soft-shell crab.

"All Lowla said was that she met an incredible policeman who loved to come visit. You know how it goes, I thought, yeah, sure. But now I see that it is true. Check please." Lloyd motioned to the waiter who came to the table as Lloyd took out his money.

"It's been taken care of." The waiter replied to Lloyd.

"By whom?" Lloyd demanded to know.

The waiter pointed at Evan. "Thank you and come back to see us," he said and left the table.

"Why did you do that? And I thought you had to go to the bathroom." Lloyd put his money away. "Don't do that any more."

"Thank you, Lowla." Rex started to stand.

"I'll thank you later," Salvatore said to Evan. "It's getting late though. I hate to be a party pooper, but I do have to be in training at eight a.m. and I'm sure it'll be tough falling asleep right away. Actually this will be the first time we have slept together. An all nighter in Hapeville is anything but sleep." Salvatore also stood. Evan smiled at Lloyd, who reciprocated in a knowing way and then they were on their feet.

The four musketeers piled into the car and went back to White Hawk Manor for the rest of the evening. The ride was quiet. Lloyd and Rex held hands in the front seat and Evan and Salvatore did likewise in the back. Once they were at the house, they went inside.

"You know where y'all's room is. I need to check on

Ruby." Lloyd went toward the front of the house.

"Good night, then," they all bid each other.

Evan and Salvatore went up the stairs. Once inside the bedroom Salvatore said, "I've been waiting for this since I saw you earlier today. How long will it take you to get dressed?"

"Dressed?" Evan said with a puzzled look on his face. "You mean, as Lowla?"

"What else? You know how you turn me on that way." Salvatore sat on the bed and rubbed his hands on his legs.

That action used to make Evan smile. This time he was trying not to show that his feelings were hurt. He responded, "It would take too long and you have to get up early." Evan walked over to his bag to get out his toothbrush and to tighten his ponytail.

Salvatore started to undress. "Well, then, just let your hair hang loose and turn out the light."

28

"Do you think they will miss us?" Rex pointed toward the upstairs of White Hawk Manor.

"If they do then what is that saying about the time they have together? Besides let's just concentrate on us. Lowla can take care of herself." Lloyd took out his keys and unlocked the Marilynmobile.

Rex put a cooler in the trunk of the car and closed it. "Okay, the suspense is killing me, where are you taking me to at three o'clock in the morning and what is in the cooler?"

"Just get in the car and shut up." Lloyd smiled as he got in the drivers seat. He looked at Rex and said, "I'm taking you to a place where I like to go to be alone. It is my special place and I have never taken anyone to it. You will be the first." He backed into the street, put the car in gear and started driving slowly. They headed to a part of the city with which Rex was not familiar. The direction was a little east of the Quarter, and Lloyd soon hit roads that seemed less traveled. Before long, the guys were at their destination.

Lloyd parked off the road and told Rex to get the cooler so they could be on their way.

"This doesn't look like a place for a picnic," Rex said, following Lloyd who was going towards the thick part of a distant woods.

"We aren't really going on a picnic. There are no tables here. Just follow me and watch where you step." Lloyd held back a weeping limb from an old tree so that Rex could pass through while he carried the cooler. "Stand aside now, and I will lead the way."

The two men carefully walked through the woods. It was dark except for the light from the moon shining through tiny openings from the thicket of the forest. There were sounds of water flowing and insects mating. Rex began to notice that the ground was getting a little damp the farther they walked. Suddenly they came upon an opening in the trees, abounding with fallen tree trunks and limbs. Plants of all sizes lined the area. Just a few feet before them lay the mighty Mississippi River. "Gosh, this is beautiful." Rex exclaimed as he stood holding the cooler, obviously delighted by the visual stimulation that surrounded him.

"It's my secret paradise. I come here to be alone and to think about life and just to enjoy nature. Put the cooler down here." Lloyd pointed in the direction of a stump. "I usually put my things here, but I rove all over the limbs and plants."

"What things do you put here?" said Rex as he put the cooler down on the stump. "And, again, what is in this anyway?"

"You'll soon find out. And you'll like it," Lloyd said, hoping to build Rex's curiosity. "Sometimes, I take off my clothes and put them here. This is where I was the first night I met you. I came here to enjoy the full moon and to pray. After I was cleansed, I left to go ride through the city. This place is peaceful, quiet, uninhabited except for nature. I feel that God talks to me here. I feel that you were an answer to my prayers that night. That is why I have brought you to my secret garden. Let's enjoy the music of the night." Lloyd started to remove his shoes. "Don't be shy, be natural. You don't want to get your clothes wet, do you?"

Rex started to take off his shoes. "Do you have this much control over everybody?"

"It's not control, Rex. This is natural." Lloyd began to unbutton his shirt. "This is like the Garden of Eden except it's Rex and Lloyd and there are no apples here. There is just us, the crickets, the trees, the birds, the river and the beautiful moon above shining down on us." He unzipped his pants and took them off. He placed them on the stump. "There are no hang-ups here. Let everything in your mind go. All you see is all there is." Once that they were fully undressed Lloyd took Rex's hand and led him to the water.

The men slowly looked around at all the beauty now that their eyes had adjusted to the darkness. Once they had made it to the shallow part of the river, Lloyd leaned over and splashed Rex with water. Rex reciprocated and soon they were playing like children. Without a hint, Lloyd took off and ran behind some trees, leaving Rex alone. Rex stood there like a lost child, afraid to move. "Are we playing hide and go seek now? I am not coming after you. I don't know your secret garden and I am not going to venture on my own in this darkness." Rex folded his arms together on his chest and in a playful tone said, "I'm going to open the cooler."

"Don't you dare!" came a voice from behind the trees. "I'm coming. I thought you'd run after me." Lloyd appeared and walked to Rex.

"So you want to be chased, huh?" Rex rushed at Lloyd, who tried to turn and run. But Rex was too fast. He dragged Lloyd closer to the river and threw him in. To Rex's surprise Lloyd leapt up and brought him into the water too. "I hope there aren't any crocodiles around here. I would hate to be someone's breakfast."

Lloyd laughed at Rex. "Not to worry, just snakes."

"That's it. I'm outta this water." Rex went to the shore as

fast as he could. Once out of the water, he went to the stump where they had put their clothes.

"There are towels in the cooler. Wait on me," Lloyd yelled as he came out of the water. He went to the cooler and pulled out two towels, one for him and one for Rex.

Toweling himself dry, Rex said, "And I just knew there was going to be fried chicken in there."

"I hope you are not disappointed. There are just towels, a liter of pop and this." Lloyd handed Rex a package which was the size of a large box of crayons.

Putting his towel down, he took the package from Lloyd. Rex held the box and replied, "What is this? Is it a present?"

"Not really. It's more of a gift. I guess it could be a present, but a gift has meaning. It's something that I wanted to give to you." Lloyd opened the bottle of pop. "Wait before you open it. Let's clear a space for us to sit."

The men cleared off the stump and Rex said, "I hope there aren't any bugs out here. I have really sensitive skin."

"I didn't think I had sensitive skin until I met you," Lloyd seductively whispered, then spread a towel for them to rest. "You'll be fine. I've been out here hundreds of times and never even got bitten by a mosquito. There, all done, have a seat, Mister Greenfield." His arms motioned to Rex as though Lloyd were a waiter. "Now you may open your box."

Rex carefully tore the plain brown paper, and a velvet-covered box was revealed. He lifted the box's lid and took out a gold ring with a garnet center stone. He looked up at Lloyd, speechless.

"That ring is really old. It means a lot to me. It belonged to my grandfather and to his father before him. It was all he had when he died. He gave it to me when I was seven and he was on his death bed. He said he wanted me to have it because I was him and he was me. 'You are the only one I see myself in,' I remember Grandpa saying to me as he put the ring in my tiny hand, smiled, and then died right before my eyes." Lloyd's eyes began to water.

"I don't know what to say. This ring means so much to you, I shouldn't take it." Rex held the ring up to the moonlight. "It shines so beautifully. I am really moved with this gesture, but . . . "

Lloyd took the ring from Rex and then took Rex's hand. The ring slid on Rex's finger as though it were made just for him. "I have never been so bold, and I thought when something like this would happen that a man would slip a ring on my finger, not me slipping a ring on your finger." Lloyd was now holding both of Rex's hands. "You said some amazing things to me the other night on the balcony in the Quarter. Remember?"

Rex nodded his head in agreement as Lloyd continued, "I don't want to take a chance to lose you or to lose out on all the things we dream about together. For once in my life, I want a partner who is my equal and who will work together with me to accomplish a common goal for the benefit of us both. I want us to be in a committed relationship. I want us to worry about what business we are going to start, not if you love me or I love you. I want someone I can count on and trust who will be there for me and that I can be there for you, also. I want to my house to turn into our home. I want to grow old with you and help you in any way I can. Rex, don't you love me the same way?"

"All I can say is that I feel the same way, except that I am grateful in ways that you might not understand. I will be committed to you." He met Lloyd's lips for a brief touching. "Thank you for such a moving moment. I will remember this for the rest of my life." Rex stared at the ring on his finger. "I will cherish this ring and protect our commitment with my life." They embraced, which led to a passionate long kiss. Lloyd broke from the embrace and lifted up the bottle of pop. The men drank from the bottle and then lay back on the huge stump to look at the stars and to hold hands. "I wish this moment would never end. I love you so much. I never thought this would happen." The wind began to blow and the trees made a swaying sound. "I want to thank you for all the help you gave me trying to find my start in this life. We have spent a lot of time on that and I know I have been a little obsessed, but I promise you here and now, that I will spent all my energy on building our lives instead of concentrating just on my problems. All of a sudden, I don't have any. It doesn't matter where I came from, I know where I am."

Lloyd sat up, "Rex, we will continue to look for your real parents. That is important to you and we will never let that go. It's just that now we have a lot more on our plate and it will get easier. Let's stay here a little while longer, but then we will have to go. I've got to get Lowla and Salvatore to the airport and I want to get home before sunrise. We will come back here again. It's our place, now." As he kissed Rex on the forehead, Lloyd sang into Rex's ear, *I Will Always Love You*. It was a song they had decided was their own and it was a song that would come to haunt them in the future, reminding them of a past which could not be repeated.

29

The flight back to Atlanta was yet another sad chapter in Evan's life. He sat beside Salvatore but that was his only comfort; it proved to be a bumpy ride for the two of them. Salvatore was fidgety during the plane trip and would look away when asked a question. He managed to answer in few words only to look back at the magazine he clutched on his lap. Mostly he looked out the window. Evan understood what Salvatore was thinking although he did not confess it. When the plane landed, they departed politely into the concourse. Since neither one of them had checked baggage, they walked toward the parking area of the airport. Before reaching the open part of the short term parking spaces, still underneath the covered walkway, Evan confronted Salvatore.

"You don't have to worry about hurting my feelings. I can tell there is something wrong." Salvatore stopped and Evan followed suit. "Just say it."

He looked past him as if to make sure that no one was within earshot. "Evan, . . . Lowla, . . .me." He pointed to Evan then to himself and with hands in the air, added, "Confusion." He put one hand back on his shoulder bag and the other he used as he spoke. "You've been good to me and I thank you. It has been a world of fantasy and fun that I could've never imagined on my own." Salvatore took the hand from his shoulder bag and placed it on the top of Evan's shoulder. "Being with you these last days made me realize that all we will ever be is a series of one-nighters. I can't give any more than that and it's not fair to you or to my obligations. I never thought we would've lasted this long." He leaned into Evan in a daring move and quickly kissed him on his cheek and let go of the grip on his shoulder. "For what's it's worth, if things were different for me, I could love you. I realized that the night we were at the Riverwalk. But it's over. I'll never call you again."

Evan froze. Speechless. Salvatore turned and began to walk. He did not look back. Evan watched him walk until he faded out of view. Evan leaned up against a concrete pillar in the parking deck. A tear fell down his cheek, joined by another and then another. Time had no immediate meaning. He didn't know how much of it had passed when he finally removed himself from the post. There wasn't even a thought in his head as he wandered in a daze until he found his truck.

On the way home from the airport, Evan could hardly see the road through all of his tears. He did not know why he was crying so much except that Salvatore reinforced what he truly believed . . . that no one would ever love him or stay with him long-term. Even though he knew the situation, he had hoped it would turn into a lasting relationship. He couldn't believe he was so desperate for love that he would take treatment of any kind from someone just to be held, especially considering the object of desire was in a legal committed marriage. The feeling that all of his relationships were doomed to be behind closed doors consumed him. The affair with Salvatore wasn't different from his other ones, except for Lowla. The one common denominator was how they ended. "I could love you, but . . ." He wasn't anything that a man would be proud to have on his arm. *Since when did sluts become really attractive?* "But I'm not a slut," he said loudly. "I'm just misunderstood and desperate for love."

The billboard by the interstate exit to his house caught his eye. It was advertising Atlanta historic tourism. The picture of the pretty blond southern belle all dressed from the old south reminded him of a movie star he had idolized when he was very young. It struck him as funny that, growing up as a boy in a small town in the south, he preferred to groom himself after a female screen icon rather than after a male role model. A small smile crept on his face as he thought of the day he was so dazzled by her beautiful clothes, her moves, her manipulations, and most of all, her voice. He thought she knew all the tricks of the trade, a funny name for love. It never dawned upon him that Mae West's movies were fiction and that one day the men would quit coming to see him rather than he being the one dismissing them. Also, he had no clue that Mae West had something he did not. He had her style, her wit, and the way she treated men down pat. The one thing he did not have was her womanhood. He could do a good presentation, but he could never fulfill a straight man completely and the gay men in his life didn't want a vixen imitation. They wanted a man which seemed to be something Evan couldn't give either as he thought he didn't have a dominating bone in his body. If it wasn't Mae West after whom he was modeling himself, it was his mother. When the innuendos didn't work, he thought cooking and cleaning for a man would. Every time he got someone hooked, his clinging chased them away. He could never understand why all these men weren't looking for what he could offer. *Didn't anyone know that nothing is equal? One has to be less than.*

He decided he had to put all of that behind him. He had to change. Driving down the street to his house, he vowed to concentrate on his talent number for the Niceville pageant. After all, he wanted to impress those people so he would have friends in the Atlanta area with similar interests. Above everything else, he wanted with all of his soul to win the pageant. He even imagined how he would look with his sash as he posed for pictures while he looked up for effect. Maybe if he got deeply involved with the Niceville group, he could change and meet someone who was single and would not have to hide behind closed doors. As he turned into his driveway, he decided that no more was he going to be a married man's — or anyone's — slut. There had to be something more in life. It was night time, for which he was glad since the neighbors were inside and couldn't see him go into the house. In his usual routine, he pulled the truck into the garage and then hurried to get his mail.

Once in the house, he checked to make sure that everything was still intact. The rooms were just as cluttered and unkempt as before. His dogs were at the kennel and he would have to pick them up the next evening. Funny, when his dogs were not there he was frightened to stay alone in the empty house. It saddened him even more to think that he had dogs not for love but to keep him company. Evan consoled himself that even though he may not pet Princess and Cher often, they lived inside the house, slept with him in the bed, and he cooked for them daily. But what are those things without love? It dawned upon him ironically that he was looking for something he did not seem to give.

Before he went through the pieces of mail, he decided to roll a joint and pour himself a glass of wine. As he opened a box containing his pot paraphernalia, he realized he would be able to create his routine for the pageant without worrying about stepping on the dogs. He couldn't understand why they would hang around when he filmed and danced. He had stepped on them accidentally many times. Surely they were smart enough to stay clear of four-inch heels. He grated the pot and quickly rolled a joint. He slipped out of his shoes and into his heels. He lit the joint and smiled, waiting for the buzz to arrive. He started to stride across the floor as he made it a rule to practice dance routines in heels. He felt that it was a more of a natural look if those stilettos looked like they belonged on his feet. The heels also provided balance for dance moves. A few tokes and he was ready to cruise through his compact discs when he remembered his mail and his answering machine. He went into the bedroom to find a big zero for the number of messages he needed to answer. The caller ID exposed calls that left no message. A few numbers he recognized as drive-by shootings that went awry for the married men. "You want what you can't have even more? Is that why you called so often while I was gone?" he said to the caller ID.

Walking back to his home-made studio of black sheets where he practiced his routines, he picked-up the mail and started to leaf through it. Mostly there were bills from the gas and electric companies and credit card offers — the usual fare. One letter caught his attention as it was from Stars and Pipes Corporate headquarters in New Hampshire. Quickly he opened the letter to read:

Dear Evan Livingston:

It is with regret that we inform you that the corporate headquarters of Stars and Pipes has decided to close the Atlanta Branch effective immediately. We have on our records that you have been with the company for sixteen years and eleven months. You will receive a compensation package . . .

Evan quit reading the letter and threw it on the chair. It was only fitting, he thought, that after being dumped by Salvatore that he would come back to an empty house to find that his job was ending soon. He took a long toke and a big gulp of wine. *This is not going to destroy my party for tonight and now that my job is ending, I guess I can call in sick tomorrow.* He decided to look on the bright side of life; maybe he could start charging for drive-by shootings or maybe even become the toast of Atlanta with his newly found drag career. He was having big dreams when there seemed to be no opportunities knocking on his door. But this would give him plenty of time to be flawless on Memorial Day, not to mention all the films he could watch all day on Turner Classic Movies, something he did every available moment since discovering that channel on his cable line-up. On his days off, he would lie in bed all day and night and eat, drink and smoke and watch all the classics they had to offer. He had come to know the stars of yesteryear as close intimate friends. Evan sometimes waved at them when he passed the television. *People would think that I am mentally ill if they only knew what I did do.* He couldn't get into the new movies of today; the male actors of the classics were men, something to which his Mae West persona could relate.

Instead of looking through his compact discs, he headed to his desk to finish the original song for the upcoming event. All he had to do was get the words to Lloyd, who would make sure the music got recorded and have Chalmette sing the song for him. His lip sync was flawless. He had tons of videos to prove it. He talked to himself out loud as he sat at his desk drinking and smoking. "Here you are trying to make yourself special again." He brought the glass to his lips and savored the liquid until it slipped down his throat. "I am special. And beautiful, too." A quick toke and a quicker sip as a prelude to the release of smoke. "After all, we all deserve to be beautiful at least once in our lives. Sometimes, twice. I just hate being beautiful all by myself. Does that mean it's wasted?" Then a great idea occurred to him. He could take his compensation money and hire some of Lloyd's hunky friends to be Egyptian slaves to carry him in for his talent number just like Lloyd had done that year in New Orleans. He was bound to win and be visually beautiful at the same time. Just as he was feverishly writing down all of his wonderful ideas, the phone rang. *It must be Lloyd making sure I am back.* He looked on the caller ID and recognized the cell phone number. He wanted to lift the receiver and ask why the caller called so much and never left a message. He picked it up hesitantly even though he vowed not to let anything or anyone interrupt his working on his pageant material.

"Hello." Trying to sound as flippant as he could. "Yes, this *is* Evan. Oh, hello. You know, *it* has been a while. That's okay, it's not that *late*." Evan walked back to the desk but did not sit down. "I've been out of town. I saw this number on the phone several times, but you never left a message. I can understand, I mean, what would *you* say? And someone might have even heard your voice. Yes, yes, I know. *One* can never be too careful." Evan picked up his glass and headed to the kitchen to refill his wine. "I'm working on a project this evening. Alone? Yes," he sighed, "I am alone. I don't know if I will take a break or not. So, you are working late this evening and you could be here in fifteen minutes. It must be time for you to get off," he said baiting the caller for a payoff. "*I meant work.*" He took a toke on his joint in a Barbara Stanwyck fashion. "I guess I'll see you in fifteen then. Bye."

Evan hung up the phone, exhaled the smoke, and cursed himself aloud. "There you go again. You are sure to get ahead in life. No wonder you live like this. Where is your respect? Just look at you and look around you and you said earlier that there would be no more married men. This will really show Salvatore." As soon as those words came out of his mouth, he realized how absurd they sounded. He paused in the hallway with his joint hand on his hip and his glass of wine in the other hand. "Well, I guess I'd better tidy up a bit." Evan scrambled to make the house look halfway decent although he knew his visitor wasn't coming over to check out the drapes. His went back to his desk and placed his fingers on the paper that contained his ideas for the pageant. "I'll have plenty of time to work on this now that I have no place to go during the day, unless of course I need to do some research in Piedmont Park." Evan lifted his glass to the air, gulped down the contents and announced, "Cheers." The glass and his life now had something in common. They were both empty.

30

"Yes, I'll hold." Rex sighed as he sat slumped on the chaise lounge in the living room of White Hawk Manor. "Yes, ma'am, I've tried them before. Who? No, I didn't speak to him." He began to tap his pen against his notebook. "What's the number, please?" He wrote down information. "Thank you." He clicked the end button on the phone then turned over to face the window.

Lloyd came down the main hall and saw Rex lying still on the chaise in the living room. He entered without being noticed. "What's the matter?" He received no response. "Hey, you! Not feeling well this morning? You never laze around." Lloyd edged to the chaise, "Or did you not get enough sleep last night?"

Rex did not turn to face Lloyd. He just sighed instead. "No help from the state's record department again. I don't exist." Still, without movement, he continued, "How could my mother not file a birth certificate on me? That's got to be illegal. What am I going to do if I need to prove who I am?" Rex said despondently.

Partially Lloyd was happy the "saga of Rex's life" was short this time. He continued as hopefully a beacon of support. "What about your social security number?" Lloyd said as he moved to stand between Rex and the window therefore blocking his view.

"I don't have one." Rex looked up at Lloyd.

"You don't have one! Have you ever had a job?" Lloyd's voice was raised with surprise at this news.

"I wasn't born with a silver spoon in my mouth, if that's what you mean." Rex's voice conveyed sarcastic aggression.

Before Rex could go any further, Lloyd quickly and proudly, even with a harsh sound, said, "Are you trying to say I was?"

It seemed as though he was having second thoughts before continuing the course of the conversation. Rex began again, this time more subdued, "I had small jobs given to me by family members and such. My mom said 'my father' gave enough money for us to get by. When she died, I found out that wasn't true, either." He put his fingers through his hair, made an effort to grin at Lloyd and then opened his notebook. He turned a page back and forth.

"Have you searched under her name? Maybe Rex Greenfield is not your real name." Lloyd took the notebook from Rex and sat down on the chaise with him.

Rex buried his head in Lloyd's lap and started to cry, "I thought of that. And I did. The only things that are on her public record are her birth certificate and her driver's license. Rita Greenfield had her tees crossed. But no one will talk with me further because I can not prove that I am her next of kin."

Lloyd just held Rex. This was different for Lloyd as he usually did not like to comfort people as it made him feel uncomfortable. A physical expression of affection had always been difficult for him, but this was a whole different feeling. He caressed Rex's head and whispered, "Everything will be okay. You'll see. I'm here. We'll get you a social security card and a birth certificate even if I have to adopt you myself." Lloyd took a handkerchief from his shirt pocket and wiped the tears from Rex's face. "I tell you what; you can help me make plans for La Moulin Rouge Carnival Charitable Event of which I am president and founder." Lloyd said. He had not previously mentioned the carnival to Rex; this was different, also. He usually told everything about himself from the start. His relationship with Rex had become a developing situation. Lloyd liked the feeling.

"What's that?"

"La Moulin Rouge Carnival Charitable Event is a real mouthful," he hooted. Then modestly and with feeling, he somberly continued. "It's an event that I started years ago to help raise money for people with AIDS who don't have insurance or a place to go. So through a lot of people's hard work and efforts, the charity raises enough money for medicine and housing to take care of twenty-five people in need."

"I don't know what to say. My life could be so much worse. What a wonderful thing to do. How did you come about doing this?"

"My father taught me the principles of a good life: do something you enjoy and be sure to give back to the community. It really got to me when I saw one of my friends totally cut off from his family because of this hideous disease. He had nowhere to go. No one to care. But he never complained. It wasn't until he was in ICU when I learned that he had been living out of his car because he couldn't afford medicine and rent. I had to help him and I wanted to help others in the same shoes. Haven't you heard of the event?"

"You know how a small town is. I don't recall ever hearing anything."

"I can't believe you've never heard of it. It's a four-day weekend the fourth weekend of August. This year it will start on Thursday, August twenty-fifth. On Thursday night, we have a silent auction of donated goods. Friday night is food and fun. Saturday is the really big party carnival day leaving Sunday for the jazz brunch good-bye. People come from all over the United States just to party at my Moulin Rouge Carnival. People love to drink for charity at any price and I love the glamour of it all. It'll take your mind off your troubles when you see how you can help others." Lloyd smiled. He hoped his philanthropy would make Rex love him even more.

Rex sat up and questioned intently, "What can I do?"

"There are tons of things." Lloyd was off the chaise with Rex's notebook and went to place it on top of the piano. "I have a board of six that plan, with my approval, the event year after year. There is no reason why we can't have another

member on the board. We'll get you in charge of something.
Trust me, the rest of the gang will love to tell you what to do."
He touched his right fingers with his left hand as he listed the
various tasks. "There is entertainment, set ups, places to rent,
invitations to be sent out, volunteers and corporate sponsors
to be found." He stopped to smile at Rex. "You'll fit right in.
But, to start, I think it would be a good idea to have the
Niceville Group perform this year during the main party on
Saturday night. And if Lowla wins this year, that will make
things even better. It will be held at the Wharf, which gives
us lots of space to create almost any atmosphere. So I will
need you to come up with something. They'll love it, I think,
because most of them have just performed for bars and small,
local pageants. This will be in front of thousands. La Moulin
Rouge Carnival is huge." Lloyd leaned on the baby grand as
though lecturing on a stage.

"What would they do? I mean, what kind of
entertainment do you have already?" Rex asked as he dried
his eyes. "I'm sure it's top drawer."

"It is, so that's where I need your help to get the Niceville
Group to fit in. We already have bands lined up and
professional dancers and acrobats also. We need to help them
ease in to this professional venue." Lloyd started to write in
Rex's notebook.

Rex got up and took the notebook back. "I'll take the
notes. We can't have the president doing grunt work."

"I think you can come up with something fun, not too
long at a time. You know, have them weave in and out.
You'll see what I am talking about when you watch the
videos. There will be a lot going on the stage at once and it
has to blend. It'll be like a circus." Lloyd wondered what Rex
was writing at the desk by the window. "What are you
putting down? You're not taking dictation are you?"

"Putting down ideas." Rex looked up and appeared to be
excited to tell a story. "You know how circuses transport
their lions and elephants, like the box on animal crackers? We

can have the circus girls and clowns transported to the event in a huge cage pulled by an eighteen wheeler or something and then have the cage opened on stage by the 'Ring Master.' That way they perform tricks around the entertainment." Rex waited for his review.

"Oh, my God. What a great idea and an easy one, too. Keep thinking along those lines and we'll steal the show because, of course, I'll be in it. I'll be the 'Ring Master.' Keep in mind, I have to somehow, some way, have a grand entrance. You remember that and you'll do great on the board. There is a meeting soon. Keep working on that and we will go out to dinner with some of the board members so you can get acquainted before the ball gets rolling. If I didn't mention it before, there are some videos of previous La Moulin Rouge Carnivals for you to watch so you can get an idea of what has gone on in the past and how fabulous I have been and how fabulous I need to be this year. I'll let you present this idea at the Niceville pageant." He walked toward Rex. "It'll be my way to show you off."

"As long as you show me off standing by my side." He always seemed to know what to say. "We can present this together. Maybe we can start a party planner business." Rex stood up and put his hands in the air as if he was reading a sign. "Rex and Lloyd's Million Dollar Parties, Incorporated."

"That's my man." Lloyd kissed Rex on the cheek. "That's enough to keep you busy while I make an appearance at school. I'm late." He said in his southern drawl. "Pity." He went to walk out of the room and stopped at the archway. "When we start working together with our own business, I'll be glad not to have to teach anymore."

"Why do you with all that you have going on?"

"Insurance, baby. You know I work all the time. See, I'm working now." Lloyd exited to the hallway.

Rex followed him and shouted, "When will you be back?"

"I'll be at school for a couple of hours and then I need to go to the club. We're auditioning some dancers today."

Lloyd picked up his briefcase off the hall tree.

"Great, I'll see you there. I told Renee that I would work with her all day."

Lloyd turned around, "You two are getting mighty close, huh?"

"I hope so. She's been really nice to me. Your whole family has. I'm learning a great deal with her too. I never realized what all it took to run a business." Rex continued to follow Lloyd to the back door.

"Oh, you're learning to run a business?"

"In a way . . ."

"As long as you don't take my place, we'll be fine." Lloyd kissed him on the cheek again.

"How could I ever take your place? You're her son and she loves you more than anything. Anyone can see that."

Lloyd stood there thinking about what Rex had just said. "See ya at the club."

Rex watched Lloyd walk down the steps to the car. Hurriedly he went back down the hallway to the living room to get the phone. He got the notebook and dialed the number that was given to him earlier. "Yes, sir, my name is Rex Greenfield and I was told you might be able to help me. Yes, sir, I'll hold." He sighed and slumped once more on the chaise lounge.

31

Speaking over the conversational noise from everyone seated around the table, the faded-looking Doris Day spoke. "Oh, I know that girls will be boys, but you must calm down. I am calling this meeting to order." Doyle-Leigh picked up a banana from the bowl of fruit and banged it gently on the table before him. "We will start the meeting without Craven Fame since he could not be here today."

"No doubt he's with his mother," Florence Tightintail said and then quickly added, "You know, they're joined at the hip."

Communal laughter emitted from the five people present.

"Oh now, we all love our mothers." Doyle-Leigh used the banana as a judge's gavel once more. "Oh, I guess y'all are wondering why I called this meeting in the first place."

"Cocktails, of course," shouted Rouge-Red, one of the original five who started the group known, only to themselves, as the "true chosen family."

"To decide who is going to be the next Miss Niceville," suggested Faux Pas, nudging Toule Lyps to his left.

"To see how much money we have made this year so the board can go to Belize? I got the cutest Speedo the other day," Florence said very sensuously.

"Oh, now girls, someone may hear you and think you're serious." Doyle-Leigh was pointing with the banana in her hand. "Everyone knows that we are all above board."

"Since when did you become a top? 'Cause you got a banana in your hand? Most everyone here is below, if you girls know what I mean. I sure would like to be below that new DJ we got for the pageant this year. He sure is handsome and sports a nice package," Faux said with a grin dripping with innuendo. "And don't squeeze that banana too hard, you might need it later." Faux Pas laughed out loud. Even though he was not an original member, he had managed to weave his way into the core five who were. He also managed to reap the benefits.

"The sooner we get down to business, the sooner we can gossip." Doyle-Leigh put the banana down and looked at Faux Pas glaringly. "Who would like to go first?"

"Since I am the treasurer of this fine group, I will. After all, that is the reason we do this every year . . . for the money we make, not to mention our own aggrandizement." Faux Pas laughed again self-assuredly. He stood. A look of self confidence graced his wide face. "This year I am proud to say that everyone has paid their dues on time. We have rented forty trailers and have one hundred and ten people attending. Each person has paid the two hundred and fifty dollars per person for lodging, food and alcohol." He looked at everyone seated, one by one. "For those of you who can't do the math, that grosses us twenty-seven thousand five hundred dollars. The cost of each trailer, with the complimentary recreational facilities, is one hundred dollars for the Memorial Day weekend. The deposit has been sent to the Niceville trailer park and we have spent roughly a thousand dollars on food and alcohol. Considering this, we have netted twenty-two thousand five hundred dollars."

They all screamed with joy.

"Now does anyone need me to do the math to see how much each one of us will get?" Faux Pas said with his arms in a triumphant pose as he slowly sat in his chair.

Rouge-Red quickly answered, "I think you should get you some new hair for that bald head of yours with your share."

"I will if you get some hair dye for your natural shade of red that you sport." Faux Pas darted back.

Doyle-Leigh stood with hands motioning for silence. "Oh, I think I should get more. After all, this was my idea when we were in college and you all said it wouldn't work. Oh, I told you all that I could sell anything, and for seventeen years now, we have been going to Niceville and crowning someone who brings more people to the show year after year. Not to mention enjoying the profits we make from my brilliance and my dedicated efforts."

"Bullshit," Rouge-Red interjected. "We all have worked hard over the years making this scheme work and we all have kept our mouths shut. All we need to accomplish at this meeting is to decide who is going to be the next Miss Niceville. I count the votes and we, as a group, decide who is going to be crowned next, for the good of the true chosen family. And that's what keeps some of those bitches coming back the next year when they don't win, no matter how good they are. Losing only makes them want it more." He put his hands over his head to suggest a tiara. "Besides what we do provides fun and prizes for those who couldn't make it in the public sector." He laughed.

"Oh, Joan Collins, you are making me sick. But I agree with you, I guess. So, girls, who is it going to be this year?" Doyle-Leigh posed.

"It's not going to be Lowla. I hear she wants it pretty bad," Florence said as he poured another glass of water.

Sitting back down, Doyle-Leigh asked, "What do you think, Toule Lyps? You've been very quiet this evening."

Toule Lyps, another original member of the group, pondered a moment before answering. "I think it would be nice if the most talented contestant won. That's the one who deserves to be Miss Niceville."

"The one who deserves to be Miss Niceville is the one we can manipulate," Florence said as he pounded his hand on the table. "Are you getting senile in your old age?"

"No, you heartless bitch," Toule Lyps said, imitating Tallulah Bankhead. "We go to have fun, right? It's not all about the money?"

"Oh, Toule, you had us worried. Of course we go to have fun." The guys broke into laughter as Doyle-Leigh got them back under control. "Now back to Lowla Lowlife."

Once more, the guys laughed heartily.

"Oh, my, that was a slip of the tongue." Doyle-Leigh laughed again. "But don't dare call her that, it's our little secret. But seriously, she needs to win Miss New Talent though. That will bring Lowla back. It will be good bait for her thirst to win. Besides, there will not be any competition since all the rest of the contestants have won that. And from her showing last month, I don't think we have to worry about the audience voting for her as a winner should the pageant be legitimate." Doyle-Leigh also got some water. "Oh, sometimes talking without a cocktail wears me out." He sipped from his glass.

Florence lifted his glass as in a toast. "Listening to you without a cocktail is just as draining."

"You are just so refreshing."

"Why, thank you, Doyle."

"I was talking to the glass, Flo. So, we have established the treasury part of the evening. Rouge, you have taken care of all the other things right?"

"Yes, Madame Chairwoman." Rouge-Red rose. He gave himself the handle of Rouge-Red because of his red hair and freckled face.   Even in his late thirties, he evoked a resemblance for a young Tom Sawyer. "First of all, my hair is natural. Let me just say the carpet matches the drapes."

Faux said rudely, "If I saw that I think I would go running for my life — or puke."

"One thing for sure is that you will never be lucky enough to see it. And, unlike you, my stomach doesn't have to be pushed back to see the full effect."

Doyle-Leigh moved between the two to referee if needed. "Now, girls, remember we all love and support each other." He danced as he sang the following words, "We're in the money."   The next words sounded like a song from the seventies, "We are the true chosen family, I got all my rich sisters with me!" He stopped dancing. "Remember?"

Rouge-Red stared at Faux Pas until he started to speak. "The food has been purchased except for the perishables which we will buy when we get to Niceville. The truck has been loaded with everything we need, like the Margarita machine and the popcorn maker. The curtain and lights have also been loaded as well." Rouge-Red sat back down.

"Oh, well, we still have some time to decide this year's winner, *which will be* Farah Dice. So let's wait until our next meeting when Craven Fame will be present to finish discussing that issue." The true chosen family nodded their heads in agreement which led to silence at the table.   "Oh, then if there is no other business, I motion that the meeting be adjourned and we make cocktails and gossip," Doyle-Leigh said taking the banana and holding it high. "All in favor say 'aye.'"

"Aye," resounded from around the room.

He rested the banana back in the bowl of fruit. "Niceville, here we come." Doyle-Leigh led the board to the bar.

32

It was like clockwork. Seven in the morning and she ran to the bathroom without waking up all the way as in previous mornings. Once again, she hugged her friend, the toilet.

Aaron called from the bedroom. "Diva, are you okay?" He got up and made his way to the bathroom to check on her. He stood by the door. "Diva?"

"I'm so sick on my stomach." She lifted her head from the seat rim. "I think I'm finished." She flushed the john. "This is some crazy flu. Sick in the morning, better in the afternoon." She extended her hand to Aaron for help.

Aaron took her hand and helped her to her feet. He took her arm and put it over his shoulders. "Can I get you something?"

"A new stomach," Beverly laughed. "Let me get to the sink and then just help me to the bed. I'll be all right in a minute." At the sink, she looked in the mirror to see him as he looked at her. His outward show of concern made her feel better as she finished her oral hygiene.

"Now don't you go getting sick on me, I'm beginning to get used to my side of the bed". In a surprise move, he picked her up in his arms and carried her to their love nest. "Besides I need my star." Aaron gently placed Beverly on the mattress. "Are you sure there is nothing I can do for you, like call the doctor?"

Those words took her from her little piece of heaven. "No doctors now," Beverly said, thinking the doctor might discover that The Diva was missing. She pulled the comforter over her body. "There *is* something you can help me with. I'm embarrassed to admit — but I forgot the combination to my safe, can you believe?" Beverly put her hands in her hair. "It must be all the excitement of you." She smiled.

He smiled in return. "You forgot the combination to your safe? You didn't write it down in a *safe* place?" Aaron laughed. "Sorry, couldn't resist. I can get it drilled out in a few days unless there is something you need out of there in a hurry."

"Just money. Thank God you have fed me these last months even though I seem to be losing it." Beverly patted her belly.

"Why didn't you say something?" Aaron sat on the bed with her. "I can't have my star wanting things and not being able to get them. Couldn't you have written a check?"

"The Diva's checks are in the safe as well as The Diva's money and The Diva did not want to be scatterbrained." She laughed heartily as she clutched her stomach tighter.

"Well, at least The Diva's man is by her side."

Suddenly it came to her that maybe the combination was her birth date. "Aaron, try my birthday would you? The safe is behind the portrait of me."

"Anything for my lady." He got up again, went to the picture, removed it, and stood in front of the safe.

"Eleven right, twelve left, nineteen right and then seventy left."

Aaron mumbled the numbers in unison with Beverly and as he dialed the last number the safe opened. He looked inside, turned back to her and said, "You're in the money. Don't forget this is now half mine."

"You deserve it. Goodness, I don't know what made me forget, and it just came back to me while I was lying here with you." As Aaron was following her instructions, she looked at him against the side wall of her bedroom. Most of the wall was windows covered with half-open, white vertical-louver shades. Looking at him in all of that light reinforced to her that he was really a ray of sunshine in her life. He had been so complimentary and loving. He had now become beautiful to her.

Aaron shut the safe door, replaced the picture on the wall,

and asked coyly, "So many differences in you. It's like you are turning into someone else before my very eyes. Is there anything else you're forgetting?"

She smiled then got out of bed to give him a hug. "Yes, of course there is, I'll correct it now. Good morning, my darling Aaron. I love you with all my heart and my body." She leaned into him.

"I love you too and don't you ever forget that." Aaron returned the kiss. "Let's go into the kitchen and you can watch me cook you breakfast. Then I have to go into the office." They left the bedroom, hand-in-hand, and walked into the kitchen. Aaron opened the refrigerator door.

"That's the strange thing, I never forget my appetite. By the way, thank you for getting groceries. You know how I hate to go to the store." She pulled a chair away from the table and sat. "Maybe I have an ulcer or something like that. I'm going to get the newspaper." She got up and quickly came back with the news of the day. Aaron cracked eggs into a bowl and started to mix them with spices. "Are you making your famous omelet for me?"

"You know it," he said as he turned on the stove and took out a frying pan. "You're still planning on visiting Evan in Atlanta?"

"Yes, if you don't mind. It's been a few years since I've seen him, but we still talk almost every day. I met him when I was eighteen." Beverly turned a page of the paper. "Can I help?"

"Mission control is under control. I'd like to see him again. I know he's been a good friend to you, to hear you tell it. I'm sure you're inviting him to the wedding?" She nodded in agreement. Aaron poured the egg mixture in the frying pan. "But I wish you'd go to the doctor before you leave."

"Aaron, don't worry. I'm not going to let anything stop me from my wedding day."

"Make that a promise." He lifted the frying pan over the fire and twirled it around. "I thought I would go ahead and move in here while you were gone. You certainly don't need any aggravation right now. After a few months, I thought we might look for another place to live." He put the pan back on the burner and took plates and glasses out of the cabinet. "Orange juice?"

Beverly turned another page of the paper. "Yes, darling, I hope you never stop spoiling me. Don't worry, I won't tell the rest of Hollywood what a teddy bear you are. And move anything you need to move even if it is out the door. Get rid of most of these mirrors now that it is you that I want to look at most."

Flipping the omelet, Aaron said, "Now I know you're sick. You want me to get rid of your mirrors?"

"Not all of them, Aaron. Most, but not all."

Aaron brought the food to the table, "Do I need to get that in writing? You won't recognize the place when you return. You'll open the door and say 'there's a man in this house.'" Aaron took her hand. "Just make sure you rest some while you are away. There's going to be a lot to do when you get back. Paramount is waiting and I will be, too." He sat at the table.

Beverly held on to his hand. They looked at each other and smiled. She never thought she'd be so happy so soon. "*Bon appetite*, my darling."

33

Evan spied Diva. She was the first to embark from the plane so he assumed she, of course, flew first class. She had probably insisted that the flight crew hold everyone from departing until her entrance could be made. In true form, a scarf and sunglasses adorned her head. He noticed that she had a rhythmic bounce to her movement as though she were listening to jazz. He gave her a few more steps, then he waved his hands in the air until she saw him. They ran to each other and hugged tightly. "I almost didn't see you from the glare of that rock on your finger."

She held her hand out for him to admire her engagement ring. "Kind of small, don't you think?"

"It's bigger than mine," he said, holding his hand out with nothing to show. "You look so good. You still look like that eighteen-year-old girl I met in New York City."

"I'll never forget that day at the hotel." She lifted her sunglasses just enough to expose her eyes. "I reported to work and you were my boss, all dressed up in that sharp suit." Beverly winked and put her shades back in place. She was a little stunned that one of The Diva's memories came to her so quickly. She was even more stunned that she felt entirely in control.

"And you were dressed all in white, even back then." His hands touched his chest, his hips and then his chest again as he spoke. "Your white jacket, white skirt and that white silk blouse." For the clincher he smiled really big and said, "And that dazzling smile that you still possess to this day."

"Stop, stop." She said modestly and then, in a conniving tone, said, "More, more." She smiled. "Those were some fun, carefree times." She gave Evan another hug.

As they stood in embrace, Evan whispered into her ear, "And you 'made it.' We both tried and you succeeded." The embrace was released and he turned to walk through the concourse.

She followed. "Don't give up hope. It's not too late."

"I'm still working on it. I guess it's better to start at this age than not at all. I feel that this pageant will help me get really motivated. I mean, this will be the first time that I've actually performed in front of an audience. Okay, it will be Lowla and not me, but I think that is where the comfort lies, you know, being someone else to give you that push to get out on stage."

"I know what you mean. Being someone else can really give you the courage you need until you can do those things exposed as yourself." Beverly tugged at his arm.

"Exactly." He grabbed her arm and stopped. "We think

so much alike." He hugged her again. "You just look so great and happy. How do you do it? It must be all that money."

"Darling, it is my old secret of baking soda and a little warm water; scrubs the years off of your face," Beverly said as they started to walk to the baggage claim area. "I can't believe I am back in Atlanta. It's been years."

"You will have to come to the premiere of your movie in Atlanta, then I can show you all of the new places in town since this will be an in-and-out trip. The city has changed so much. Are you ready for the ride to Florida?"

"As long as I can sit in the front," Beverly laughed as they got on the escalator. "I have already been sick today."

"Sick? Did you get motion sickness on the plane?"

Stepping off the escalator, she said, "No, not motion sickness. I don't know what it is. I've been sick every morning." She looked around and saw her destination. "Over this way." She pointed to the baggage office of Delta. "You know, The Diva's luggage will be picked separately and not delivered on some conveyer belt." She got close to Evan's ear so no one would hear her say, "I threw up in the barf bag though, how embarrassing. First class has its advantages. I was escorted to the restroom right away. But I still managed to have lunch." Beverly laughed again, and reached into her purse. "Here are my claim tickets. Be a dear and get The Diva's bags."

He curtseyed. "Just like old times. I'm at The Diva's disposal." Evan went to get the luggage and in seconds they were out the door en route to his truck. "You didn't mention you had been sick on the phone. How long has this been going on?"

"For a couple of weeks, at least."

"For a couple of weeks, every morning?" he repeated.

"At least."

He glanced at her with a knowing smirk. Gallantly he opened the truck door. Beverly got in her seat and settled before he closed the door. Evan placed her bags in the back and then got into the driver's side. "Lloyd has rented a van for us so we can be comfortable. I have so much stuff it wouldn't have fit into the bed of the truck anyway." He put the keys in the ignition. "You don't have the usual seventeen bags. You must be sick. Your make-up usually takes at least three cases." He cranked up the truck and proceeded to get out of the airport parking lot.

"The Diva is delighted to travel light these days. I'm so happy, Evan, that you will get a chance to perform. I know it is a dream of yours. And dreams should come true." Beverly pulled down the visor mirror to check her scarf. Even seated, her bouncy movements had continued and when she wasn't speaking, she hummed. "I hate wearing this thing, but you never know who might want to snap my picture. By the way, did you tell your friends who I am?"

"No, that was part of our deal. I gave them 'Beverly Heels' like you told me to do. By the way, hello, Beverly, it is nice to meet you." Evan extended his hand.

"Pleased to make your acquaintance. I've always wanted to know what it felt like to be someone else." She shook his hand in return.

"It's a great feeling. When I am Lowla, I have confidence. What amazes me most is that people do not recognize Evan as Lowla. It's like they can't believe she is me or I am her since we are so different looking."

"You used to do my make-up, remember? You were always were great at painting a face."

"Great at many things, but fabulous at none." He had put his hand on his heart; then he began to toy with her. "Not that it is any of my business. But since you've told me all about Aaron and that you are madly in love and that he is sleeping with you . . . I am assuming you are having sex? After all, you did tell me he threw you a bone. I figured you did more than chew on it," Evan said with a grin.

"And I led you to believe it was the baking soda making me look so young!" She flashed her brilliant smile.

"Diva, are you on birth control?"

"No. Why? You know The Diva can not have children."

He mocked her accent. "Nothing shall ever stand in The Diva's way of success." In his regular southern accent, he continued, "This is Evan, remember? I know that is what The Diva told her men so you would never be in the position to be a mother because you wanted to pursue a career." He boldly inquired, "Is he using condoms?"

"What are you getting at, Evan?" Beverly crossed her arms as a look of panic ran across her face. She had thought The Diva had told the truth about conceiving.

Evan pulled up to the booth to pay for parking. "Well, Diva, I know you have never been any good at math, so listen closely. One plus one plus sex equals three." He paid the attendant. "And you have been sick in the morning. Ever hear of morning sickness?"

A look of seriousness joined the look of panic over Beverly's face. "What was I thinking? It never occurred to me that I might be pregnant."

"Bingo, you can add. There is a drugstore on the way home. I think we should stop in and get us a pregnancy test. What do you think?" Evan said, blending the truck into the traffic.

"I think perhaps we should, and then if it comes back negative, I can rule that out. If it comes back positive . . . "

"At least you have a wedding around the corner," Evan said.

"But I've got a film. What will The Diva do?" Beverly dramatically questioned as she placed one hand on her stomach and the other on her forehead.

"Hollywood can figure out how to work around you. It happens all the time. Madonna was pregnant when she filmed *Evita*, which upset me greatly because I could have played that part without moving up the film's schedule in order to accommodate an unplanned pregnancy. *How unprofessional!* Besides, I could play your part in the film."

Evan laughed at what he thought was clever wit. The drugstore was right by his house so it took no time to get from the airport to where the fated test was purchased, then on to his house where Lloyd and Rex were waiting.

The fellows were outside enjoying the beauty of Evan's yard, which contained an array of plants and bushes. It was easy to get lost in the rose bushes, the Lelands, the overgrown crepe myrtles, and all of the low-hanging limbs from the old pecan trees. They came to greet the truck as Evan pulled into the garage. The Marilynmobile and the rented van were pulled on the grass in the back yard. Lloyd ran around the truck to open the door for Beverly. Before she stepped on the paved driveway, she looked at herself in the visor mirror once more, closed it and then took off her sunglasses.

"Diva!" Lloyd screamed. "It is so good to see you. How come you will come down to perform in Florida and not do my Moulin Rouge Carnival?"

"Working me already. You haven't changed, Lloyd." They embraced. "And who is this handsome young man?" Beverly looked at Rex. "Is this your brother?"

Lloyd placed a hand on the back of Rex's neck. "No, this is Rex Greenfield. Rex, this is The Diva."

They exchanged polite first hugs. "I just love your book. I brought it for you to autograph, if you don't mind," Rex said.

"Not at all. I just love those kinds of comments. It makes me happy that people appreciate my works. Hopefully, the masses will come to the movie after it is filmed and released and not stay at home like they did for 'The White Elephant.'" She batted her eyelashes.

Rex appeared to be very excited. "That's great, I can't wait."

Lloyd took her hand. "Oh my God, Diva, how ever did you get that accomplished? I want to be in it! Really! Congratulations!"

"The Diva will see what she can do. Right now, I'd say

Rex has a good chance to be in it." Beverly looked at Rex. "You remind me of a character from my book."

"I hope it's Carlos," Rex said with anticipation at her answer.

She smiled as she replied, "It is. We will definitely have to exchange our thoughts on the subject this weekend."

"Hey, you two, remember." Lloyd pointed to himself. "I have to be in it. I'll bet Lowla has been bugging you to be in the movie, too."

"Unlike you, he hasn't even asked." She smiled at Lloyd and then touched Rex's arm. "I hope I didn't insult you when I thought you two were related. You look alike. Of course, you're handsomer," Beverly said as she walked out of the garage. "Lloyd, do you notice anything different about me?" She waved her left hand in the air.

Evan took her luggage out of the back of the truck to put it in the van. "You'd have to be blind not to notice."

"Oh my, look at that ring," Lloyd said. "What did you have to do to get that?"

She chose not to acknowledge that comment. "Yes, The Diva is going to be married. Thank you for asking," Beverly shot back at Lloyd.

"So am I," Rex said. "Look at the ring Lloyd gave me." He showed off his gold ring with the garnet stone that Lloyd had given him in their secret place. "He was so sweet when he proposed."

"Oh, congratulations yourself." Beverly said as she hugged Rex. "Marilyn, I just knew you would be the one to wear white on your wedding day." She laughed and gave Lloyd a hug also. "Did all of your drag fit into the van?"

"What drag?" Lloyd said sarcastically to Diva.

Diva looked at Lloyd quizzically. "You proposed. You have no drag. My, you have changed. I guess The Diva shouldn't call you Marilyn anymore?"

"You can call me Lloyd. Marilyn has temporarily left the building."

Evan was beginning to get antsy about the weekend. "Let's save the conversation for the road. We've got to go. Lloyd and Rex are in the Marilynmobile and we are in the van." Evan opened the door for Beverly to get in. "Does anyone need to go to the bathroom?"

They all shook their heads.

"I can't wait to hear all about you, Rex," exclaimed Beverly, getting into the van. "You guys don't drive too fast. I am assuming we will caravan there. And don't get mad when I have to make frequent stops, either. The Diva has to take ultimate care of herself."

"Did you lock up the house for me, Lloyd?" Evan said, holding his hand out for the keys.

"Rex did it. Do you know where your Egyptian slaves are?" Lloyd asked as he handed Evan the keys.

"Yes, they left yesterday, as you well know, to have fun in Pensacola. Now don't mention them again. It's supposed to be a secret." Evan got in the van and shut the door. Lloyd and Rex pulled out first, then Evan. He stopped the van so he could get out and lock the gate behind him, and then got back in the van.

"Look at all of this stuff. What are you going to do, build a pyramid? And what did Lloyd mean about slaves?" Beverly questioned Evan, who was trying to keep up with Lloyd.

"Too bad I didn't think of that . . . or the Sphinx to build . . . and it's Egyptian slaves, Diva. The theme *is* 'Midnight at the Oasis.' I hired four hunky friends of Lloyd's to carry me in during my talent number. And it's a secret, so keep it to yourself."

"If there is one thing The Diva can do, that is to keep a secret," Beverly responded.

The van and the Marilynmobile made their way through the Atlanta traffic headed for an adventure to Niceville, Florida.

34

The sun was shining brightly from above, revealing the hues of green foliage and reflective metals that dotted the area. The country highway which led to the setting was lined with palm trees and huge pines that had Spanish moss decorating the limbs as though it were garland on a Christmas tree. All during the day entertainers and spectators from around the country arrived at the Niceville Trailer Park, some in car caravans with few stray vehicles here and there. Some flew to the closest airport and had to be picked up in nearby Pensacola. Most drove since each performer had to bring his own drag and props if he was going to perform. Each person and group of arrivals had to go to the recreational center to pick up trailer assignments and keys. From there, they would park in front of their small trailers for the holiday.

The sounds of laughter echoed as new attendees met the ones that had come to Niceville for years while others got reacquainted, chatting about their pasts of this meaningful weekend. Regardless of the reason, there was a buzz of one-liners and salutations in the air. People were unloading their cars and moving into their temporary homes. Clothes, costumes, fans, and food were among the items carried into their quarters. Once people had settled in, some ventured out and explored the surrounding area of Niceville and Fort Walton Beach. Others sat in front of their trailers and drank and talked about the fun they would have as the weekend progressed. However they spent chosen past-times, all had to be back by eight in the evening. That was when the event started and instructions and rules for the accommodations would be given . . . and more introductions made. Friday night each person was on his own as far as gathering a meal. The bar opened immediately, but the catering did not start until Saturday breakfast. There were chips, dips and such the whole weekend from start to finish.

Evan and his gang had arrived at the archway that

welcomed all visitors to the trailer park around six that evening. The campground trailer park looked as though it belonged in the 1950's rather than the twenty-first century. Lloyd drove straight down the road between the silver, blue and tan colored trailers which led to the rectangular brick building called the recreation hall to get their sleeping and living assignments while the others remained in the car and van. He came out with keys. "Follow me." They drove to their trailers, parked and took their things inside.

While he and Beverly were unpacking in their trailer, Evan said, "Gosh, this is a lot nicer than I thought."

"Not bad, a little tight." Beverly scanned the space. "But it isn't Melrose Place, child."

"Well, you might fit in if you turn out to be pregnant," Evan said as he put the last of their stuff on the counter. "At least it's just you and me. I'm glad that Lloyd and Rex are next door. This may turn out to be a good time. Speaking of a good time, do you want to take that test now?"

"No, not now. I just want to relax and enjoy the evening," Beverly said as she took off her scarf and specs and retrieved her wig out of her bag.

"Just make sure you don't drink tonight. Just in case." Evan went to help Beverly with her wig.

"There is something I need to tell you, Evan." Beverly pulled the wig down over her head. "I haven't told anyone and I figure I could tell you. Now don't freak out on me, but I haven't been The Diva lately."

The door to the trailer flew open, Lloyd stuck his head inside. "Come on; let's go get something to eat before the night begins. I need to eat!"

"Okay, we'll be right there. You don't mind driving, do you?" Evan looked at Lloyd. "I hate to drive when I am stoned. Just can't handle it at this age."

"I'll drive, but smoke later. I don't want you to miss a thing and you need to mingle with the crowd and campaign for votes." Lloyd shut the door.

He gave Lloyd a moment to get out of earshot. "What is it, Diva?"

"The Diva has gone away," she said defiantly.

"So," Evan looked at her, perplexed, "where has The Diva gone?"

"Sit down, Evan." He sat on the tiny chair beside the kitchen counter as she continued, "I'll be brief and we can talk more in detail later. Are you familiar with Dissociative Identity Disorder?"

"Do you mean schizophrenia?"

"No, if I were schizophrenic, The Diva would have killed you by now," she laughed. "It's called DID for short. It's when a person has two or more personalities and only one is in control at the time."

Evan looked at Beverly, confused. "Diva, are you trying to tell me that you are someone else?"

She extended her hand. "Evan, I would like to make *your* acquaintance. My name is really Beverly Heels."

"You have got to be kidding," Evan said as he shook her hand in return. "No wonder you had a name ready for me." He glanced from the floor then back to her eyes. "You're not rehearsing for a role or something are you? I mean, you're serious?"

"As serious as having a child."

"And is there someone else, or just you?"

"No, just me, Beverly."

"Would you even know?"

"I think so. I know about The Diva . . . and she knows about me. If another shows up, please be so kind to let me know."

Evan stood and paced in the tiny room of the trailer. "Some people have all the luck. When I was younger, I hated myself so much that I used to pretend that I had a split personality. And I never got any attention for it either. Not even a 'what is your name again?'" He stopped and looked at her. "I thought there was just a little something different about you. I guess all of the humming and moving you have been doing is the Beverly bounce?"

"That is so cute, Evan. I like that." She did a quick bounce and a hum.

"You seem to be a little more relaxed. How long has Beverly been in existence?"

"For a while. I'm really not sure. Some time had passed before I started keeping track of my appearances. But it's been about a couple of months now that I have been steady at staying out. Before it was an in-and-out situation, you know like most love making. But now The Diva is definitely dormant. It could be an explosive situation if she were to reappear since I am involved with Aaron and maybe pregnant. She let me know she didn't like to be touched."

"Oh, she let you know? What did she do, write you a letter?"

"Now, Evan, I know this may be a little difficult, but save your humor for the stage. Let's just say that it was a mind communication type of thing. There are times when I hear her voice. I think I was born because deep down The Diva is unhappy and doesn't know how to let go or doesn't want to face an unsuccessful future. She was banking everything on a new movie. I'm here to make a difference."

"Has The Diva mind communicated with you that she is unhappy and unsuccessful? You sound like old friends. It seems to me that you two ought to be able to sit down and talk this out like two adults."

"I know this sounds strange, but believe me when I tell you that The Diva will not bend once her mind is made up."

"You don't have to tell me that. I've known her forever. She is quite rigid when it comes to changing her mind."

"I'll do her hidden impulses because I have nothing to lose. I've thrown all caution to the wind."

"Oh yeah, what about your existence? That sounds like a lot to lose to me." Evan hoped he wasn't being too difficult for her. He had to know if she was on the level. This was one time he was stumped at reading a face. The one thing he felt he did know was that she was somehow a changed person. "Does anyone else know?"

"No one else knows. Let's keep this between us. It's hard enough trying to remember when to be me and when to be pretending to be her."

"Not even Aaron?"

"Especially not Aaron, I'm trying to have a successful future. Do you think The Diva would be getting married? I mean, if the movie doesn't work out, at least The Diva will not have to work, being Aaron's wife. Hello, are you listening?" Beverly said as she took the pot out of a knapsack that Evan brought with him in order to roll them a joint. "Time for Mary."

"I'll puff to that. I must say what a grand idea to be involved with Aaron so that no matter how the dice rolls, you can't lose no matter who you are."

"But . . . I do love him."

"That makes the wager even sweeter. You really can't lose and I suppose The Diva wouldn't have come to Florida either. Even as Beverly you should know that I am just crazy enough to get along with you. Thanks, Beverly, I need you here this weekend, I think. Are you sure you don't want to go ahead and take that test?"

"I don't think I need to take it. I think I know the answer, but I'm going to wait until bedtime. That way I can recuperate by morning if necessary," Beverly said as she pulled at her hair.

"Recuperate overnight? What are you going to do? Hide your feelings like The Diva does? I thought you were supposed to make a difference in her life?"

The door opened again. "I should have known you two would be smoking. Do you want something to eat or not?" Lloyd said angrily.

"Yes." Evan got up quickly. "You know how time flies when you hold a joint in your hands." He turned back to

Beverly. "And you can't smoke until you take that test either." He took the pot away from her and hid it in the cabinet. "Let's go. By the way, Lloyd, we have changed Diva's name to Beverly. Beverly Heels."

"How clever. What test are you talking about taking and why did you change your name? Are you going to do drag?"

"Lloyd darling, The Diva will explain everything to you later." Beverly giggled.

"Well, then. Let's go eat. Surely there is a Popeye's or a KFC in this town." Lloyd turned to leave followed by Beverly and Evan. While driving the seventeen miles to Fort Walton Beach, Beverly clued in Lloyd and Rex as to Diva's new name and the possibility of an arrival in the months to come along with the necessity to keep it all private. They had excited chit chat as they ate at a local diner and then headed back to Niceville so they would not miss any of the festivities. As soon as the Marilynmobile was parked under the trailer canopy, Evan hurried to his neighboring trailer to smoke. The rest of the gang went to the recreational hall and started mingling with the crowd that had already gathered. Evan finally arrived, smelling like marijuana, and immediately noted that the hall looked like most bingo parlors: rows of tables and chairs with the stage being about four feet above ground, located in the rear of the huge room.

Out of the crowd, Doyle-Leigh made his way through as he acknowledged everyone like a politician at a fund raiser. He marched up onto the stage slowly and deliberately as he stared into the gathering of hopefuls, has-beens, and those just seeking a fun and crazy weekend.

Evan whispered into Lloyd's ear, "Oh, there is our Doris Day. I hope to God he doesn't sing *Que Sera Sera.*"

With microphone in hand, he shouted, "Hello, everybody, my name is Doyle-Leigh, what's yours? And I am your emcee for the weekend. I would like to welcome everybody to this seventeenth annual Memorial Day extravaganza of the Miss Niceville pageant." The crowd applauded which made him smile even bigger. "As your emcee, I want to go over with you some of the rules, regulations, and duties for the weekend. Now, I know you all are excited, but you must be quiet and listen to me." He took a sip of his cocktail. "Yes, listen to me while I make sense. As the evening progresses and I drink more, I will make less and less sense and I will become more and more pretty to you."

The crowd gushed a patronizing laugh.

"Now where was I? Oh yes, sipping my cocktail." He sipped from his glass again. "Rules, duties, and regulations, oh my! We have these issues to discuss because we rent this facility and we want to be able to come back next year. So keep your trailers neat, and clean them when you leave on Monday. You are responsible for your own maid service. There are washers and dryers right down the hall over there." He pointed to his left. "That means wash your sheets. Also, over yonder on the left are sign-up posters for you to sign up for duties. The duties are meal preparations and such. Oh, before I forget, do you all have on your name tags?" A faint response was heard. "What? I can't hear you. Now when I ask a question, I expect an answer, damn it. Do you all have on your name tags?"

"Yes!" they all yelled.

"That's more like it. Don't make me come off this stage."

"Oh please, do us a favor!" one of the people screamed.

"It's crowded in here, but I recognize that voice and I will punish you later." Doyle-Leigh sipped from his glass once more.

"What are you going to do, perform?" the voice said again.

The crowd roared with laughter.

"You know it's a shame when you can't even take your own boyfriend out of the fucking house." He guzzled more cocktail down his throat, then said into the microphone, "No wonder they say a dog is a man's best friend. Oh, keeping on track, I think, I was talking about tags. Please wear your name tag as everyone doesn't know you yet but they will before the weekend is over 'cause we are," he said as he extended his arms, "one big chosen family." He smiled a presidential smile to his constituents.

Applause erupted from the group.

"Thank you, and now for my next number. Just kidding. Will someone bring a lady a cocktail?" Doyle-Leigh handed his glass to his friend, Jamie. "Thank you, darling. Now, I know it is confusing that most of us have two names. So just concentrate on the girl names and when we say her, we mean him, but bitch applies to everybody, especially Faux Pas." He acted as though he was hit in the back. "Oh, was that a dagger between my shoulders? Just kidding. Faux Pas is actually a nice person. Just kidding. Oh yes, listen up, most important, stay away from the water when you are drunk. That includes the beach and the bay. And do not drink here and then go drive your car somewhere. The cops hang out all weekend on the highway just looking for an excuse to handcuff one of us and not just for sex. Lowla, I hear you can tell us all about handcuffs and sex later. Apparently she has experience with law enforcement."

Evan's face reddened as laughter and "ooohs" came from the group. "Now if y'all are quiet I won't be on this stage long." Suddenly a dropping pin would have reverberated through the room. "This group is a real riot this year. Okay, okay, okay where is my drink?" Jamie handed him a refilled glass. "Thank you, Jamie. Everybody, let's hear it for Jamie." The crowd applauded. Doyle-Leigh took a sip of his cocktail. "Oh, this is delicious. Where was I? Oh, yes, Friday nights are special here because we get to meet all of you and show videos from the past. There are drinks the entire evening and chips and what-not. The food schedule is as follows for Saturday and Sunday: breakfast at eight a.m., lunch at noon and dinner at six p.m. If you don't like what we're serving, go get your own damn food. Remember to take your turn for kitchen duty and sign up on the sign-up posters so I will shut up." He put out his hand to the crowd. "Don't go there. Just don't go there because if you take me there, I will stay. On Monday, the day of your departure, breakfast only will be served. Make sure you turn your sheets in on Monday at the laundry room located by the washers and dryers and be sure to take your trash to the dumpsters. Not your lover, but your trash." He took another sip. "Am I pretty yet?"

"Hell no," people yelled.

"Well, keep drinking," Doyle-Leigh continued. "Saturday you can do whatever you want unless you are in the pageant. Contestants, listen up. We will meet in here at ten a.m. to start working on the stage. You may rehearse your number if you like and talk with the DJ about your music. The rest of you need to stay out until show time at eight o'clock and those of you who have been here before know we all start on time." He laughed at himself. "Whoever is crowned Saturday night will be the guest of honor at the Sunday breakfast and will lead off the Sunday night show. Now anyone can perform on Sunday. You must sign up with our stage manager, Alex. Alex, honey, wherever you are, stand up and take a bow."

Alex stood up and bowed to the applause of the crowd.

"Moving professionally along, if I have left anything out, tough shit. Let's all mingle and party, and welcome to Niceville Seventeen." Doyle-Leigh put the microphone down and headed off the stage.

Through the rest of the evening, the crowd talked, laughed and drank. It was about ten in the evening when Evan noticed Beverly was not in the recreational room. He found Lloyd and told him he was going back to his trailer and that he would see them in the morning. He left the recreational hall and headed to check on Beverly. He opened the door and found Beverly laying down crying. "Oh my, did you take the test?"

"Yes," Beverly replied.

"Was it positive?" Evan said going to her.

"Positively!" Beverly sobbed. "I don't think I can handle this. I think I have to let The Diva come back," she murmured hopelessly.

Evan sat on the couch with her. "Beverly, this situation is new to me, but you really have been a lot of fun and from the looks of everything, I think you've been good for The Diva. Can't you two just get along?"

"That's part of it, Evan. If I go away, we will integrate and become one. I'm not sure how we would mix. I'll never be totally back or in control. I would do it in a heartbeat if I knew most of my personality would prevail. But you know how The Diva is: self centered, vain and scared. I never meant to hurt anyone, and now if things backfire I will hurt Aaron, our child, The Diva and myself."

"Beverly, I hope you don't mind, but I need to smoke a doobee on this one." Evan opened the cabinet, got out the pot and rolled a joint. "The one thing we don't need to do is to freak over this. So, I say a big 'congratulations' to you." He took out a lighter and lit the joint.

"Thank you, I guess. This may be the end of my world," Beverly said in a pitiful voice.

"No it's not. I have been at the end of mine at least once a month. You will never go out when you think you are. God will not take you away just because you don't want to face tomorrow. He'll take you when you do. Come on, girl, get that hair off your head and let me tuck you into bed. It will seem different in the light of the day." He helped her with her wig, got a blanket and placed it on her. "I've seen you in worse jams; you always come out on top. I promise it will be better in the morning. I won't leave your side. I'll be here all night watching over you. I promise."

"You promise?"

Evan shook his head yes, leaned over, gave her a kiss, turned out the light and proceeded to smoke in the dark.

35

Little stirred in the trailer park when the sun rose in the east above the tiny town of Niceville. All of the drag queens, performers and spectators were nestled in their trailers. The trailers were lined up like dominos on each side of the road that passed between them. Sounds of snoring or music playing — or silence — would have hit passersby. Every unit came equipped with a small den, a tiny kitchenette, and a bedroom to the rear. Two could sleep in the bedroom and two could uncomfortably share the pull-out sofa. The patrons of the pageant event did not seem to mind. To many of them, it was more important to have a get-away place where they would feel as though they belonged somewhere.

As the morning progressed, the place was abuzz at the breakfast tables with talk of plans for the rest of the day. Some would go to the beach while others would paddle canoes along the bay. The contestants would obviously be busy getting the recreational hall ready for the big event of the evening. The trailers did not come with air conditioning so most brought their own fans. It was the sound of the fans that allowed Evan and Beverly to sleep through breakfast. Evan awoke and realized he had less than half an hour to get to working on the set. He entered the den and saw Beverly, still asleep on the sofa bed. He wondered where Lloyd and Rex were. Lloyd was usually up very early in the morning. He turned to go out of the door and ran into Lloyd, who was about to knock.

"So, you decided to knock this time?" Evan said as he rubbed his eyes.

"Yeah, I figured I'd better get here and see what you two were up to. You know it is almost ten o'clock. I thought I would see if Beverly wanted to hang with us today since you have chores to do," Lloyd said, following Evan back into the den.

Beverly was sitting up by this time and greeted the two.

"Good morning, guys."

"Good morning to you," Lloyd said. "You want to hang with Rex and me today? We're going shopping and then to the beach for a swim."

"Do you feel up to it?" Evan questioned as he picked up a doughnut from the assortment of food they had brought along with them.

"It's really amazing. I slept really good last night and for the first time, I don't want to puke my guts out this morning," Beverly replied, throwing the covers off of her. "I'd love to go, if you'll allow me to take a quick shower and make a phone call."

"No problem. Does The Diva think she can be ready in a half hour?" Lloyd said, looking at his watch.

"No problem. The Diva knows she can be ready in a half hour."

"Lowla, you'd better get a move on." Lloyd left the trailer to head back to his.

"I'll bathe later. I guess I don't smell." Evan ate his doughnut and went into the bedroom to change his clothes. After putting on a clean tee shirt and short pants, he came out and gave Beverly a hug. "I am assuming you are going to call Aaron." He released her from his grip.

"Yes, we are going to face the music somehow," Beverly said, getting her cell phone out of her purse.

"We?"

"It's time for Beverly and The Diva to get together. Now that we are going to be a mother, we need to set an example."

"Please, if it is a girl name her Lowla," Evan joked as he grabbed his music and turned to leave. As he left he heard Beverly on the phone.

"Hello, Aaron, this is The Diva, the woman you love so much that you would do anything for and I know that it's early . . ."

And that was all he heard as he closed the door, allowing her privacy to tell Aaron the good news. Walking into the recreational hall he realized he was the last to arrive. Everyone there was sitting in attention with the current Miss Niceville, waiting on instructions from the queen.

"It looks like everyone is here now and we can get started," he said as he looked at Evan. "I am Crown Jewel, your current reigning Miss Niceville and I am looking forward to crowning one of you tonight. Most folks call me a lot of things but you can just call me Jewel." He moved to the center of the room. "We have a curtain to hang so I will need a volunteer who is not afraid of heights for that. The other things are easy, just the placement of props that I have already painted and put together. I have everything drawn out, so you will know where to put each backdrop or plant." He held up a poster-sized drawing of his creation. "Just remember, we are building an oasis. Also we will need to create the dressing area which will be over there." He put down his drawing and walked over to the right. "You can still see the nails in the molding. We left them there from a couple of years back hoping they would be here the following year. It makes it easier that way." Jewel pointed to the molding. "We just need to tie a piece of rope to the nail then string it to the portable Maypoles that are in place. Then we will drape sheets over the ropes and before you know it, we will have us a dressing area. Okay." He paused to look at his notes. "We will need to help the DJs so they will make us sound good. There is a lot to do, *but* it will get done. If you have any questions, please ask. Don't piss off the reigning Queen who is about to become news of yesterday. First we need to move the first four rows of tables and place the chairs for theater seating." Jewel motioned toward Alex. "This is Alex, our stage manager. He will be very valuable to you, making sure you are on stage when you are supposed to be. Over yonder are Ashley and Marc, our music maestros who also run the spotlight and the video cameras."

The maestros waved to the contestants.

Jewel placed her notes on a nearby table and picked up a

hat. "I will now have you draw a number out of this hat and that will determine your contestant number. Once you have your number, you need to write it on your music and then give it to Ashley now so there will be no confusion later as to what music goes with which contestant. That is how you will be introduced. Example, let's welcome contestant number one, Jewel. Everybody got that? Good." He moved from contestant to contestant as each one picked a number out of the hat. "Do all you girls have a number? All right, starting with you, I'd like for you to stand and say your name and your number. Wait a second and let me write these down." Gathering his paper and pen, he pointed to the first person to his left.

A rather large hopeful stood. He looked like a normal guy with brown hair possibly in his late twenties or early thirties. "My name is Farah Dice and I am proud to be contestant number one. And I am very happy to be here and I wish you all the best." He took his seat as the next in line began to rise.

"Hello, my name is Lowla de la Vie and I am contestant number three. Thank you." Evan returned to his seat quickly. He was already nervous and could not muster any chit-chat at the moment.

"This is your contestant number four." He stood up exposing his tiny frame and long blond hair. Evan couldn't get a make on his age as he was really thin which probably made him look older. "And my name is Petula." He grabbed the seat in front of him for support. When he was at Doyle-Leigh's house, Evan had heard that Petula was on some kind of medication which made him look muscular but emaciated. *Maybe he should give some of that medicine to Farah Dice.*

The next contestant was very polite. He waited with a smile on his face as Petula slowly sat. A very Spanish-looking Montgomery Cliff-type of young man stood up, spun and declared, "I am Tehaira. Contestant numero cinco." Evan could not imagine him in drag since he was so handsome. He couldn't resist looking at him and tried not to let his eyes stay on him too long.

"And all the way from Cleveland, Ohio, I am contestant number two, Moana Leesa." Moana Leesa looked every bit like the painting. It was easy for someone to know how he got that handle. Evan was amazed. Even his black hair was parted down the middle without one curl. The hair was straight as a stick.

As soon as the introductions were completed the contestants wrote their numbers on their music and handed it to the DJs. Then they all headed back to Jewel who directed them through the course of the show, then assigned them duties to perform in order to change a simple recreational hall into a "Midnight at the Oasis." It was fun, but it was a long, grueling day until everything was completed. The contestants talked as they built the oasis and when they were finished, a sense of pride came over them.

"The stage and the audience arena look perfect," Tehaira said to Evan. "I can't wait to perform."

"It does look like paradise," Evan answered.

"Did someone call my name?" Farah Dice came to where Evan and Tehaira stood.

Evan was disappointed to be interrupted with his first chance of the day to have a one-on-one with Tehaira. "We were just admiring our work when I said it looked like *paradise.*"

Jewel came from the dressing area. "Y'all have done a great job. This is the best stage I have ever seen at this pageant." He stared at the stage. The look on his face was undeniably happiness. "Would someone lower the main curtain?" Alex waved from behind the side of left stage and lowered the black theatrical curtain as requested. "Now let's go eat. Be back here by seven-thirty and you can bring your stuff to the laundry room . . . I mean dressing area. By all means, get made up in your trailers. The show will start at eight. I mean it. Break a leg, ya h'ar!" Jewel blew them all a kiss and then was out the door.

Tehaira smiled at Evan. "Good luck to you both."

"I hope you win!" Evan gushed to Tehaira and hoped he didn't sound silly.

"I wish you luck, too," Farah Dice replied.

"See ya in a few." Tehaira grabbed his things and was out the door.

"Are you ready to eat?" Farah Dice said to Lowla.

Now that you have run off Tehaira, do you want to make me sick, too? "I'm way too nervous and it takes me forever to get ready so I'm going back to the trailer now. See you in our dressing room," Evan answered.

"Yeah, see ya in the laundry room," Farah Dice laughed back.

Evan stopped and looked back at her. "Good Luck."

"Yeah, you too."

Evan rushed to his trailer to begin enchantment. All of the dancing, singing, and filming he had done so faithfully for so long surely would pay off this evening. All of the times he had created Lowla out of his face did not seem to give him comfort. He was nervous. His hands shook as he touched his face. *Is my life so empty that winning tonight will determine if I get knocked down or if I'm left standing up? Or do I think this is my big break? In this trailer park?* He did not dwell on his thoughts. Evan started drinking wine and smoking pot as soon as he hit the door. Between the combination of the two, he figured he should be able to make it through the evening. He had never showered or shaved as fast as he did this night. After getting out of the shower, he wrapped himself in a cloth robe and moisturized his face as he mouthed the words to his talent song. Once the lotion set, he put on the pancake base and then lightly powdered. Before continuing with the make-up, he went over everything he needed to make sure it was all there. Indeed the checklist was complete.

The den door swung open and in walked Lloyd, Beverly and Rex. "We missed you at dinner. Where were you?"

Beverly said all grinning.

"I was showering and shaving. Are y'all ready to help me get ready?" Evan pondered to his friends.

"I'm leaving Rex and Beverly at your disposal. I'm going to get them Egyptians you hired."

Evan almost shouted in desperation, "Be sure to keep them hidden and make sure they are dressed in their outfits."

Lloyd gave Evan a look of hopelessness and said, "I'll do my best." He slammed the door leaving the three to get ready for the show.

"How did your phone call go this morning?" Evan asked Beverly. "I thought about you all day." He was placing part of his headdress in a bag to carry to the recreational hall.

"Everything is great and you can call me Diva, just plain Diva. Beverly and I got together this morning and it is a win-win situation. And if this baby is a girl, her name will be Beverly Lolita Archer," Diva said, helping Evan place the needed items.

Evan stopped what he was doing and hugged Diva. "I knew it would work out. And I will live on."

"We had a busy day." Rex picked up Evan's wig. "Diva can tell you all about it while we help you. What can I do?" he wondered.

"Pray," quipped Evan.

The hour flew by and Evan was ready to perform. He and Rex listened as Diva explained how wonderfully things had gone with Aaron, and that he was flying into Pensacola Sunday afternoon so he and Diva could get married on Monday. Instead of shopping and swimming, Lloyd drove them all over the town of Fort Walton Beach to find a preacher that would marry them in the trailer park. During supper Lloyd and Diva had secured the help of the Niceville group. The buzz of the wedding was getting bigger than the crowning of Miss Niceville.

Evan had his wig on and his face completed. He was wearing a moo-moo when they left the trailer with costume, gown, props and wigs being carried by Diva and Rex. They made it to the converted dressing rooms which were blocks of areas divided by hanging sheets and drapes as walls. Rex went to meet Lloyd and to help maneuver the Egyptian slaves. Diva stayed with Evan to be his assistant. All of the other contestants were behind their individual sheets, dressing up in their best harem outfits.

"Okay, girls, the pageant is going to start in about twenty minutes. Get ready for your presentation part," Jewel, wearing a decorative bra and a sarong, said as he twirled through the contestants, giving hugs to each one. After that, Jewel went backstage to get ready for the curtain to be opened. As the current Miss Niceville, he was the first to be presented on stage. They could hear the pageant begin and the music start. The audience clapped when the curtain was drawn, exposing palm trees, camels and pyramids as the backdrop. The dimmed lights were brightened as a familiar tune began to play. Then the crowd went wild. Crown Jewel had made her way to the footlights with all of the former Miss Nicevilles as back-up dancers as they sang and danced to *Walk like an Egyptian*. Halfway through the song, the music was played continually without words. Crown Jewel got the microphone and began to talk over the music while he introduced each Miss Niceville. "Ladies and gentlemen, welcome to the Miss Niceville Pageant. I am your current Queen for the night, Crown Jewel. All right, girls, line up." He snapped his fingers as the former titleholders got in line as they walked like Egyptians. "Please welcome Miss Niceville 1988, Doyle-Leigh." One by one, the formers bowed until the last was introduced. It was easy to tell if the crowd liked someone or not by the amount of catcalls and applause. Since the only thing separating the contestants from the audience was cloth, they experienced the full effect of the crowd's cheers or jeers.

This added a lot of pressure to Evan. His imaginary audience in *White Trash from Hapeville* always loved him and begged for more. He hoped that he would get the same reaction in Niceville. He sat motionless as Diva reassured him he looked great. He felt his heart beating harder when he heard Crown Jewel come out to start the presentation part of the pageant. The first contestant, Farah Dice, strutted on stage dressed as a female Julius Caesar and began to recite the famous *Veni, Vidi, Vici*. Evan thought, *How brilliant.*

The next contestant to grace the crowd was Moana Leesa. He rolled out onto the stage a large picture frame while he posed behind it. Keeping with reality, he was dressed in Leonardo's creation as he lip-synched two minutes of Nat King Cole's *Mona Lisa*. Evan and Diva had peeked through the sheets. They stepped back, looked at each other and rolled their eyes. In an instant, it was Evan's time to go on stage.

"Our next contestant has been to the desert before. She likes palm trees and loves to sit on pyramids. She knew she was gay the first time she saw Cleopatra's Needle. Ladies and gentlemen, I want you to put your hands together for our contestant number three in her presentation debut, Lowla de la Vie and her dance of the seven veils." Jewel finished the introduction and Lowla stormed the stage and danced wildly to a Middle Eastern beat as her veils spun around the floor. The crowd's response was very favorable, he thought, as Jewel introduced the next contestant, Petula, for presentation.

Back in the dressing area, Diva assured Evan that the crowd went wild for him. Evan answered, "A drunken crowd goes wild for everyone." Before he changed into his talent garb, he waited until it was Tehaira's turn for presentation. Again, he and Diva watched through a hole in the sheets.

Crown Jewel came back to the front of the stage while the curtain was being lowered. "Last, but not least, is our contestant number five, Tehaira. The thing Tehaira likes about the desert is the rare Farafra Oasis where comfort and beauty can be found. Tehaira also has a fondness for camels. I wonder what that means." Crown Jewel imitated thinking for a moment. "I wonder if camels are hung like a horse. I'm sure that has nothing to do with it. Let's give a 'hump' to our contestant number five, Tehaira."

The curtain rose and revealed Tehaira dressed as Nefertiti. He was stunning. His moves were very professional as he interpreted Steve Martin's *King Tut*. Evan winked at Diva and then started to get ready for his talent part. Evan heard all of the other songs the "living legends" — what the former winners of Miss Niceville named themselves — were performing. As he was lining his lips, the final touch, he was calmed by hearing Florence Tightintail's choice of music. He was performing as Judy Garland doing *Somewhere Over the Rainbow*. Evan had to look through the sheets once more. Florence looked good, he thought, emoting feelings in a dark blue suit with a black hat. One of the star's trademark outfits. After the song was over, he went back to his hand-held mirror. He, along with the audience, was stunned to hear two living legends do the same Judy Garland number back-to-back. He ran to the spot he had stood to watch so many times during the evening to see Faux Pas dressed as Dorothy in the *Wizard of Oz* doing his take of *Somewhere Over the Rainbow*. Faux had the back-up of the scarecrow, the tin man and the lion. He even had a small dog in a picnic basket. The audience was really eating up this version as Faux had wonderful choreography and site gags with his stage mates. It wasn't a nice scene when Faux Pas and Florence Tightintail met in the dressing area after the latter Judy performed. Each was cursing the other and vowing vengeance. *It's nice to be chosen family*, Evan thought.

As had been done earlier in the evening for presentation, the contestants were called out once more. This time it was for the talent competition. Evan stood still listening to the first contestant. Farah Dice entered the stage and attempted to wow the crowd with Bette Midler's version of *Paradise*. The crowd became louder every time that word was sung. Evan decided not to listen to the next contestant. However, the cheering seemed to be as favorable for Moana Leesa as it had been for Farah Dice. He refused to look at their performances so he did not know if they were really good or not just by listening. This had proved to be an easy crowd to please. The curtain came down on contestant number two as his moment of truth arrived. This was his chance to become a star. Evan was dressed to the nines as Lowla in his Cleopatra outfit borrowed from Lloyd. The hunky Egyptian slaves he had hired were waiting in the wings to carry him on for him to lip synch his original song. The music was a sultry beat with heavy drums. A taste of Cairo hung in the air as the music played. Crown Jewel was on the stage, ad libbing and trying to be funny as Evan was hoisted up onto the guys' shoulders. His heart was beating so fast with anticipation that this was real and not just a fantasy in his bedroom.

"Ladies and gentlemen or whoever you are. Our next contestant has a little treat in store for us with an original song. That means, children, one you have never heard before. Even the music is original. It was written by Lowla and recorded by a good friend. Put your hands together and give much love to Lowla de la Vie." Jewel hurried off the stage.

The disco Middle Eastern music started and the four hunky slaves brought Lowla onto the stage amid screams and shouts from the crowd. They paraded her around the stage to the beat of the music. Twelve bars of music passed before they put Lowla down. The crowd screamed even louder when they saw the full effect of Lowla's costume. Evan spotted Lloyd, who gave a "thumbs-up" gesture. He was all in proportion with golden asps in his hair and on his arms. Even the pyramid tits bounced to the beat of the music. Two of the slaves were behind him and the other two were in front kneeling on one knee so Lowla could sit as the standing slaves held his arms, spread out like an ancient Ibis. He opened his mouth and started to sing *Our Love is like a Mirage*.

I'm walking through the hot sands of life
My heart is on fire

I'm thirsty for love
You're standing in the distance
Holding a loving cup for my parched lips
When I get to you
The cup is dry
Our love is like a mirage
From a distance it is beautiful
Plentiful for us both
When I reach out to touch you
Everything evaporates into thin air
Walking for miles and miles
Through the desert of love
You appear to be loving
You appear to be kind
Our friends think you are wonderful
That I am out of my mind
That you are everything a god should be
And yet they don't know
You really don't want me
Our love is like a mirage
From a distance it is beautiful
Plentiful for us both
When I reach out to touch you
Everything evaporates into thin air

The crowd was on their feet as Lowla was being taken away by the slaves. As soon as they were out of sight, Evan thanked each guy for a great job and hoped they enjoyed the rest of the weekend in Pensacola. Back in the dressing area, Lloyd rushed in and whispered, "Lowla you are going to win, and that was great. I didn't think you had it in you. But you were really, really good. Almost as good as me. The other contestants suck so far. Farah Dice did not even know her words and was too drunk to dance. Everyone is saying that was the most professional act they had ever seen." He quickly exited as only contestants and their helpers were allowed in the dressing rooms. The words Lloyd uttered solidified Evan's thinking that he just could not lose.

"You were really great," Diva said. "I watched you from the wings and that song, you tore it up, child, and no other contestant even comes close. I can't believe that was you." Diva helped Evan get ready for the evening-gown competition. All the contestants would strut their formal stuff, one at a time, then all together. They remained in their evening gowns as the voting started. Everyone in the audience was given a card with instructions to circle the name of the contestant for best talent, best presentation and best costume, and of course, for the overall winner. Once the voting was over, the cards were gathered and counted by Doyle-Leigh and Rouge-Red as planned to ensure that the counting appeared to be fair. Until the votes were counted, there were many more performances by past Miss Nicevilles. After Jewel's special guest, Craven Fame, had performed, it was announced that the tabulation was complete. Finally the moment had arrived . . . the moment that Evan's fantasy life had prepared him all those years. The light would shine on his face.

The contestants were gathered back onto the stage, and in a gesture of camaraderie they all held hands as if they wished each other the best. "What a show. What talent, ya'll were all so fantastic," announced Doyle-Leigh as he staggered taking center stage while Jewel held the crown ready to put on the new Queen's head. Faux Pas was standing by her side with a white sash that was printed with *Miss Niceville* in maroon. Rouge-Red was also stood in attendance with certificates of placement.

The certificates for the lesser awards were handed out. Evan did not win any of those. He thought it was because he had won the pageant, which would be enough. Best talent went to Farah Dice, best presentation went to Moana Leesa and best gown went to Petula. Doyle-Leigh had the microphone in hand. "And now the moment you have been lusting for, let's hear it for your fourth runner-up, Lowla de la Vie," Doyle-Leigh shouted. Evan smiled as best he could and took his fourth runner-up certificate from Rouge-Red and got back in line. "Your third runner-up is Tehaira." Applause from the crowd. "Your second runner-up is Petula." Catcalls were heard throughout. "Now, Farah Dice and Moana Leesa come forward. One of you is the new Miss Niceville and the other will be our new Miss Memorial Gay. Now if something should happen to Miss Niceville, then Miss Memorial Gay will have to take over. Drum roll, please, Mr. DJ. Your first runner-up, our Miss Memorial Gay, is Moana Leesa. Our Farah Dice is your new Miss Niceville. Let's give it up." There were lots of cheers and kisses and well wishes while Farah Dice was crowned and the sash was put on him.

As soon as he could, without seeming rude, Evan got to the dressing room, where he and Diva scooped up his stuff and headed back to the trailer. He opened the door to the trailer and said, enraged, "I hate these two-faced bitches. I know one thing for sure. I will never come back here again. Tehaira and I were robbed. We lost to someone who didn't even know her words. Chosen family, my ass. Get me a joint." He slung off his wig, buried his head in his hands and started to cry.

36

Lloyd shook Evan. "It's breakfast time, sleeping beauty."

"And why would I care?" the waking Evan said. "I'm not going. I've got food here."

"Now don't be that way, Lowla." Lloyd sat on the bed.

"Watch me." Evan pulled the covers over his head.

"It was Farah Dice's seventh time to try to be Miss Niceville. Don't take it personally. I guess I just wanted you to win so badly and you should have won." He tried to pull the covers from Evan's head but met resistance. "You were good, really good, and I am proud of you. You've definitely proven that you need to be seen as an entertainer. I should have known it takes a while to get in with these people. Miss Niceville is just like any other pageant. The best doesn't always win. It's the staying power and putting your talent in front of an audience that counts." Lloyd successfully pulled the covers from Evan's face. "Besides, Rex and I are going to present the Moulin Rouge Carnival idea this morning at breakfast. We would like for you to be there. You'll always be queen of that to me."

Evan spoke with a voice full of emotion. "It's just that . . . I wanted to win. I wanted to be noticed. With a life full of no direction, I felt as though winning would give me the push I needed. You know, like a try-out that really didn't count."

"Lowla, if you are a good entertainer, it doesn't matter where you perform. Besides what you did here does count. Being entertained is entertaining."

Evan knew Lloyd was right. "These people led me to believe I had a good chance."

"You did have a good chance."

"What, the chance to come in last, like I did?" Evan sat up in bed. "This would have made me feel special and talented. Instead, I have to sit at the back of the bus."

"Don't you feel special and talented when you come to New Orleans?   Haven't you been on the stage during the carnival in front of thousands of people?"

"Yes, but only as a background performer."

"Look, I brought you a joint this morning to make you feel better." Lloyd pulled a reefer from his shirt pocket.

Evan took it from his hand.   "I know I must sound ungrateful." He leaned over to pick up the lighter from the side table and looked back at Lloyd. "I can't expect you to understand. You have never sat on the back of the bus. You've always been in front. You've always been a crowd pleaser and you always get the man."

"Lowla," Lloyd said defensively, "that's not true."

"Yes, it is and let me finish. Just be quiet. Please sit on the back of the bus just this one time and I'll never ask you again." Lloyd folded his arms as Evan continued. "You've always been handsome. You're educated and talented. You are everything that I will never be . . . and yet you love me and you make me a part of your life." Evan's eyes began to mist. "You always make me feel special. You've given me clothes to wear and generously paid my way too many times." He expressed with his hands the excitement in his revelation to Lloyd. "I even got to ride a float all by myself in your parade. You crowded a whole dance troupe of thirty on one. But me! All alone. There I was, Marilyn Monroe in a pink satin outfit that you had Chalmette make me, sitting on a black coffin, flowers draped all around me while being pulled through the Quarter by horses. You've introduced me to society, circuit parties, parades, and travel beyond my vivid imagination. You've given me more than the Moulin Rouge. Everything in consideration, you've given me the Moulin Huge."

"The Moulin Huge?" Lloyd questioned with a disgusting look.

"Yes. The Moulin Huge. I was thinking about it last night. Moulin for the constant circular motion in our lives, like the windmill, and huge for everything else you've done for me in my life." Evan lit the joint and took a toke. "My favorite breakfast." He exhaled.

Lloyd sat and watched. He seemed to be moved by Evan's words.

"The trips to Egypt and to Europe. All of the Moulin Rouge Carnivals you've done and let me be a part of. The times on Troubled Waters, the times at *Le Oui-Oui*. The times you have tried to get me a husband. All of our Confederate soldiers that you got. How you have taken care of the friends I have brought down with me to New Orleans. If I had never met you, all I could talk about is how to grow a really big tomato in rural South Carolina. You've given me the world and you don't even know it." Evan grabbed Lloyd and hugged him tightly. "Thank you for the Moulin Huge. I love you so much."

"Then get your ass out of this bed and let's go to

breakfast. Then we have to go get Aaron at the airport. We have a wedding to plan. It's about Diva now." Lloyd got off of the bed and stood by the window. He pulled back the curtains in the trailer. Evan reacted to the sunshine by putting his forearm over his eyes while he smoked with the other hand. "That's my Lowla. Get ready and come to my trailer." A hand rose to his face. "That sounds so like something I never thought I would say. You'll be Miss Niceville one day; don't turn away from a fun time. Rex and Diva are sitting outside laughing and talking and you should be right there with them."

"You really love Rex, don't you?" Evan said as he put the joint out in the ashtray.

"It's hard to believe, but yes." Lloyd sat back on the bed. "I thought when Torch left me I would never survive. Looking back, I see myself as such a hopeless piece of work. All I did was live for the scraps of attention he would give me. With Rex, I have become stronger because he needs me to help him in emotional ways and not material ones." Lloyd got up and peered out the window to look at Rex and Diva sitting under the canopy. "He helps my mother and my grandmother. He is never condescending to me and treats me like a king and all my life I thought I wanted to be treated like a queen." He turned back to Evan. "It is really different."

"I can tell. I noticed a difference in you when I was last at your house. I'm sorry I wrote you that note saying that you were on your own when you needed me most. I just didn't see how distraught you really were at that time. And thinking of myself, I didn't want to move to New Orleans just to help you keep an eye on Torch." Evan started to take off his shirt.

"It was wrong of me to expect you to give up your house and your job just to come be my house spy. Thank God I can see now how desperate I was, and thank God Torch left me. I still have his things if you want them." Lloyd turned to Evan. "But now that you are unemployed, I think you should consider moving back to White Hawk Manor. Rex and I are planning to open our own business and there would be room for you, too. Rex really likes you. He knows you have been one of the few people in my life that love me for me and not my money."

"What money? You never seem to have any." Evan hugged Lloyd again. "Thank you for that and remember no matter what you do or how big you become, you'll always be Marilyn to me — that skinny kid with stars in his eyes that I met twenty years ago at an audition. We should have known it was fate for us both to try to get a part in 'Dames At Sea.'"

"Enough of this, you know I'm not mushy." Lloyd pulled away at arm's length.

"All right, I'll get dressed and be out in a minute."

Lloyd left the trailer to join Rex and Diva. They engaged in conversation with the people who passed by en route to the recreational hall for the Sunday breakfast. "Is that real or faux?" Lloyd asked of a passerby.

"Faux?" He laughed. "Miss Niceville only wears the real thing." Farah Dice slowly turned around, showing off his black full-length fur coat. "It is such a cool and windy morning for the end of May. Don't you think?"

They all laughed as Lloyd added. "Congratulations!"

"Yeah, congratulations!" Evan appeared out of the neighboring trailer and joined the gang.

"Thank you all." Farah Dice gave Evan a hug. "Congratulations, yourself. That was quite a show, girl. I couldn't sleep last night, all excited, so I watched the video of the pageant. Lowla, you are going to love how good you looked."

"Why, thank *you*. That is very sweet." Evan could not help but grin as he looked at his friends.

"Join me please; I need a following as I make my entrance to the breakfast honoring the Queen."

"I just love to stroll with royalty." Diva got up out of her seat and they all walked to the recreational hall for breakfast.

Facing the people wasn't as hard as Evan had thought it would be. More than a few made their way to him to tell him how much they enjoyed his performance and how talented he was, not to mention that he really looked beautiful. Many of them pulled him to the side and told him not to give up, that he soon would be Miss Niceville. There was excited chatter during breakfast with people talking about what they were going to do that evening in the Sunday show.

Farah Dice stood, in his fur coat and his sash garnished with the crown-on-head, took a spoon and hit it against his glass. "Good morning, everybody. First of all, thank you very much. You have no idea how much being Miss Niceville means to me. Where else except in America can a fat girl like me become queen of the trailer park?" Laughter and applause erupted from the tables. "Seriously though. I am looking forward to representing our chosen family this year. I promise to each and every one of you to make this a year to remember." His arms spread wide as more applause was heard. "Now, on to business. I hope you all have put your names, addresses, email addresses and birthdates, no years, on the master register. I am planning to get *The Niceville News* out every month and I want to be able to mail it to you all. I will also need all the help I can get for the newsletter, so let me hear from you soon. Also, I will be mailing everyone a copy of the address list with the first mail-out. Remember it is not too early to tell me you are going to be a contestant for the next Miss Niceville pageant. This year's contestants were divine. Could all last night's contestants please stand?" The previous hopefuls stood. "Let's hear it for Lowla, Tehaira, Moana Leesa, and Petula." The crowd stood and after a polite length of applause, they all sat. "Pay attention. I promise next year's crown will be bigger." Farah Dice touched his own crown on his head. "Any crown is a good crown. I will be announcing the theme in the months to come. You'll have plenty of time to come up with wonderful ideas just like every year. It amazes me all of the talent I have seen in this trailer park. Before I turn the floor over to Lloyd and his handsome Rex, I want to remind you to sign up for the show tonight. The poster board is located stage right. You will perform in the order that you sign up. Number one will go first and et cetera."

Doyle-Leigh interjected. "Oh, sorry to butt in, but I want to remind you that your linens must be put in the laundry room before you leave. Check out time is ten a.m. Be sure to empty your trash, again, not your lover but your trash, and clean your trailers. It wouldn't be fittin' for us to be run out of this trailer park. Oh, thank you and have a nice day." Doyle-Leigh sat down, relinquishing the floor to Farah Dice.

"Thank you, Doyle-Leigh; you are always a fountain of information. We have some excitement headed this way for all the Nicevillites. Please give a big round of applause to Marilyn and Rex."

He had told Farah Dice not to call him that on their way to breakfast this morning. Lloyd tried not to let it show that he had been rattled by being called Marilyn as he and Rex got up and headed to the front of the room. "Hello everyone." He put his hand on Rex's neck, a position that seemed to have become his favorite spot for touching Rex when they were in public. "This is Rex. He is mine. Hands off!" He laughed. "We love being here. I tell everybody I know about this place and hopefully more people will continue to come. We would like to extend an invitation to everyone here this morning." He went on to explain about the charitable organization known as La Moulin Rouge Carnival. "The four-day weekend is jam-packed with things to do." He looked at Evan. "La Moulin Rouge Carnival is huge. *Really huge.* It is everything. The event brings over tens of thousands of people to New Orleans and we're giving you a chance to perform in front of them on Saturday night, the big party," Lloyd told the wide-eyed captive audience. He went on to tell them that this year's theme was the circus, and that he needed "circus people" to accent and interact with the talent which has already been booked. "You'll be taken through the streets of New Orleans in a huge cage only to be let loose on stage in front of thousands of eyes watching you." The Niceville attendees hooted, applauded, and cheered.

"We will provide lodging and passes to the events," Rex said in a very business-like tone. "All we need from you today, or let's say by next Sunday, is a commitment and how you would like to present yourself as a circus person if you already know. We need to have some kind of a plan for our costumes and figure out how we will get us all on the same page. If you have any ideas, please let us know. You will need to provide your own transportation to New Orleans. Your new Miss Niceville will be the liaison between you and La Moulin Rouge Carnival to coordinate travel and keep you abreast of the activities. Or a thigh, if you prefer."

A voice came from the breakfast crowd. "When did you say this was?"

Rex smiled. "Oops, I don't think we did. La Moulin Rouge Carnival is the fourth weekend in August. This year, it will start on Thursday, August twenty-fifth, 2005. It will be an event you will remember forever. You can check it out on the web at La Moulin Rouge Carnival dot com." He gestured with his hands. "Also, just for the Niceville group, as a gift from Lloyd's family, the Rochelles, each one of you will be treated to a champagne brunch in your honor on Sunday. The brunch will be held on the one and only showboat 'Bridge over Troubled Waters.' Yes, *you* will be wined and dined while floating on the Mississippi River enjoying the breathtaking beautiful scenery. Also, as an added incentive, there will be an entertainer, well, let's say a star that you all would love to meet. But *her* celebrity identity will remain a secret until that day." Lloyd looked at Rex as though he were equally surprised.

The crowd roared, screamed and applauded. Rex and Lloyd had made a home run with the group. People started getting out of their chairs and heading to the front to sign up for the event. "There is one more thing. Listen up," Rex added. "For those of your who haven't heard, there is going to be a wedding here tomorrow at nine a.m. Diva, are you out there?" She stood and bowed. "Come on up here."

Diva made her way to the front through the crowd. "Thank you. First, I would like to say what a wonderful time I have had and how nice you have been. And best of all, you've treated me like family."

"We love you," Craven Fame screamed.

"Ah, and I love you, too. Oh, thank you. So, I would like to extend an invitation to everyone tomorrow to be a part of the happiest day of my life, my wedding day. And I would like to thank Lloyd with all my heart for the work he did in arranging my special day. He went above and beyond the call of duty." She took his hand. "I am very grateful." She dropped his hand. "Now back to me! This wedding was planned, but for a future date, so I am kind of at a loss to as to what to do. But from what I have seen here last night, I am hoping that you will help me with pictures and with bridesmaids. For those of you who have always wanted to be a bridesmaid now is your chance."

Farah Dice came to Diva's side. "Isn't this just going to be a Memorial Day to remember? Soon our pictures will hit the tabloids and we need to give 'em somethin' to see." He turned to Diva. "I pledge to you, Diva, that we will have you a wedding you will never forget."

"Child, I will never forget this weekend and I can assure you that I will never forget this wedding. Who would believe it? One day this weekend is going to be on film. I think this experience would be a great vehicle for me. And I am sure I could work a few of you in the film as well." More applause came from the group.

In his best Ethel Merman, Farah Dice crooned. "Well, who could ask for anything more?" He laughed then immediately showed his serious side. "Okay, we've got a lot to do today, girls, so anyone who wants to help me with this wedding please make your presence known now."

The front of the room was bombarded with volunteers for the wedding and with people signing up for the carnival and for the Sunday evening performances. All four friends were sought for questions regarding the events about which had been spoken earlier. About an hour later, Diva, Evan, Rex and Lloyd left the recreational hall to go pick up Aaron. Before they all piled in the Marilynmobile, Lloyd pulled Rex aside. "What were you talking about earlier? What star?"

"Great idea, huh. It came to me when I was standing in front of the crowd. I just pulled it out of the air," Rex said with a sheepish grin. "I know you can find someone."

"We'll discuss this later, maybe they won't remember." He yelled back to Diva and Evan, "Okay let's get this top down and get a move on."

Diva and Rex sat up on the back seat, waving to the people as they passed under the wrought iron arch inscribed "Welcome to the Niceville Trailer Park."

It was a tearful reunion at the airport when Aaron arrived. The group made their introductions and gave congratulations. Everyone in the car seemed to be filled with joy. Even Evan managed to give a smile or two although in his mind he was the once again oddball out and the only one who would return to gloom and doom as he watched his friends bloom with happiness. Maybe he could give Tehaira his phone number and they could get together. *Just maybe, if Diva was serious, I could be in her film about the Niceville Memorial Day pageant.*

They made it back to the trailer park and Evan moved his things to room with Lloyd and Rex so that Aaron and Diva could be alone. The rest of the afternoon flew by quickly. Lloyd and Rex joined Evan in a walk around the bay. They did not investigate any of the woods around the park as Evan had thought he might do. Instead they sat in the sunshine and enjoyed each other's company. At dinner time, they headed to the hall to find that Diva and Aaron were already there, surrounded by a multitude of well-wishers and Hollywood seekers.

It did not take long for the group to discover who Diva and Aaron were and with the mention of a possible movie, many scrambled to be noticed and hopefully cast. This did not seem to bother the soon-to-be Mr. and Mrs. Archer as the Hollywood couple appeared to be so happy. "We are glad to not have to worry about reporters. We feel very relaxed and content just to be away from the Hollywood community. And to be able to wed in private, so to speak," Diva said, smiling at Aaron.

"The press that we are going to receive from getting married, secretly, in a trailer park is going to be phenomenal. This is pure genius," Aaron assured her earlier in the day as they discussed what a "publicity coup" had hatched for them.

After dinner, the group all hurried back to their respective trailers to get ready for the night. Hours later, various country stars like Patsy Cline, Tammy Wynette, Shania and such made their ways to the hall for a gala of fine entertainment. Farah Dice, emcee of the evening, opened the festivities and the action began. There was serious drag and comical drag. There were even a few poetry readings. Some people expressed disappointment that Lowla did not perform. Evan replied he was saving himself for Diva's wedding. As he watched everyone perform, he regretted his stubborn decision to pout. *What fun I could've had tonight.* It soon became Diva's turn to get up and perform. She had told Aaron and Evan that she was nervous as she had never done stand-up before and was afraid to bomb. They reinforced to her the love she had in the audience.

It came time for her introduction. Farah Dice was center stage. "Ladies and gentlemen, boys and girls, cross-dressers and gender benders, winners and runner-ups, have we got another treat for you tonight! Our next performer is not a legend in her own mind like the rest of us. She actually *is* famous. She has appeared in films and has even written a

book. I would tell you the title but I know no one here knows
how to read. Give up much love for Diva." Farah Dice
clapped her hands together as Diva entered the stage. Farah
Dice gave her a hug, handed her the microphone and then left
the stage.

Holding the microphone, Diva looked at it peculiarly.
"How do you work this thing?" Laughter. "Thank you, that
may be my only laugh except I warn you I will laugh at
myself." She laughed at herself. "Come on; don't let me be
the only one." The audience laughed again. "It's great to be
here tonight. Really great. I can't believe I came together for
this event. There was a conflict of personalities and I don't
mean the performers. Are you guys having a good time?"
The crowd roared yes. "Well, it's over now." She laughed at
herself again and then stopped and looked at the audience,
who laughed in return. "You guys are probably wondering
what I am doing up here. I'm not doing a song or dancing
and I don't need the money. We do get paid, don't we? And
believe it or not, I am a real girl." More laughter came from
the crowd. "Please, do I need to prove it? Just ask half the
men in West Hollywood, but then again, how would they
know? I'm here as a testimony to sickness. My life has been
one sick episode to another. Actually I thought it was
sickness until I discovered I had a bullshit magnet in my
body. It's true. I was so relieved. All these years I thought I
had 'fool' tattooed on me somewhere." She looked around at
her body. "All the creepy men I went through before I met
my prince." She motioned her hand toward Aaron. "I should
have known that when men come to you with their hand out
that it is not to hold yours. You know, I thought I had the
greatest plan to get a man. I would mold myself to what he
wanted for the moment and then I would be the best at it. It
never occurred to me that a short-term theory would never
work for a long-term relationship. So, when it didn't work
out, I changed the man, not the plan. Sometimes the man
would change me. He went running for his life, saying, *that*

bitch only knows one speed. But I followed my plan like a recipe: one cup sweetness, two cups loyalty, three cups happiness, four cups whatever he wanted, five cups wait on him hand and foot, and fifteen pounds of sex." She paused. "Of course I always forgot to mix in three cups my identity and three cups self respect." The crowd applauded and Diva was on a roll. She kept them in stitches and it was obvious that her stand-up debut was a good thing.

After finishing her routine it was time for the Sunday night awards to be given out. They had various awards for the weekend from the Newest Living Legend of the group to Miss New Talent which was given to a new person who showed promise. There was also an award for the best comedy and an award for the worst behavior.

Farah Dice spoke into the microphone. "Gentleman and ladies of the evening, this year's recipient of the Miss New Talent award goes to," as he opened an envelope, "Lowla de La Vie!" Evan was really delighted when his name was called. The audience enthusiastically applauded as he was handed that award. That was the first thing he had ever won. A feeling of electricity flowed through his body. He, at last, had light upon his face. Little did he know that the award would give him so much hope for the future.

37

An array of fresh peonies adorned the table in the center hallway at the Rochelle Mansion. Fine art paintings hung on the walls throughout the house, complementing the Italian-marble statues placed at strategic locations. Her home was overdone as only a *nouveaux riche* person could decorate.

Renee was lying on the couch, reading peacefully, thinking all was right with the world. The environment around her was serene and still until the ringing of the phone broke her meditative mood.

She felt happy and refreshed as she rushed to answer the beckoning call with, "Good afternoon." She placed her romance novel on the table.

"You sound very happy, Miss Renee."

"And why shouldn't I be, Johnston?" she said into the receiver.

"I don't see any reason for you not to be, ma'am." Johnston, a southern import from Mississippi, arranged papers in a file as he spoke. "I have completed my report on the alleged Rex Greenfield."

"And you implied you did not see a reason for me not to be happy." She clutched her heart. "I am so relieved. He has turned out to be, well, an angel. He takes me places, he watches after Miss Ruby, and he is always at the club helping me. Rex is more attentive to me than my own children."

"Miss Renee," Johnston said in his matter-of-fact voice. "I want to talk with you face to face to discuss this file." He closed the file folder and laid it on his desk. "When is it convenient for us to meet?"

Renee took in a breath, "So you have bad news, after all? I've misunderstood."

"It's not necessarily bad. What I have to say may turn out to be a good thing in the end."

"Is it necessary that you meet with me today? I'm alone and I don't want to take a cab to your office." Half hoping she could put him off as a sense of dread was beginning to envelop her. "Can it wait until tomorrow?"

"No, Miss Renee. I think you'll want to know this as soon as possible. I don't mind coming to your house. How long will you be alone?"

"For three or four hours at least. Johnny, June and Johnny Ray are having dinner on the Troubled Waters Showboat. They just left." She placed her hand on the table for support.

"Do you mind if I come over, then?"

"No. I'll be waiting for you, Johnston."

"Good. I'm on my way."

Renee put down the phone and walked back to the couch in a daze, wondering if she should be worrying or if she should be happy. It had to be really something for Johnston to want to see her in person. She had initially hoped that the Mississippi Investigator would have found something on Rex's record. Now, she wanted everything to be okay. She slipped her shoes back on her feet to walk to her dressing room. She thought toying with her teased hair would calm her nerves. Upon seeing her reflection in the mirror, Renee decided not to mess with perfection. Instead, she would have a pot of tea waiting for the bearer of the news of the day.

38

From a distance, it looked like an unidentified flying object. A radiant glow of white jetted into the sky with streamers which blew in the wind. The archway to the trailer park was covered with white tulle and white balloons. Never had there been such a festive site at the entrance of the Niceville Trailer Park. Standing underneath the extravaganza were the preacher, Aaron and his best man, Rex. In a stark contrast to the archway, the preacher was dressed in black. Aaron and Rex were in white dress shirts and madras shorts. Except for the bridesmaids, the rest of the wedding party were in shorts or dresses, waiting for the moment when Diva, the new Niceville sweetheart, would leave the trailer and walk down the dirt road to matrimony.

"You look so beautiful, Diva." She smiled at him. "I am so happy for you," Evan said as he pinned white tulle to Diva's hair. "I can't believe that this trip has turned into so many things including a wedding."

"I can't believe I'm getting married in a sheet," Diva said, briefly looking back at herself in the mirror.

"Yes, but you look fabulous." Evan lifted up a piece of the tulle and sprayed it with instant starch. He held the piece in place. "I remember growing up I used to make dresses out of sheets all the time when I was locked away in my room. But don't worry, yours is safety pinned where mine was tied together and would come loose when I danced," Evan laughed and let go of the tulle. "But there is one thing I would like to ask you before you get married today."

"Yes, Evan?"

"Are you sure that you are Diva?"

"Why would you ask me that?" Diva stared at Evan's reflection in the mirror. "Don't you believe me?"

"I don't know." He continued to pin her veil. "I want to think that everything is okay, but you never let go of anything so quickly." He put his hands on her shoulders and looked at her reflection in the mirror. "You're leading me to believe that you have just let go of 'The Diva' and became 'Diva' while Beverly left in the night without a fight. That right before my eyes you have gone from one person to another and then become one with a snap of your fingers." He began to snap his fingers. "I'm snapping my fingers and nothing has happened for me. Just like that, you have let go of your rigidness and all of a sudden you are free and easy and under control." Evan put his hands back on Diva's shoulders while she sat silently. He went for the attack. "You're getting married in a sheet in a trailer park with a bunch of sissies and you are letting people take your picture with your drag bridesmaids which will wind up in some magazine and all is right in your world." He put his arms in the air. "What have you got up your sleeve? Your image meant more to you than anything."

Before Diva could answer, Doyle-Leigh was at the trailer door. "Knock, knock," Doyle-Leigh said as he opened the door and handed Diva a bouquet of wild flowers. He was dressed in a simple one-piece white dress with a pillbox hat on his head. "Oh, this is for you, sugar. I picked them this morning. Make sure I get this when you throw it."

"I will never forget your kindness." Diva took the bouquet to smell the fresh wild flowers.

"Are you ready?" Doyle-Leigh asked. "Your flower girl and bridesmaids are all waiting."

Diva looked back to Evan. "Yes, I'm ready." Diva got up.

After a knowing glance, they hugged.

"One minute, let me puff the dress." Evan puffed and mended a part of the sheet with a pin. "There. Your dress is ready."

Doyle turned to Lloyd who was behind him and nodded. As Lloyd walked to the archway to take his position as ring bearer, a hush came over the wedding party which had lined up on both sides of the road. Once Lloyd was in his place alongside Rex, the preacher nodded and the Niceville group started humming *Here Comes the Bride*. The bridesmaids were waiting in Lloyd's trailer, listening for their cue. When the humming was heard, Craven Fame, the flower girl, started making his way from the trailer to the archway. He threw wild flowers from a basket along the journey. All of the bridesmaids, Farah Dice, Rouge-Red, Faux Pas, Crown Jewel, and Toule Lyps, were each uniquely dressed in full wedding drag. Doyle-Leigh joined in the procession as they passed Diva's trailer. The Niceville Living Legends marched in step with their wild flowers in hand until they made it to the archway and divided up in even numbers on each side.

Diva made her appearance out of the trailer with Evan, behind her, holding the excess of the sheet so it would not drag on the ground. Diva's dress was made out of four white sheets and looked like it belonged to a spread in *Vogue*. The walk down the road was short. She had her head held high with her eyes focused on Aaron until she got to the preacher.

The preacher welcomed all to the ceremony of marriage and asked for everyone present to bow in prayer. "We are gathered here together today for a joyous occasion. We ask that God bless Aaron and Diva and everyone present." After the prayer, he began the ceremony with the usual sayings. The time arrived for him to ask the feted question, "Who gives this woman to this man for holy matrimony?"

"Her friends and I," Evan said, lifting the tulle to give Diva a kiss. Then he stood next to Lloyd.

The ring was requested, and Lloyd gave it to Aaron.

"Please take this ring and place it on her finger." The preacher cleared his throat.

"Do you, Aaron Alan Archer, take Diva Aneicia Borro to be your lawfully wedded wife?" The preacher looked at Aaron.

"I do," he barely got out.

"Do you, Diva Anecia Borro, take Aaron Alan Archer to be your lawfully wedded husband?"

"Oh, I do," Diva declared.

"By the power vested in me, I now pronounce you man and wife. Everyone, I give you Mr. and Mrs. Aaron Archer." They kissed and embraced to the cheers of their new friends. Diva relaxed her embrace then threw her bouquet to the waiting attendants. As fate would have it, Doyle-Leigh caught the bouquet as he pushed aside the ones around him.

After the ceremony it was time for all to depart so they took advantage of being together at the archway to initiate the goodbye process. All the participants of the weekend started cheering and laughing and hugging as they were all saying their farewells and posing for pictures. Evan said to Aaron, "You be good to Diva. I have never seen her happier." Aaron patted her belly and they kissed once more. "Diva, who would have ever thought all those years ago we would still be together and that I would not only give you away at your wedding, but also design and make your dress."

"I will cherish it forever."

"I love you and I am so happy for you." He leaned in and whispered in her ear, "Remember, you can call me for anything. I hope to discuss further our conversation that was interrupted before you got hitched, 'cause you are headed for trouble."

"Thanks for everything, Evan. I love you," Diva told Evan as they hugged each other. The wedding attendants started to throw confetti. Diva and Evan parted as she held Aaron while posing for more pictures. Tehaira, Moana Leesa, and Petula started to decorate the car that was to take Diva and Aaron to the airport.

Lloyd was standing with the newlyweds as he heard his cell phone ring. He flipped the phone and saw on the caller ID that it was his mother. "Hello, Ma. Hold on and let me go to where I can hear you." He leaned over and gave Rex a kiss, and said, "I'll be right back." Lloyd moved far enough away from the wedding party so he could hear. He walked to the back of a trailer and then spoke into his cell phone, "Hey, Ma, sorry I haven't called you today but I was waiting until we got on the road to tell you we were on our way. Is everything okay?"

"I think so, darling. But I want you to promise me that you and Rex will come here as soon as you get back into town. What time do you think that will be?"

"Ma, what's wrong, you sound upset."

Renee tried to sound normal. "Nothing is wrong, Lloyd. I just need for you two to come here. There is something I want to tell the family and I want everyone present, including Rex."

"You're not planning to hurt Rex in front of everyone are you?"

"No, Lloyd. I wouldn't hurt Rex for the world. I love him just as I love you."

Lloyd didn't know what to say or how to take that remark. He knew he should be happy that his mother had said that about Rex, but there was a part of him that was jealous and suspicious. "Ma, you're not sick, are you?"

"No, Lloyd. Just get here. Call me when you get on the road."

"Okay, Ma, I love you."

"I love you, too, son, and tell Rex that I love him, too."

Rex had made his way to Lloyd and saw that Lloyd had a puzzled look on his face. "Is everything all right?"

"I don't know. Ma says for us to get home and call her when we are on the road."

"Well, then let's say our goodbyes and hit the road."

"I've got to remind Diva and Aaron not to forget us when it's casting time. I've got to be in that movie. Rex?"

"Yes."

"Ma told me to tell you that she loves you."

He took Lloyd by the hand and said, "Finally." The guys continued to hold hands as they mingled back into the crowd. This time Rex led the way.

39

The residents of White Hawk Manor put the top down on the Marilynmobile as they navigated the back roads of Florida until Interstate Ten was in view.

"Are you worried?" Rex yelled with his hands cuffed around his mouth so that Lloyd would hear him over the noise of the wind blowing as they sped along the highway.

"No," Lloyd screamed back, "just curious. I can't imagine what is up. I hope Ma is okay."

"Me, too. I don't think she would ambush us by telling us she loved us." Rex was searching through a small bag for a cap. Putting the cap on his head, he said, "There. Now my locks won't blow and I'll be presentable when we get to your mother's."

"You'd look presentable soaking wet."

"You may get your wish. It's very cloudy in the west, pardner. You want a hat?" Rex rambled through the bag again.

"No, let's stop and get gas and put the top up. I can't even hear myself think." Lloyd spied an exit, put on the blinker and turned right off the exit ramp. "I'll pump and you go get us something to munch, and for me a can of cold ice tea, please."

When Rex returned to the car, he found that Lloyd had topped off the tank and had secured the top of the Marilynmobile. Back in the car on the road again, they both laughed as it started to rain. Rex turned on the car stereo and turned up the volume.

"You're playing our song . . . again? Don't you ever get tired of listening to it?"

"Never, I could listen to Zapp and Roger's version all day long." Rex said as he started to sing along, "I – I – I will always love you."

Lloyd grabbed Rex's hand and joined in with the vocals. They sang songs and laughed and talked about their future. Both guys were in agreement to create the party-planning business in the Crescent City. Now that their relationship had been established for a while they felt it would be a good move for the both of them. Lloyd was prepared to say goodbye to school teaching and the nightclub and Rex was ready to abandon his search for his parents. They felt their energies and efforts could best be spent building something they could share together, something that would belong just to the two of them.

After a couple of hours of travel they finally arrived at the bridge to New Orleans, which exposed a breathtaking view of the city. Dusk approached and the city's lights were brightly shining. "Look at those city lights. Just like the night we met when I saw them from the Troubled Waters office. Bright and full of hope. I can't believe that I came to this city not knowing what to expect, and look what I found. More happiness than I have ever had. Since we are going to start our business, I think it would be a good thing if I sold my mother's house in Plain Dealing. That way I would be on more of an equal footing with you." Rex took off his cap and looked into the car's mirror so he could comb his hair. "I don't want to go to your mother's looking like a rag doll."

"If you really want to sell your mom's house that is up to you. Just know that I think we are equal now, but I will never let you go back to north Louisiana and we can buy a house together or you can buy into White Hawk Manor." Lloyd slowed to exit off the interstate.

"You'd actually let me buy into White Hawk Manor?" Rex smiled and flipped up the car's visor mirror. "That's a great thought, but unless I make lots of money, it wouldn't be right. Let's find a way to buy a house of our own on the avenue. That way nothing could come between us."

"What do you mean? What could possibly come between us?"

"In case you didn't love me anymore or something."

"Rex, I – I – I will always love you – u – u – u." He laughed at his attempt to sing the song. "We're here." Lloyd pulled into the driveway and kissed Rex passionately. He held Rex's face with his hands and said, "Seriously, remember, I will always love you."

"And I will always love you." They both exited the car. "I forgot your mom's present." Rex returned to the car and got a bag out of the back seat. "I hope she likes sand dollars."

"She'll love it because you thought of her. I didn't get her anything."

Rex nudged him. "Silly, I signed the card from both of us."

Lloyd took out the key to his mom's house, knocked on the door, and opened it to enter. As they walked into the hallway Lloyd announced, "Ma, your boys are back."

Renee came into the living room from the kitchen, looked at Lloyd and Rex and started to cry. She fell into Rex's arms and sobbed heavily. Her embrace was intense and her hair almost blocked his view.

"Ma, what is it?" Lloyd's voice came from behind Renee.

"I was just in the kitchen trying to make y'all something to eat. It didn't work out," Renee said without moving her position.

"Ma, you know you can't cook." He touched his mother. "What's wrong?" Lloyd was surprised that Renee fell into Rex's embrace and not his. "I thought you said it wasn't bad."

As she took her Kleenex and wiped her tears, Renee pulled from Rex and said, "It's not the end of the world. I hope it will be the beginning." She held the boys' hands and walked them over to the couch. "Sit down. I have a story to tell."

After they were seated, Renee sat in the chair across from them. "I would sit between *my boys*, but I need to see your faces."

"Where's everybody else?" Lloyd asked. "You said you wanted everyone here."

"After thinking about it, I thought it best it was just the three of us. I have already told Johnny."

"Oh, great. I am always the last to know."

Renee looked at her son then blew her nose. "I know that over these months you two have become very close, and I am happy about that. I hope that you will always stay close and have a love for one another and I hope you don't hate me," she said as she wiped the tears from her eyes, "but I didn't do it. I didn't know something was missing. I mean, I knew what was missing, but I didn't know it hadn't really gone. That what I wanted was within arm's reach if I had only listened to myself. It was a hard time in my life."

"Mom, please get on with it. What are you talking about?" Lloyd looked at his mother, who returned a smile aimed at him and at Rex. "The suspense is killing me. I don't know what is coming next. What do you mean, hate you? For what? What is missing?" Lloyd started to move from the sofa.

"Lloyd, please sit down." Renee motioned with her hands and then toyed with her hair. "This is hard enough and the transition may be hard on each of us all for a while to come. Precious time has been wasted and there is so much to say and do."

Rex sat there on the couch and looked as though he sensed something heavy was about to happen. In order to maybe cheer up Renee he said, "Here's a present that Lloyd and I got you at the beach." He got up to hand it to Renee. She took the bag out of his hands and removed a card and a pretty wrapped box.

"Just tell us first before you open the present. It really is from Rex anyway. It was his idea," Lloyd said as he ran his fingers nervously through his hair, thinking maybe the family fortune was gone.

Renee ignored Lloyd's command and opened the card. Reading the inscription, she started to cry again. As the tears were falling down her checks, she didn't bother to wipe them. She opened the box and found a lovely rare sand dollar inside. "How beautiful and how thoughtful you are, Rex. I knew there was something about you when Lloyd first brought you here. I didn't know if it was a good thing or a bad thing. I thought I would ride it out and now I am glad I did." She wrapped her gift up and placed in the bag and sat the bag in her chair. Looking at Rex, she said, "Honey, please sit down. We're going to be fine."

Rex returned to the sofa by Lloyd. "Have I done something wrong?"

"No, my darling. You have done nothing at all." She wiped her cheeks once more and blew her nose again. You've both been patient and I'm asking you to not interrupt me. Save the questions for later, not that I'll have all the answers but we can work on that together. You must understand that this hard for me and a little unbelievable. I'm very nervous and perhaps a little bit shocked."

Lloyd and Rex looked at each other, then back to Renee. "Okay," they both uttered without prompting.

"Lloyd, you know your father and I had our ups and downs. More so than I realized. Years after you were born, we were almost at the brink of divorce."

"Ma!"

Renee cut Lloyd off with the wave of her hand. "We were on the brink of divorce when I found out I was pregnant again. Since I had lost a child only six months before, Anthony decided not to leave me, although I wish he would have. But," she sighed, "he stood by me and he also kept his lover on the side. Mistress, if you will. I thought in my own way, that maybe things would work out. They didn't. I spent most of the nights alone except for you and Johnny. I think there were days when I lost my mind. One night it was storming, like tonight; I had just put you to bed, Lloyd. Johnny was with Ruby. I couldn't take care of myself by myself, let alone two young boys."

The tears welled up in Renee's eyes. "I was headed down the stairs when a bolt of lightening struck the front door. I remember screaming and then nothing until I woke up in the hospital." She got up and walked around her chair. "I remember waking up, frantic that something had happened to you, Lloyd, and that I lost my baby. Lying in the hospital bed, I knew that I wasn't pregnant anymore."

"Can I get you something?" Rex tried to be of comfort Renee.

"Honey, please sit down and let me finish." Rex obeyed as Renee continued, "I grabbed the nurse call button and pushed and screamed, 'where are my babies?' The nurse comes in and tries to calm me down. The only thing she could tell me is that Johnny and Lloyd were okay and that she needed to call my husband immediately and for me to relax." She walked from the chair to the bookshelves. "I tried to get up, but I was strapped to the bed. A couple of hours later, your father arrived and told me that I had lost the baby from falling down the steps." She turned back to face her captive audience. "A baby boy. Another one." She spoke as she walked back to her chair. "I thought, *why is God doing this to me*? Once I heard that, there was no talking to me, especially your father. 'If you had been there, this might not have happened,' I screamed to him over and over again. He agreed and vowed to be faithful to me and give all of us a happy home."

She sat back in her chair. "I resigned myself that I was being punished and spent the years following in a depressed state, which Lloyd knows all too well."

"Ma, what is the point of all of this? How does that night

fit into today? What's going on? Why does Rex need to hear all of this?" Lloyd asked his mother in a low, almost embarrassed tone. He remembered in his youth listening to his parents fight. Hearing his mother talk of the past made him feel uncomfortable as memories of yesterday flashed in his mind. The Rochelles kept their laundry to themselves. This was not a customary type of behavior from his mother.

"Lloyd, let your mother finish," Rex said in a scolding voice.

"Soon you will know everything," she continued with a shaky voice and shaky hands. "Other than slowly getting over the loss of a child, I've had no other reason to revisit those years. Your father kept his promise and stayed with his family. I've been happy and content for years now and forgave your father, until yesterday."

"Yesterday? Daddy's dead."

"Yes, and at this moment I could drag him from the crypt and slap him." The tears began to flow again. "Where was I? Oh yes, I was happy with my family and my life and we were comfortable. No money worries, I could buy what I wanted. I felt like a whole fulfilled woman. The only thing in life that troubled me, really, was that you seemed unsettled, Lloyd, and susceptible to people using you. I blamed that on myself since I depended on you so much when you were growing up. Not that I thought Rex was using you, but I had a mother's intuition to find out more about him on my own."

"More about me?" Rex questioned. "Hey, I would never hurt . . . "

"Rex, please forgive me. I had Johnston investigate you and your past."

Lloyd was up and mad. "How could you do that? Aren't you ashamed to admit this in front of Rex? And here you are telling us some sob story just so that you could get sympathy first. I could have told you he was okay."

Rex calmly took Lloyd's hand and pulled him back to the sofa. "From what I have heard about Torch, I don't blame

Renee. Getting into this family would be a temptation for a lot of folks. I mean, y'all are rich. *Really rich.* She was doing what a mother should do. She was protecting her son. She didn't know me."

"But I should have known you. I should have known my own son!" Renee screamed out hysterically.

"What?" Lloyd and Rex blurted out in surprise. "What?"

"I didn't lose my fourth child. Your father paid off the hospital and let me believe my son was dead so he could give a child to his mistress who couldn't have children, just to keep her quiet since he wouldn't leave me." Renee gasped for air and said, "Her name was Rita Greenfield."

Rex stood, obviously shaking. "Renee, what are you saying?"

"I am your mother." Renee barely got those words out as she extended her arms to Rex. "You are my baby. *My* baby boy."

"Ma, this is not funny. Is this some kind of a joke?" Lloyd said, clutching his heart at the thought that Rex was really his mother's son along with the obvious implications.

Renee and Rex held hands in a brief, awkward moment. "No, no joke. God has found my son and brought him back to me. I never believed he was dead. Rex is your brother, Lloyd." With more emphasis, she said again, "*Your brother.*" She brushed his face with her hand. "Rex, I am your mother. This is your family. This is where you belong."

Rex looked at Lloyd with a half of a smile. His shakiness seemed to have vanished. Renee stood and fell into Rex's arms as Lloyd sat on the sofa in shock.

40

Evan returned to Hapeville emotionally drained from the Memorial Day weekend. All the way home, he kept thinking about the pageant and how good he felt to have performed in front of an audience. Even with the positives of the experience, he still was glum. At least by winning the pageant, he would have had a direction. Newsletters, trips, appearances, and his pageant the next Memorial Day could have made for a full year ahead. But he didn't win. Pulling into his driveway he said, "That's show business." He parked the van by the front door so he could move his things inside easier. He went into his empty house carrying a suitcase. After getting everything into the living room, he walked from the dining room to the kitchen to the bedroom and back to where he started. Evan wondered if he would ever be as happy as Diva and Aaron or Lloyd and Rex. He was so miserable that he knew the hearts of those who hated him must be filled with joy. He never, ever meant to hurt anybody. But he had. He had not understood the concept of love and had broken hearts unnecessarily. Not that he understood it now; he thought he was being punished for being a fool . . . a fool because he had set his standard so high that no one could meet it. When a potential mate failed the test, he would hate them instead of working it out. He assumed that was why he was lonely in his life today.

Looking at all of his stuff on the floor, he knelt and took out his Miss New Talent Award and proudly placed it on the mantle. The award was an Oscar imitation and it seemed to bask in the light. He smiled as he went to check his answering machine. No one had called. He took the receiver with him back to look at his award on the mantle again. He had planned to call his friends to make sure they made it home okay. First, he sat in the chair in front of the fireplace and stared into the silence. He didn't even have the energy to listen to music or sing or dance . . . or to roll a joint or to get his mail or even care if anyone saw him getting his mail. The only energy he thought he could muster was to take an overdose of pills, but a microscopic glimmer of hope in his soul that one day he would make it prevented him from doing that. He just sat there sinking into oblivion. Slowly he fell asleep.

He walked into a restroom and didn't recognize his

reflection. He saw men he recognized but didn't know their names. They asked him what he was doing in there. "Looking for a urinal," he responded as he pushed through the line of guys blocking his way. He stormed past the blockade and found them all gone except one, totally naked, posing in front of Evan, enticing him to have sex. Just as the man had both hands caressing his face putting pressure on each one of his cheeks as to pull him down, Evan's father appeared.

"Have you come to get me?" Evan asked of his father, hoping this would be the end of his meaningless life. There was no answer. His father went into the hallway and motioned for him. Evan got up out of the chair and eagerly followed after his dad. He walked behind him and was led into a shop. At first, he could not make out where he was or who the people were around him. One at a time, objects and textures came into focus. The first thing he noticed was the high ceilings and the one brick wall which lined one side of the rectangular shaped shop. It appeared to be the Christmas season and the shop was very busy. But the merchandise was not all seasonal. Mostly, it was antique furniture, lamps, pictures and unique gifts inspired by the great places in the world like Italy, England and Greece. He saw most of the things he had collected over the years mixed in with new items. He wondered what his things were doing in this store. On the brick wall were framed photographs that he had taken along side his "masterpieces" he had created with his computer. On the far end was his version of the "King Kong" poster. Nestled in the array of art in the middle of the wall was a large picture of Lloyd and Evan sitting side-by-side with the silhouette of the Sphinx in the background.

All of the brilliance dazzled him as he turned to seek his father, who was standing next to him. His father didn't speak but pointed to a picture on the wall behind the checkout counter. Evan traveled to it and squinted to read, *Keep in public view.* The next line read *this is a business license for home furnishings and gifts.* The line below that read, *this is a business license for* and then in bigger letters read, *THE MOULIN HUGE, a gift boutique by Lowla.* Evan reached for his father, but he was no longer there. Evan moved all over the store trying to find him to share with his dad the good feeling he had and how happy he was. What he then heard he perceived as Christmas chimes that hung from the ceiling of his shop, but it was actually the telephone ringing which awakened Evan. He was still in the glow of the dream when he looked at the caller ID on the phone and saw that it was an Atlanta cell phone number. A smile came over him as he didn't answer the phone. Something in his heart had changed. He leaned back in his chair, looked at the Miss New Talent award brightly shining on the mantle and determined that he had worth. Suddenly he felt he was Lazarus who had risen from the dead only to walk again among the living. This was a second chance and a divine inspiration from his father. The meaning of the dream finally dawned upon him. Leave the search for love and sex and use your talents to prosper and grow. Then you will love yourself and be able to love others. The phone continued to ring. Evan ignored it and lusted for the day when "The Moulin Huge, a gift boutique by Lowla" would become a reality.

Evan smiled. He was actually daydreaming about something other than performing a song that wasn't his. As he shut his eyes to maximize the ability to concentrate so he could start to develop a plan, there was a knock at the front door. Evan's heart felt as though it had sunk to the bottom of the ocean. He naturally thought it was a neighbor wanting to complain about something so he just sat there. The knock came again, this time louder. *What the hell? Why do I care? If I am going to open my own business, I have to quit being afraid.* He put the phone down on the side table and got up and opened the door. "Salvatore?"

He pushed by Evan with force and said nothing. Salvatore stepped back to the door, pulled Evan away from it and slammed it forcefully. He stood there, glaring at Evan with the look of a wild man.

Not sure how to handle the situation as he knew that Salvatore was upset, Evan said, "What's wrong?" He continued to glare at Evan. "Did you come to see Lowla?" He remained silent. "Can I help you with something?"

Salvatore looked at Evan with piercing eyes. "You can get me my wife and kids."

Evan tilted his head slightly as his eyebrows moved closer together.

"Don't stand there like you don't know."

"I don't know wh—"

Salvatore slapped him across the face before he finished the sentence. "Apparently my wife's hair dresser is one of your *gay* friends that you told about me at some fuckin' party."

The heart that had sunk deep in Evan's body was now fully beating high in his chest. His face still stung from Salvatore's slap. "Give me a chance to defend myself." Evan said caressing his face. "I don't know what you're talking about."

"I guess you are going to tell me you don't know Todd Thompson?"

"Todd? I don't know a Todd."

Salvatore stepped closer to Evan. "Do you know a Doyle-Leigh?"

So, the hoity snob is a hairdresser and a bitch. After the shock of hearing that name, the first thought that popped into his mind was to run out the back door and call the police. But what good would that do? Salvatore *was* the police. Evan wanted out. He had been in tight spots before, but this one felt different. There wasn't a good lie surfacing in his brain. Without thinking, Evan leaped out and pushed Salvatore as hard as he could and turned to run without looking back. He got halfway across the room before Salvatore grabbed his shirt. He had only grabbed the material so he did not have a good grip which allowed for a struggle. The two men's arms seemed to be engaged in a wild ritual dance that resembled something other than a fight.

Salvatore's strength coupled with Evan's feet getting tripped paved the way for Salvatore to have Evan pinned on his back on the floor. Salvatore towered above his face. He screamed at Evan over and over again, "You did this to me, you fag, and now you are going to pay. You lured me and you seduced me and you made me lose everything I own." He screamed louder, "You did this to me!" He slapped Evan once more.

Evan made one last attempt to knock Salvatore off of him when Salvatore reached into his back pocket and pulled out a switchblade. Evan's first thought was that he would slice his face in order to make him permanently disfigured. Instead, Salvatore raised his hand high and with all of his strength buried the blade deep into Evan's side. The pain was excruciating as he gasped for his breath. He began to yell for help as he was stabbed deep in each thigh. As Evan throbbed with pain, Salvatore got up and ran to the window shades and frantically cut the pull strings leaving little drops of blood on the blinds. He went back to Evan and tied his feet together. Although it was difficult to do, Evan still tried to fight back and yell for help. Each time he yelled, Salvatore slapped him either on a wound or in the face. Rolling him over to his side further smearing the blood on the floor and himself, he tied Evan's hands behind his back and then stabbed each arm. He stood over Evan, breathing heavily.

"Please," Evan spoke in a desperate manner, "don't let me die. I didn't mean to cause you any pain." He continued with a hint of hysterics, "I'll tell her it wasn't true—it didn't happen."

Salvatore flared his nostrils and then ran into the kitchen. Seconds later he came back with a dish towel and stuffed it into Evan's mouth. "Just shut up! I hope you bleed to death, *Lowla*. You know I bet you always wanted to have bled like a real woman." He picked his knife up and braised it across the front of Evan's pants.

Evan lay on his hardwood floors as he looked up in disbelief and in shock.

Something in Salvatore's expression changed as though he realized what he had done. His look of anger and hatred had changed to disbelief and horror. He brought his knife to his side and folded the blade back into place. He took a long look at Evan tied up and bleeding. He turned to leave. He stopped by the side table and picked up Evan's phone. He took the phone and opened the door. He did not look back. Salvatore went out and slammed the door behind him.

Evan knew that he was going to die. Not only was he going to die alone, he would die tied up and stuffed. He could only imagine the newspaper headlines: *Cop Goes On Rampage — Drag Queen To Blame*. At last, he would get the widespread attention he thought he deserved except he would not be around to enjoy it. It hurt him that all of his videos of himself, and the one with Salvatore, might be viewed by an unappreciative audience just looking for evidence and would not understand his quest for talent and love. More than that, it anguished him deeply that his relatives would come to find out how he lived and died. He couldn't let that happen. He had to make something of his life in which to be proud. He began to struggle to get free but with each movement, he lost energy. Luckily he was able to push the dish towel out of his mouth with his tongue. "Help!" he shouted as loud as he could as he tried to move his feet to loosen the cord. As he struggled, he started to pray aloud. "Oh God, please help me. I'll never pray for a silly thing again. I'll change. I swear, oh God." If he didn't survive, he hoped that he would soon see his father and his grandmother come to get him and not die in evil darkness. "Please let there be eternal light and not eternal darkness. Please forgive this stupid human who wasted all of the precious gifts You gave me. Please, oh God, I beg of You to be with my mother and take care of her." There was one more attempt to get free as the room began to get brighter. *If only I could get to the brick at the fireplace and rub the string against them.* Slowly, he made contact with the inside of the fireplace and used his feet and pulled himself closer. He got close enough to grab the brick. He pulled himself up as he ignored the pain to be on his knees. As he looked out at the room there seemed to be a mist cloud of moisture that hung in the air. His attention made him turn his head to the direction of the bedroom as he thought he heard the faint echo of a show tune. He took one look around and fell to the floor, passed out.

ALSO FROM DIVACITY PRESS, A THOMASMAX COMPANY

A Kept Promise
Debra Ann Barré, $ 11.95

The author draws on her experiences to explain that there's more than just power in positive thinking. When combined with spirituality, there's a promise of a bountiful life.

OTHER GREAT BOOKS FROM
THOMASMAX PUBLISHING

After Midnight In Savannah
B. Forrest Spink, $ 12.95

A gay crack addict, convicted in Savannah in 1993 of the murder of his Nazarene minister mother, maintains more than a decade later that the real killer was his crack cocaine supplier, a female impersonator. Non-fiction. Includes family photos, trial transcript.

Crackajack Love
Bill Jackson, $ 18.95

Brokeback Mountain meets the U.S. Army and Tinseltown in this romantic yarn set in the early 1960's. Serving Uncle Sam and dreaming of being Hollywood's next leading man (although he's a complete unknown), South Georgia farm boy Alex Price falls in love twice, first with a fellow soldier, then with the daughter of a TV star.

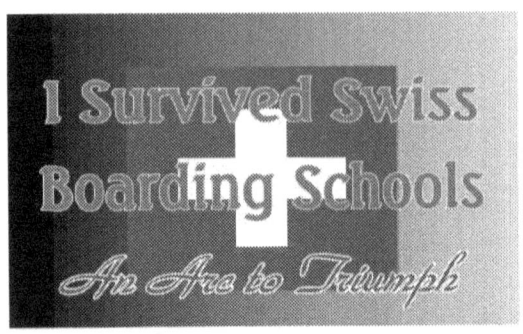

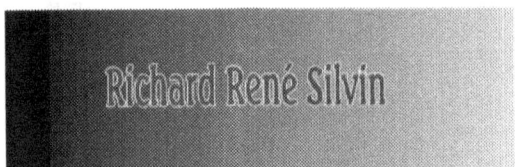

I Survived Swiss Boarding Schools
Richard René Silvin, $ 14.95

He rubbed elbows with celebrities and royalty, but at his first school he learned only to avoid beatings and to evade a pedophile woodcutter. At esteemed LeRosey, he was molested by an older student and was disgraced as "a fairy" when standing up to his molester. His resolve in overcoming humiliation makes the book's title an understatement.

Since You're UP!
Linda Ward Wilson, $10.00

Southern cookin' and other recipes from the family archives of the late Thomas William Ward Sr. Includes family photos and anecdotes, sections on entrees, desserts, cooking for large crowds and others.

All ThomasMax and Divacity Press books are available at bookstores or online. If a store doesn't have the book you want in stock, ask the store to order it. Or order from internet sellers such as BarnesandNoble.com, Amazon.com and others. You may also purchase books directly from the publisher through your PayPal account at thomasmax.com.